DON'T LEAVE

JENNIFER SUCEVIC

Don't Leave

Copyright© 2015 by Jennifer Sucevic

All rights reserved. No part of this book may be reproduced in any form or by any electronic or mechanical means, including information storage and retrieval systems, without written permission from the author, except for the use of brief quotations in a book review.

This is a work of fiction. Names, characters, businesses, palaces, events, locales, and incidents are either the products of the author's imagination or used in a fictitious manner. Any resemblance to actual persons, living or dead, or actual events is purely coincidental.

Cover Design by Mary Ruth Baloy at MR Creations

Editing by Andie Edwards of Beyond the Proof

Home | Jennifer Sucevic or www.jennifersucevic.com

1

CASSIDY

"Wake up, babe." Cole kisses his way across my naked shoulder. "We've got class in an hour."

Still sleepy, I stretch against the firm length of his body. "Not yet," I mumble, "we don't have to get up just yet."

Twenty-five minutes. That's all we need to roll out of bed and still have roughly thirty seconds to slide into our seats for Psych 201. Unable to pry my eyelids open, I turn in his arms as my palms find the solid planes of his chest before stroking over them. It isn't long before my wandering fingers descend down his body.

Have I mentioned just how amazingly hard and cut he is?

Hours spent on the ice and lifting in the gym have made him into the chiseled god that he is. A few heartbeats later and my hand is delving into his boxer briefs before gliding over the rigid length of his morning wood.

Well, hello there.

"Looks like we won't be making it out of bed on time after all," he growls, warm breath feathering across the outer shell of my ear as he rolls me onto my back. Before I can offer up a response, his lips crash down on mine as my fingers caress his thick erection and then slide further down to play with the only soft part of him.

Squeezing, petting, and teasing.

God, I love the feel of him.

The barely harnessed power that hums beneath the surface of flesh, bone, and muscle. It's something that used to make me nervous. But I know Cole would never use that well-honed strength against me. After what happened last year, being touched or manhandled can send me spiraling into a panic.

I hate when the icy tendrils of anxiety flood through every cell of my being before wrapping around me. My heart jackhammers a painful tattoo against my chest. Nerves careen and skitter across my flesh. Nausea churns in the pit of my gut...

Until I can't breathe.

I.

Can't.

Breathe.

But I've been working on that with a psychologist and it's getting better.

I'm getting better.

The attacks don't happen as frequently as they used to. I'm controlling it instead of being controlled *by* it.

Cole is always so careful and patient with me. Right from the start, he was gentle and kind. It's probably the reason I fell so easily for him.

Well, maybe not *easily,* because in the beginning, I fought against the attraction. Fought against getting to know him. I tried to shut him down at every turn. But the guy is seriously persistent.

After my life imploded last year, it was important I get myself back on track. And a boyfriend, or even a hookup situation, wasn't part of the plan.

No distractions.

That was my mantra.

What I've found is that the best laid plans never turn out the way you expect them to. If you'd asked me a year and a half ago, I would have told you that I'd be dominating on the ice at Dartmouth. Succeeding academically, because that's what I'd always done. I had worked hard my entire life to get to a Division I school. I'd sacrificed friendships and a social life to make that dream come true.

Instead of taking Dartmouth by storm, I'd crashed and burned spectacularly.

Too much pressure and stress.

I ended up losing everything.

Including my family.

It's the way Cole's tongue tangles with my own that pulls me from those dark thoughts. Instead of allowing me to get stuck inside my head, he forces me to be present by hovering over my body and caging me in beneath him. I love the way it feels to be surrounded by him. We've spent hours in bed, exploring one another. Learning what the other likes and doesn't like.

I curl my fingers around him, stroking his hard length in a way that drives him to distraction. I may be new to this, but I've caught on quickly. With a groan, he slips his fingers into my dampened panties.

"You're so damn wet." He sucks my lower lip into his mouth before nipping at it. "So fucking hot," he groans.

A whimper escapes from me when his fingers drift over my heated flesh before sinking inside me. His tongue and fingers move in tandem, driving me higher. And then higher still.

My hand tightens around him, pumping harder.

Faster.

Cole tugs my pink tank top over my head before tossing it to the floor. His heated gaze holds mine for a heartbeat before kissing his way down my body until he can suck my nipple into his mouth. He continues the onslaught until I'm shifting beneath him, needy for more. With a soft pop, he gives the other one the same attention.

I love the feel of his hot mouth as it roves over my naked body, and the way he makes me feel when we're wrapped up in each other. It's as if the world around us shrinks down until everything else ceases to exist.

Releasing the other stiffened bud, he sinks lower until he's nipping at my navel. His lips ghost over my belly before reaching my hip bones and peppering me with kisses. Anticipation spirals through me as he reached the elastic band of my panties. Instead of stripping off the cotton material, he presses his lips against my throbbing heat.

I shift restlessly beneath him, desperate for the thin barrier to be ripped away. All I want is to feel the heat of his mouth as he brands me. It drives me crazy when he teases me like this, and he knows it.

But that's just part of the fun.

When he presses another kiss against my damp panties, I groan and arch toward him. I'm precariously close to begging for it.

For him.

The chuckle that escapes from him is deep and low as if he knows exactly what he's doing to me right before his finger slips beneath the edge to brush over my slick heat. He yanks the panties aside until the material stretches across my exposed flesh. A moment later, his mouth descends, warm breath feathering against me until I'm aching with need.

It's always like this between us.

Hot and explosive.

There are times when it's slow and gentle, and others when it's fast and hard. With anyone else, that would scare me.

But not with Cole.

Never with Cole.

He's like a drug careening through my system and I crave only what he can give me. Every thought swirling through my head disappears as he laps at my pussy until my entire body trembles with the need he's ignited to life.

A month ago, this kind of intimacy would have freaked me out. It would have unleashed the anxiety I keep tightly under wraps. That's no longer the case. I love surrendering to him. I love the way he makes my body throb and pulse.

Most of all, I love that Cole Mathews is mine.

And I'm his.

"You like that, baby?"

"You know I do," I whisper as he strokes his tongue over me, playing my body like a fine instrument. I arch, wanting to feel him buried deep inside my body, filling me to the brim. The ache within is growing. Pulsing and throbbing until it feels like it could consume me.

I've never felt anything like this before.

"Cole, please…" Desperation bleeds from me.

"Please, what?"

His voice is raw, scraped low with just as much pent-up desire as mine. His tongue dances over me before plunging deep inside and making me moan. That's all it takes for me to teeter at the edge. My hips move restlessly against him as need floods through every cell of my body. I'm panting and pleading for him to push me over the edge and into oblivion.

I'm.

So.

Close.

So close to shattering into a million little jagged pieces.

With an orgasm poised to crash over my body, his mouth disappears. I gasp, my eyelids flying open as his warm breath ghosts over my pulsing flesh.

"Cole," I ground out. "I'm so close." Desperation threads its way through my voice. My neediness should embarrass me, but I don't give a damn. I want to scream in frustration.

I can't but arch toward him, trying to close the distance. Even though he's intent on teasing me, I know how affected he is by my body. He tells me all the time how much he loves being buried deep inside me.

And I love his hard length filling me up, and how perfectly we fit together.

None of my drunken hookups ever came close to feeling like this. What we have is special.

A hungry look fills his eyes as he stares down at me. "One more taste."

He thrusts his tongue deep inside me. As a whimper falls from my lips, he pulls away for a second time.

"Stop teasing!" I growl.

With a soft chuckle, he crawls up my body before pressing a kiss against my mouth. "Delicious." There is so much intensity filling his eyes. "And I love teasing you. It's my new favorite pastime."

As soon as those husky words escape from him, he flips me over onto my belly before dragging my body to the edge of the mattress. My underwear is quickly stripped away. His hands sink into my hips as he pulls my backside into the air. I groan as his fingers glide over me, swirling around my entrance before sinking deep inside. He keeps up a steady rhythm until I'm pushing against him, the orgasm once again beginning to build. Whimpers fall from my lips as he forces me closer to the edge.

Just when a wave of pleasure crests inside me, his touch vanishes.

"Cole," I groan as tears of frustration prick my eyes. "Please, I need you!"

The sound that escapes from him is strained around the edges as he moves behind me. The blunt head of his cock teases my slick heat, stroking against my lips, caressing them gently. I can just imagine what he looks like, holding his thick erection in his hand as it glides across my flesh. That picture is branded onto my brain forever.

When he finally sinks inside me, my eyelids feather closed as I strain against him.

He's buried so deep.

And it feels so good.

But then again, it always does.

Hovering over me, he wraps his hard body around mine. His hands drift across my ribcage until he's able to palm my breasts. He toys with my nipples all the while thrusting inside me. After a few moments, one hand trails down my body until he's able to play with my clit. I whimper as an orgasm builds with each flick of his fingers and stroke of his cock.

We stand at the precipice before careening over the edge. I have to bite down on my lower lip in order to keep the screams locked deep inside as pleasure streaks through my body. It's so tempting to let go and release the intensity. Instead, I resist the urge. I refuse to suffer through the shit-eating grins, sly looks, and obnoxious comments from a houseful of his hockey teammates over a bowl of cereal at the kitchen table.

Been there, done that.

As the last aftershocks reverberate through me, exhaustion takes hold. Cole relaxes against me, his bigger body curving around mine.

"I love you, Cassidy," he whispers before pressing a kiss to my back.

"I love you, too."

2

CASSIDY

As I leave Mackenzie Hall, where my Economics class is held every Tuesday and Thursday afternoon, my feet grind to a halt and a shiver of dread slithers down my spine. Luke Wellington is sprawled out on one of the stone benches along the walking path.

His gaze sweeps over the exiting crowd. A pit the size of Texas grows in my belly as he studies the mass of students leaving the building. Unsure of who he's searching for, I duck my head and hope that my long curtain of black hair will shield me from his view so I can escape.

Most of the girls on campus would be ecstatic to catch Luke's eye. He's tall, probably around six feet or so, with broad shoulders. He's muscular from skating hard at practice and lifting weights in the gym several times a week. He's handsome with blond hair and blue-gray hazel eyes.

But that's not what I see when I look at him.

I see someone who has the power to resurrect my past and bring the fledgling success I've found at Western crashing down around my head.

The moment his gaze locks onto mine, my skin prickles with

unease. All thoughts that this is simply a case of paranoia vanish as he rises to his feet and pushes his way through hundreds of students who are trying to flee the building. As much as I want to pretend that I don't see him, it's pointless.

Instead of darting away like every instinct inside is screaming for me to do, I straighten my shoulders before forcing my feet to shuffle forward.

My muscles tighten as he eats up the distance between us.

A million memories somersault unwantedly through my head as our gazes collide. I can't help but remember how he came to my rescue and fought off the three guys who'd pinned me down. He'd wrapped a shirt around my naked body, all the while murmuring soft words before gathering me up in his arms and carrying me to his truck. A heavy silence had fallen over us as I sat huddled in the front seat during the short drive to the dorms. He'd stayed in my room with me until I'd fallen asleep. The next morning, I'd tried to make myself believe that it had been a terrible nightmare, but I knew the truth. Could see the bruises on my wrists.

My life had been spiraling downward for months. What had happened that Saturday night at an off campus house party was the rock-bottom.

Heat and shame flood my cheeks as our eyes stay locked. Luke is a stark reminder of the mistakes I'd made last year.

The reason I'd come to Western was for a fresh start.

A clean slate.

A do-over.

I'd wanted to move on and leave the past where it belonged—in the past. At Dartmouth. A good five hundred miles away from where I am now.

But how could I do that with Luke here?

How could I forget about everything that had happened when he alone had the power to dredge it all back up again? When he could shatter the fragile peace, the hard-fought success, I'd found over the last two months?

His expression remains shuttered, making it impossible to decipher what he's thinking. "Do you have a few minutes to talk?"

The way his gaze probes mine makes me feel as if he's silently feeling me out. Picking through all the secrets I've locked deep inside.

I'm tempted to shake my head, but I need to know what he wants. This isn't the first time he's sought me out. But it needs to be the last. Maybe if I give him a few minutes of my time, he'll leave me alone. It feels like everywhere I go, there he is. I want to believe it's a string of coincidences, but something tells me that's not the case.

My teeth sink into my lower lip as I reluctantly say, "I only have a couple of minutes and then I've got somewhere to be."

That's a lie.

I'm done with classes for the afternoon, but don't want him to know that. If nothing else comes out of this, he needs to understand that there is nothing between us. And there's certainly no reason for us to speak again. As that thought slams through my head, guilt swiftly follows.

Because he saved me that night.

Saved me from ugly, unspeakable things those three guys were intent on doing.

Things I can't bear to dwell on. If I do, anxiety will flood my system and my chest will constrict. Nausea will churn in my belly, perspiration will spring to my palms, and my thoughts will race as fast as my pulse.

And then I won't be able to breathe. It's like I'm being choked from the inside out.

For the past ten months, those debilitating feelings of anxiety have been a constant companion. I've only started to master the symptoms through relaxation, breathing techniques, and regular sessions with my psychologist. I can't—no, I *won't* allow someone from my past to show up and derail all my hard work.

As much as I want to forget, there's a tiny part inside me that wonders if maybe it's something I need to remember. This is the one person who came to my rescue when no one else did.

Without him…

I can't finish that thought.

"That's fine," he murmurs. "Want to go to the Union? Maybe grab a coffee?"

I'm already regretting this decision. "I guess."

Ten minutes.

Fifteen tops.

That's more than enough time to figure out what he wants and then, hopefully, we can both move on with our lives.

Separately.

The three-minute hike to the Union is made in awkward silence. As soon as we step inside the one-story building, we head straight to the coffee shop. Once our drinks are in hand, we find a table buried in the back that offers more privacy—away from the pool tables and groups of people who are relaxing between classes.

I take a sip of the scalding hot drink and wait with hunched shoulders for him to delve into this conversation. Nerves prickle along my skin before settling in my belly.

A long stretch of silent moments slips by as I shift on my chair.

Just as I'm about to shoot to my feet, he clears his throat. "You remember me from Dartmouth, don't you?"

Everything within me stills.

For a second or two, I consider the merits of lying. Then I can get the hell out of here. But I'm tired of all the lies and the secrets.

It takes effort to force out the response. "Yes, I remember."

God knows I don't want to. I've done my best to forget everything that happened. With him sitting across from me, his eyes pinned to mine, that's impossible. It's all so fresh and vivid.

And I hate it.

I hate that he's able to bring it all rushing back to the surface again.

A slight tremor racks my body as my mind tumbles back in time.

It's a relief when his gaze drops to the steaming cup of coffee before flicking back up again. "When we were dancing at that party, I didn't realize it was you." He corrects himself. "Not right away."

I hadn't recognized him, either.

We were just dancing, having fun at some off campus fraternity party. A few days after that, Cole and I ran into him at a restaurant, and he told my boyfriend that he knew me from a different school. When he'd mentioned Dartmouth, everything had clicked into place.

The realization had rocked me to the core. Ever since that happened, I've been terrified he would spill all my secrets.

I'm knocked from those thoughts when he says, "At first, I thought I was imagining the likeness." He lifts his eyes to mine before sifting carefully through my shuttered expression. "I tried to find you after that night. I wanted to make sure you were okay, but you disappeared from campus. Not knowing what happened to you only made it worse."

It's a little surreal to sit across from someone who is a stranger and, yet, will forever be intertwined with my story.

Almost tentatively, he reaches across the table that separates us before covering my hand with his own. "I've spent the last year wondering what happened to the girl I found up in that bedroom. The more I tried to push you from my mind, the more you stayed with me." His lips quirk at the corners. "Part of me wondered if I'd conjured you up at that frat party." His gaze scours my face as if he's still trying to convince himself I'm real. "You look different than last year."

My heart jackhammers as my gaze falls to our clasped hands. "I'm in a much better place than I was before. I'm a lot healthier."

Some of the tension disappears from his expression as he nods in agreement. "You look great." A slight flush hits his cheeks as he corrects himself. "I mean happy. You look *happy*. It's nice to see."

"I'm a lot happier now than I was at Dartmouth," I admit.

I don't want to think about what a mess I'd been last year. Anxiety. Depression. Out-of-control drinking. Indiscriminate hookups.

It never occurred to me that he would be affected by the night in December our lives collided. I assumed he'd forget about the incident. Or that I would be the fucked-up-girl story he laughed about with his friends in the morning. Our interaction had been so fleeting and random.

Even though I hate talking about what happened, maybe he deserves to know how it all unfolded. He's the only one who helped me the entire semester I spent at Dartmouth. It's a harsh truth my mind continues to shy away from.

As I stare into his eyes, I realize it might be cathartic for both of us. For me to release the words and for him to hear them. Unsure of what else to do, I start at the beginning and tell him what it was like to play hockey growing up, and how my dad mapped out my high school and college athletic career. I talk about the pressure to push through to the next level, and how I'd given everything else up—including a social life—so I could focus on getting a scholarship to play at Dartmouth.

My life consisted of extra practices, a strict workout schedule and diet, private skating lessons, as well as advanced placement classes that would make me academically competitive. I may not have been an Olympian or a professional athlete, but I trained like one.

By the time I started my freshman year in mid-August, I was a stressed-out and burnt-out mess. And it was all downhill from there. Without my dad there to structure my time and activities, I felt strangely lost. Almost from day one, I found myself buried under an avalanche of coursework. Instead of excelling, I was failing across the board and drowning in a sea of unknown faces.

Rather than seek out help, I fell into a pattern of binge-drinking and hooking up with random guys to numb the pain and forget about the issues I was struggling with. It's what eventually led to the disastrous night Luke found me up in that bedroom at a house party. Even thinking about it is enough to have a shiver snaking down my spine.

I'd been fooling around with a guy, and we'd been on the verge of having sex when two others walked in. They'd wanted to watch. Uncomfortable with the idea, I'd tried to leave but they wouldn't let me go. They'd held me down and even though I'd been drunk, I knew how the night was going to end. That's when Luke burst in and found me.

The entire time I talk, he holds my hand, squeezing it every once in a while when there's something particularly painful, as if he wants me to understand I'm no longer alone. Even when I wish his penetrating gaze would stray, it stays locked on mine.

When I finally purge it from my system, I sit back in my chair, emotionally exhausted. Strangely enough, it also feels as if a few more of the shackles that bind me to the past have fallen away.

The hand clasping mine rises before stroking over my cheek. I still, frozen in place by the tender slide of his fingers and the unexpected shiver that races across my flesh. More bizarre is that there isn't the normal spike of fear or anxiety gripping me, sending my senses into a tailspin.

I gulp. It's something else entirely, and that frightens me more than anything else. It doesn't make sense that someone other than Cole could have penetrated the thick, protective armor I've shielded myself with since that night.

"I'm relieved that you're okay." As his fingers glide over my skin, it barely feels as if I'm able to breathe. "I don't know how we both ended up at Western, but I'm glad we did. Now we have an opportunity to get to know each other."

In the back of my brain, I realize I shouldn't allow him to touch me so intimately. It's almost as if there's a strange bond connecting us in a way I couldn't have imagined. It's what prompts me to lean back until his hand is forced to fall to the table.

As much as I want to glance away and break the link, I can't.

This is starting to feel...

I shake my head to dislodge the uncomfortable thought before it can take root inside me and do permanent damage.

"I'm with Cole," I blurt. As soon as the words escape, I feel like an idiot. Heat crawls over my cheeks. He hadn't exactly been flirting. But his touch and the way he'd been staring had felt uncomfortably intimate.

I'm no longer used to allowing people in so easily.

For the last ten months, I've worked hard to keep everyone at a distance. It's disconcerting to feel so at ease in Luke's presence.

Instead of making light of my outburst, his voice dips. "I know."

The way he watches me only strengthens my suspicions that I haven't misinterpreted the vibes he's putting out there.

They're real.

Silence falls over us before he breaks it. "I wish you weren't."

When he rips his gaze from mine, everything within me collapses.

Barely do I inhale a shaky breath before his gaze locks on mine again. "I can't explain it, and I know it doesn't make sense, but I feel protective of you."

As soon as the unwelcome thrill slides through me, I snuff it out. Even though I don't fully understand what's happening here, it feels like I'm betraying Cole. I lean away from the table to put some distance between us.

"I'm much better now. There's no reason to worry about me."

"As weird as it sounds, I've thought about you so many times over the last year. I had no idea where you were or what happened to you. Now that you're here and I know that you're all right, I'm not sure if I can just turn it off."

His brow furrows and, for a moment, he looks as confused as I feel.

I bite my lower lip before blurting, "Have you been following me?"

When his eyes widen, embarrassment surges inside and I feel ridiculous for even asking the question. Of course, he hasn't been. Why would he?

"I did show up at your practice the other night. I remember you from the girls' team last year, and you were such a good player." There's a pause before he adds, "I'm glad you didn't quit."

Warmth blooms in the pit of my belly as I reach out and cover his hand with my own. "I've been playing on the intramural team for a few weeks now. It's turned out to be a lot of fun and there's no pressure. Not like there was before. Like I said, you don't have to worry. I have everything under control." With one final squeeze, I pull my hand away so we're no longer touching. The physical connection between us feels somehow dangerous.

Like a match strike to kindling.

The last thing I want is for something to explode between us.

The way he searches my eyes for answers to questions he has yet to ask scares me, because I can't give him anything more than friendship.

"I'm glad you're doing so well."

I lift my lips into a smile, hoping to reassure him. "I am."

Is it possible I've overreacted to the situation and the peculiar feelings that have sprung up between us?

After today, Luke will go his way and I'll go mine. Maybe, at some point, we'll run into each other on campus or at a party. When we do, I won't feel the need to avoid him. We can be friendly.

Or maybe we can be friends.

Who knows?

That's when I realize I'd actually like to be friends.

How ironic is that?

I've tried so hard to run from him these past couple of days, and now that we've sat down and cleared the air, I realize our shared history has unexpectedly bonded us together.

"Does Cole know what happened to you?"

Breaking eye contact, I jerk my head into a tight nod. "I didn't tell him right away."

It doesn't take long before my gaze shifts to his. "He hadn't known that night you'd said something at the restaurant." There's a pause before I push the rest out. "That's why I lied about it. Lied about knowing you."

He tilts his head and clarifies, "But he knows everything now?"

"Yes."

When I'd met Cole two months ago, I hadn't been looking for a relationship. I hadn't felt emotionally equipped to deal with one. The last thing I wanted was to explain my past to someone who might turn around and judge me for the mistakes I'd made.

In hindsight, I should have realized he wouldn't think any less of me. But still...stripping yourself bare is a scary prospect. And divulging my past—all my mistakes and failures—hadn't been easy.

Luke's eyes turn fierce, and something within me constricts. "You have nothing to be ashamed of. You know that, right?"

I give him a forced smile. The truth of the matter is that I'm still embarrassed about everything that transpired last fall. I made a lot of mistakes.

Failing out of school.

Losing my athletic scholarship.

Getting kicked off the hockey team.

Drinking.

Sleeping around.

All of which led to a fractured relationship with my family.

"I'm still working on that part." On forgiving myself.

"Everyone makes mistakes," he murmurs. "None of us are perfect."

"I know. It's just..." My voice trails off before I admit, "It's hard to live with."

"Regret is always difficult to live with."

We fall into silence as those words hang suspended in the air between us.

"Look, I understand you're seeing Cole," there's a pause as he shifts on his chair as if uncomfortable, "but there's something between us." His gaze flickers away as he drags a hand over the back of his neck before skewering me once more with a well-honed stare. "Whatever this is, I've never felt anything like it before. It's unnerving to feel so strongly about someone I barely know."

I nod, feeling the same way. It's where the confusion springs from. I'm unsure what to do with all these strange emotions that career unwantedly through my body.

Before sitting down with Luke today, I'd been angry that he was trying to intrude upon my new life. I was afraid he'd tell Cole all the ugly details he had firsthand knowledge of. I was embarrassed and ashamed that he'd witnessed me at my absolute worst. He'd seen me naked and wasted, being held down by three drunken guys. A thick shudder slides through me as that night rears its ugly head in my memories.

Like a kaleidoscope, my perspective has shifted, morphing into something different. Even though it doesn't make sense and I'm not entirely comfortable with the realization, Luke feels like the opposite end of a magnet I find myself being drawn to.

There is a string binding us, and I have no idea how to cut it.

Gaze locked on mine, he leans forward, attempting to close the distance between us. "I feel like we're meant to be in each other's lives." With a shake of his head, he plows his fingers through his hair as if he's agitated by his own words. "For fucks sake," he whispers, "that makes me sound like a stalker."

I'm not going to lie, it kind of does. Under normal circumstances, I'd already be walking—no, make that running—toward the nearest exit. Everything he's just given voice to sounds much too intense.

I draw air into my lungs before holding it captive for a few seconds and then releasing it as I try to wrangle my thoughts and make sense of them. "No, I feel it, too."

How is it possible for something to feel both right and wrong?

My heart constricts to the point of pain as Cole pops into my brain.

That's all it takes for me to shoot to my feet. I need time and space to think about everything that's happened with Luke. I have no idea how to define this new relationship that has sprung up out of nowhere.

His eyes widen as he rises. There's a strange intensity marring his expression. "I'm sorry. I shouldn't have said any of that. I didn't mean to frighten you."

I glance away. "I'm not sure what you want from me and that makes me nervous."

Whatever is unfolding between us, it needs to be straightforward. There can't be any room for ambiguity. Luke needs to understand that we will never be anything more than friends.

He takes a hesitant step toward me. Instead of retreating, I stiffen my shoulders and hold my ground. Perhaps that's a mistake. When I refuse to retreat, he takes another careful step until he's invading my personal space.

"I'll take whatever you're willing to give. For now, maybe that's just friendship. Later on, it could be something more. All I know is that I need to be a part of your life."

"I love Cole," I whisper.

His eyes darken. "I know." His hands drift across my cheeks before tipping my face upward. "I can be your friend. If that's what you want —what you need—then that's all we'll be."

A thick lump settles in the middle of my throat as his quiet words wash over me. Their meaning feels immense, and I'm unsure what to do with them.

"But you want more," I press.

He hesitates before admitting, "Yes."

My tongue darts out to moisten my lips. "I can only offer friendship."

"Then I'll be content with that."

The way his gaze softens, becoming almost tender, sets off alarm bells inside my head. "I really do love him."

Cole is everything I never thought I'd find, and I refuse to throw that away.

Even though I don't understand the bond that has been forged with Luke over the course of an hour, I also realize I can't walk away from it.

His lips lift into a smile before he presses a kiss against my forehead. "Then he's a lucky guy."

"Thank you." My muscles loosen at his easy acceptance of the situation. As we stand, almost embracing, my heart twists under my breast. "I should go."

My emotions feel strangely tangled. Not only do I need to physically distance myself from him, but emotionally as well.

His hands fall from my face before he takes a step in retreat. As he does, I suck in a deep breath and try to clear my thoughts.

With shaking fingers, I gather up my bag and turn to say goodbye when a blur of movement from the corner of my eye catches my attention. As I turn, my gaze collides with Cole's. His golden gaze holds mine for a painful heartbeat before slicing to Luke who still stands next to me.

His expression darkens before he swings away, stalking through the crowd.

Everything inside me seizes, spurring me into motion. "Cole, wait!"

My heart clenches as his name rises above the din of the Union. If he hears me, he doesn't stop.

All I can do is hope I haven't ruined the best thing in my life.

3

CASSIDY

With my heart lodged somewhere in my throat, I finally catch up with Cole outside the building. He's already made it down the cement stairs to the pathway that snakes through campus. Even though I yell his name, begging him to stop, he ignores me. It's like I'm not even there. When I'm close enough, my fingers wrap around his arm, biting into his flesh.

I've never seen him this angry. The Cole I know is always calm and in control of his feelings. But that's not the case right now.

What I hate most is the hurt that flashed in his whiskey-colored eyes. I don't want to lose him over a fledgling friendship with Luke.

"Cole," I plead, "please stop and talk to me."

In that moment, it feels like he's slipping through my fingers like sand. Allowing Luke to touch me was wrong.

"It's not what it looked like."

Those six words have him grinding to a halt before wheeling around to face me. The movement happens so quickly that I slam into his chest. His fingers bite into my shoulders to steady me. As his eyes collide with mine, I catch sight of the anger and uncertainty simmering within their golden depths.

"What do you think it looked like?" Even though his eyes flash, his voice remains devoid of emotion.

I gulp before forcing out the words. "I'm sure it looked like something was going on between us." And in all honesty, maybe it had been. Maybe we crossed a line.

I'm not sure.

What I do know is that I can't lose Cole.

"It had looked like he wanted to kiss you." His eyes scrutinize mine before he says with even greater calm, "And it had looked like you wanted him to."

Had I wanted that?

Had I?

I bite my lower lip, remembering the feelings of confusion that had spiraled through me before shaking my head.

No, I didn't.

Not really.

The last thing I want is there to be any misunderstandings. It's the reason I was honest with Luke about my relationship with Cole.

"We were talking about," my gaze slides away, "what happened last year."

For some reason, I'd assumed my explanation would smooth everything over. It would give him insight as to why our conversation had looked so intimate. Instead, he stares at me in confusion. It takes a heartbeat for me to realize that I've made a tactical error, but it's much too late to backtrack now.

"You don't even know him." His brows pinch together as hurt weaves its way through his voice. "You really shared all that with him?"

Tears prick the backs of my eyes as I shrug, silently wishing Cole could understand that a strange connection has been forged between us. It's not romantic or sexual in nature, but there's still *something*.

"He's the one who got me away from those guys and out of the house. I don't even like to think about what would have happened had he not been there," I whisper.

He blanches, tugging me into his arms before wrapping them around me. "I know, I know." His voice is thick with unspent emotion as he presses his lips against the crown of my head. "I'm thankful that he was."

I release the pent-up breath from my lungs. "It felt good to sit down and talk to him. Even though we don't know each other, I feel connected to him. It's not something that makes sense." As scared as I am to force out the rest, I need to be honest with him. "Those feelings aren't just going to disappear."

His muscles stiffen, and for a long moment, he remains silent. "What does that mean for *us*?"

"It just means that Luke and I are friends. We're in each other's lives." There's a pause before I add, "After what he did, I owe him my friendship."

He draws in a deep breath before releasing it. A steely quality enters his voice. One I'm not used to hearing from him. "You don't owe him anything, Cassidy. Did he make you feel like you did?"

"Of course not." I pull away enough to search his eyes. "It wasn't like that at all."

I suck the corner of my lower lip into my mouth before carefully considering what I say next. How do I convince Cole that he has nothing to worry about?

"I want us to be friends. I know he feels..." My words trail off.

"He feels what?" There's a beat of silence. "Because I saw the way he was staring at you. The guy wants more than friendship." Cole tilts his head as his eyes search mine. "You realize that, right?"

Unable to hold his gaze, mine skitters away before I force it back again. For weeks, I tried to keep my past hidden and now that he knows, I won't lie to him.

About anything.

Instead of answering the question, I say, "I told him that I loved you, and that we could only be friends."

His fingers bite into my flesh as his grip intensifies. "Do you really think he's going to be satisfied with that?" Frustration wafts off him in heavy waves.

"It doesn't matter, because I'm yours," I whisper. "I love you. There's nothing he can say or do to change that."

Even though he still looks skeptical, Cole jerks his head into a tight nod before pulling me against him. Only then am I able to fully relax in his embrace.

We're okay.

Relief slides through me at that thought.

Still wrapped up in Cole's arms, my attention locks on a figure standing near the entrance of the Union. Luke. Our gazes lock and hold for a long stretch of moments before I blink and rip mine away. An odd prickle of unease blooms in the pit of my belly. It feels as if I'm standing on the cusp of a decision.

But that doesn't make sense. I've made my choice. Luke is nothing more than a friend. That's all he'll ever be. Once we settle more into our friendship, he'll come to accept that.

4

CASSIDY

"Dr. Thompson is ready to see you, Cassidy."

I smile at Wendy before passing by the reception desk.

After my life imploded last December, my parents decided it would be best for everyone involved if I lived with my grandparents. They didn't want my bad influence to rub off on my younger sisters, Lexie and Miranda. I'd been so depressed and riddled with anxiety, that my grandmother suggested I work with a local therapist. Then, after I moved to campus in August, I found Dr. Thompson.

I drop down in my usual spot on the couch as she settles onto the chair parked across from me. Even though we've only been working together for a few months, I feel really close to her. She's a great psychologist and it's doubtful I would have made such a smooth transition to Western without her support.

"Cassidy," she says warmly, "you're looking well. It's been more than a week since I last saw you. Tell me how everything is going."

"It's going well." With that, I launch into what had been discussed during my last session. "I took your advice and spoke with two of my professors about changing my courses for next semester, and they gave me some great suggestions. I'm probably going to drop my

History course for a Sociology one instead. I've also made an appointment to speak with my academic advisor about the majors I'm interested in exploring."

She nods approvingly. "That all sounds great. It seems like you've got everything under control. That must feel good."

"It feels great." A smile tugs at the edges of my lips.

"I'm sure the Sociology class will help with your decision to pursue a career in psychology," she adds. We've spent time discussing possible majors since I'm currently undecided. I've narrowed it down to psychology and education, since math and science are two of my stronger subjects.

"That's what I was thinking. Professor Mullens also mentioned a couple opportunities for me to assist her grad students with their experiments next semester."

Her brows rise as she nods. "What a wonderful, not to mention valuable, experience."

"Yeah," I agree, "I'm really excited about it. I'd love the opportunity to help out with, or even participate in, something like that."

"That all sounds amazing and if nothing else, you'll get a better feel for that particular area of study."

I beam. "That's what I was thinking."

"And classes are still going well? Are you feeling overwhelmed now that we're two and a half months into the semester?"

I do a quick mental rundown of each class and the assignments coming due before shaking my head. "No, everything is going smoothly. There's a lot of reading, but I'm staying on top of it by doing a little each day, and that helps to keep everything manageable. I still have A's in all my classes."

"Tackling small chucks at a time is a smart way of staying on top of your classes." She takes a few quick notes. "Tell me how you've been doing otherwise. Any anxiety since we last spoke?"

I shake my head. Now that I don't have to worry about Luke sabotaging me at Western, it feels like a massive weight has been lifted from my shoulders. Sitting down and discussing the past with him made me realize that he probably needed closure. Even though I'm glad we were able to do that, I'm worried this new relationship with Luke will cause problems with Cole.

"Have any other issues popped up?"

"No," the whole Cole-Luke situation flits through my head, "not really."

"Not really?" Her brows arch in question as she picks up on my hesitation. Have I mentioned that Dr. Thompson is really good at what she does?

"Well," I nibble on my lower lip, silently debating whether or not to tell her about Luke, "there's someone here who knows me from Dartmouth."

"Is that going to be a problem for you?" she asks.

We both know how much I've struggled with my failure and the fight it took to get back on track. It's something I'm still working on. Any setback has the potential to send me spiraling back down the rabbit hole, and I've worked too hard to allow that to happen.

"I don't think so. We grabbed a coffee yesterday and talked about everything."

Surprise flickers in her eyes. "How did that go?"

I blow out a steady breath as our conversation replays through my brain. "Better than I could have expected. When I realized who he was, it made me sick to my stomach that someone from my past could dredge up my mistakes and spread them around." I fall silent before admitting, "Someone who could destroy the new life I've created for myself."

Her dark eyes fill with both understanding and compassion. It's one of the reasons I feel so comfortable talking with her. "Now that you've had a chance to sit down and face your fears, do you still think that will happen?"

"No, I don't." I think about the fear that had swamped me over the previous week. "The guy who is now here is the one who rescued me from that bedroom."

If Dr. Thompson is surprised by what I've just revealed, she never allows it to show in her expression. "I see."

"Yeah," I agree with a small smile. "He wants to be friends."

Her smooth brow furrows. "Are you comfortable with having a relationship with him?"

I take a few moments to turn the question over in my head before nodding. "Yeah, I am. After we began talking, I realized he wasn't here to hurt me. He was genuinely concerned about how I was doing. Even though we don't know each other, there's a bond between us. I ended up telling him everything that transpired throughout the semester leading up to that night. As strange as it was, it felt good to talk about it with him because," I gulp in a breath, "he was there."

With a nod of understanding, her expression turns thoughtful. "Striking up a friendship seems like it might be good for both of you."

"I think he's interested in being more than just friends." As soon as the words escape from my mouth, I wish it were possible to suck them back in again. I don't know why I mentioned that. It doesn't matter what Luke wants.

With a tilt to her head, she asks, "How do you feel about that?"

I nip my lower lip, pinning it in place as I consider how truthful to be. If there's one place where I can admit the unvarnished truth and lay myself bear, it's in this office.

"Confused," I whisper.

"Why do you think that is?"

I shrug, not understanding it myself.

"Before we sat down to talk, I wanted to avoid him. Seeing him was an ugly reminder of what had almost happened."

"But it no longer feels that way?"

"No. Talking everything out with him felt...freeing." I glance away for a moment, attempting to wrap my mind around the strange thoughts and feelings that course through me. "The entire time I was at Dartmouth, he's the only one who tried to help me."

"I suppose that's true." She picks up her notepad and jots down a few things. "Even though your interaction was fleeting, it was enough to forge a connection between you two."

"Yes," I admit, relieved that she understands, "that's exactly the way it feels."

How could it not?

How could I not feel something more than friendship for him?

I suppose that's exactly where the confusion stems from.

"It's not uncommon for people who have a shared traumatic experience to end up befriending one another and becoming involved in each other's lives." She allows those words to sink in before asking, "What kind of feelings are you having for..."

She looks at me, brows raised, waiting for me to supply a letter.

"Ah, *W*."

For Wellington.

Luke Wellington.

Since Dr. Thompson works with a number of students on campus, she'd previously asked me to use a letter when I referred to someone in our sessions.

My code letter for Cole is *M*.

For Mathews.

Cole Mathews.

"What kind of feelings are you having for W?"

My fingers twist together in my lap as I consider the question. It's a nervous habit I picked up within the past year. "I'm not sure." There's a pause. "I want us to be friends but..."

When I remain silent, she encourages, "But?"

I shrug, not wanting to verbalize my feelings. It's as if releasing them into the atmosphere will be a betrayal to Cole. And I don't want to do that. Not even here in this office.

"We barely know one another, and yet, I feel this strange closeness to him. It doesn't make sense."

"Is that necessarily a bad thing?"

"I don't know." I glance away, my gaze getting drawn to the window. "It makes me feel guilty."

"Guilty?" she prompts.

"Because of M."

She asks what I've been too afraid to think about. "Are you sexually attracted to W?"

I shift in my chair as my fingers play with the hem of my shirt. "A little bit," I whisper.

A slight smile tips the corners of Dr. Thompson's lips as she says, "There's nothing wrong with finding other people attractive. It's what you do with that attraction that matters."

Doesn't she understand that I don't want to feel attracted to him at all?

"I think I'm drawn to him because of this strange closeness I feel." The fact he feels the same way makes it even worse.

Luke isn't trying to bury his feelings or maintain a distance.

That scares me more.

"You shared a very personal experience with him, something that ties you two together in a very intimate way. It would be difficult *not* to feel connected to him."

As I release a steady breath into the atmosphere, I silently wonder what the best course of action is. It would be so much easier if Dr. Thompson could just tell me what to do. But I know she won't because this is something I need to figure out on my own.

All I can do is follow my heart and hope no one gets hurt.

5

CASSIDY

"You know that what you're wearing is the antithesis of sexy, right?"

I glance at the blue scrubs and fake stethoscope dangling from around my neck before arching a brow at Brooklyn. Her assessment of my Halloween costume isn't off target.

"I wasn't going for sexy." Unlike a certain someone who shall remain nameless, I'm not trolling for a little hookup action tonight.

Brooklyn, who happens to be a champ at multitasking, adds the finishing touches to her smokey eye before huffing, "Mission accomplished, Nurse Ratched. No one will mistake you for sexy."

My brows snap together. "That's Dr. Jameson, to you."

Her only reaction is to roll her eyes. After two and a half months of rooming together, I'm more than used to Brooklyn's attitude. In fact, I'd go so far as to say I'm barely affected by it.

My roomie's costume, on the other hand, is sex personified. She's poured her curvy body into a tight, black bodysuit before adding a pair of midnight-colored cat ears on top of her wild mane of blonde hair. There's a long tail pinned to her ass, and black whiskers painted on her cheeks.

I'm almost afraid of the trouble she'll find tonight.

31

And the comments…

My god, the comments.

I can almost hear them now.

"Is there any way I can talk you out of wearing that?" I ask in a tone filled with hope.

She swings toward me with a grin lighting up her face. "Nope." The word comes out sounding more like *nooooooope* before popping the P at the end.

My face scrunches. "There'll be no end to the pussy comments you'll have to endure."

Her green eyes turn decidedly sly. "As long as they're made by hot, muscly-type football players, I'm perfectly fine with it."

Ugh.

Bad answer.

"Fine," I grumble. "Let's get this over with."

A few girls from our floor catch a ride with us as we pile into Cole's electric blue Mustang. I love his car. It's just as sexy as he is. Apparently, I'm not the only one lacking in creativity tonight, because Cole is wearing his hockey jersey with a pair of jeans. The pads make his shoulders look even bigger and broader than normal.

The party is at a house on Greek row. As we turn onto the street, it's difficult to tell which party we're hitting, because there are about seven or eight others already in full swing. Tons of costumed students crowd the streets as they stagger from one party to another. Brooklyn and Cole both warned me about how crazy it gets on Halloween.

I guess they weren't kidding.

With my fingers firmly ensconced in Cole's larger hand, we wind our way through the thick press of bodies. Brooklyn is behind me, talking with Olivia, a girl from our floor. It takes about five minutes to push our way into the kitchen, where the lighting is dim but decent. Cole grabs us a couple of waters because he doesn't drink during the season, and after the debacle that was last year, I've lost my appetite for alcoholic beverages. Once in a while I'll have a drink, but that's about it.

When he offers one to Brooklyn, her eyes go flat as she narrows them at someone across the room. "I'm going to need something a hell of a lot stronger than that to make it through tonight."

There's only one guy who's capable of eliciting that kind of response from her.

And that would be her ex, Austin.

I scan the sea of revelers. Sure enough, Austin is standing on the other side of the room with a drink in one hand and a girl tucked under his other arm. My gaze flies back to Brooklyn who looks frozen in place. Wanting to offer a bit of moral support, I slip my arm around her waist.

Even though I keep the question buried inside, I can't help but wonder what she expected.

That he was going to keep pursuing her?

All she's done is shut down every attempt he's made since their breakup two weeks ago.

He's tried calling, texting, explaining what happened the night she caught him kissing one of the puck bunnies, but Brooklyn refuses to have anything to do with him. It was only a matter of time before Austin decided to cut his losses and move on.

I have to wonder by the look in her eyes if that's what she really wants. Even though Brooklyn and I have been friends for years, living with her has given me glimpses of a different side of her.

A stubborn side.

"Are you all right, Brook?" I ask, dropping my voice so only she can hear. "Do you want to get out of here?" There are plenty of other parties we can crash tonight. And they're all the same. Loud music, drinks a-plenty, and tons of costumed revelers.

She rips her gaze from Austin before pasting a smile on her face as if not bothered in the least. If I didn't know her as well as I do, I'd think maybe she wasn't. But I'm not fooled by the façade she's putting on.

"Of course not, I'm fine. There's no reason for us to leave."

I give her a beseeching look. "Are you sure?"

When her smile turns brittle, I get a sinking feeling that tonight has the potential to go off the rails. "Absolutely."

Cole returns with a red Solo cup filled to the brim with beer. As soon as he hands it to Brooklyn, she tosses it back, sucking down at least half the contents in ten seconds flat.

Yup, it's definitely going off the rails.

With wide eyes, I meet Cole's confused gaze. Before I can clue him in about what's going on with my roommate, Brooklyn drains her cup and stalks off, muttering something about finding the keg.

And a hot guy.

Not necessarily in that order, either.

Still looking perplexed, Cole's gaze tracks Brooklyn's movements before quirking a brow at me. "Do I even want to know what that was about?"

"Probably not." There's a pause before I add, "Austin's here and he isn't alone."

This explanation only seems to confuse him more. And I can't say I blame him for it. Cole was the one who had to sit Austin down and tell him to back off. I think the words *restraining order* were used during that conversation.

Multiple times.

"I thought that's what she wanted."

As I stare after Brooklyn's retreating form, I realize that I'm not the only one. At least four pairs of eyes, including Austin's, follow her black swishing tail as she vacates the room.

"I'm not sure if Brooklyn knows what she wants." Or maybe she just wishes she didn't want the person who carved out a place in her heart.

Cole captures my distracted attention when he slips his hand into mine. I smile as he gives my fingers a squeeze before leaning down to brush a kiss against my lips. Needing more, I grab the front of his hockey jersey and pull him down for another. As our lips continue to linger, someone clears their throat from beside us. We break apart only to find Austin.

One brow is cocked as he glares. "Can't you two keep your hands off each other for five freaking minutes?"

Cole's lips lift as he wraps an arm around my shoulders and tugs me closer. "Nope."

Even though I should mind my own business, I nod toward the girl who had been snuggled up against him a few minutes ago. "Who's that?"

His expression doesn't change as his gaze flickers toward the female in question. She perks up before smiling brightly and giving him a wave.

Austin lifts his chin in acknowledgement. "Just someone I know."

I make a noncommittal noise deep in my throat but remain silent. His attention shifts from the tall blonde who'd been clinging to him to where Brooklyn is just visible in the other room. I realize that *just someone I know* bears a striking resemblance to his ex.

Austin's face darkens. "I need to get back to Eva." Without another word, he stalks to his Brooklyn look-alike. What's obvious is that neither of them are completely over the other.

Cole brushes his mouth over mine before whispering, "I think my lips were right about here when we were so rudely interrupted."

My belly dips as his eyes darken. That one heated look is enough to have the thick crowd surrounding us fading into the background.

Have I mentioned how sexy Cole is in his hockey jersey?

His lips lower until they're able to brush over mine again. "Is there any chance of getting a physical later on, Doc?"

"Yup. And it's going to be *incredibly* thorough."

"I like the sound of that. Maybe we should get out of here now. What do you think?"

I press closer before nipping at his lower lip and tugging it between my teeth. "Let's dance for a bit and then we can slip away."

"Sounds like a date." He winks before grabbing my hand and towing me through the gyrating throng to the living room where everyone is dancing to the loud pulsing beat. A strobe light flickers, illuminating all the costumed students. It takes only a moment for us to lose ourselves in the music. Brooklyn and one of Cole's teammates, Alex, join us. Alex is wearing a giant condom costume.

It fits him well.

The guy is all about hooking up.

His face sticking out of the made-for-her-pleasure latex is hilarious.

Watching him attempt to put the moves on Brooklyn is even funnier, because she's not having any of it. She shuts him down at every turn. Even though my relationship with Alex started out rocky, we've slowly become friends.

All right, maybe the term *friends* is a bit of an overstatement. *Acquaintances* probably sums up our relationship rather nicely. Cole was right when he said Alex was harmless.

He is.

The guy is built like a brick shithouse and is a real goofball. I've got to hand it to him—for someone so enormous, he's incredibly smooth on his feet.

After about an hour on the dance floor, we're all sweaty messes.

Brooklyn yells over the music, "Let's find the bathroom."

Before I can nod in agreement, she's dragging me away from Cole and toward a long stretch of the hall. I let Cole know what's going on as I'm towed behind her. It takes effort to shove our way through all the zombies, ghosts, and sexy devils packing the hallway. The line for the bathroom is ten deep, and it takes at least fifteen minutes before we're able to lock ourselves in the small space.

As Brooklyn uses the toilet first, I turn toward the mirror to assess the damage. Like I assumed, it's bad. My face is all red and sweaty from dancing. I look like I've just run a marathon. I'm glad I decided to wear scrubs and nothing heavier. Even though it's the end of October and there's a chill in the air, it's hot as Hades in here. All the people crammed inside the house don't help matters, either.

After Brooklyn finishes up, we change places. She checks herself out in the rectangular mirror hanging over the sink. Unlike me, she's not all sweaty or red-faced. I narrow my eyes. Instead of sweating, she looks more like she's shimmering.

Or glistening.

Bitch.

"So," I clear my throat, "Austin…" Unsure of how to finish that sentence, my voice trails off.

Her expression becomes pinched. "What about him?"

"Does it bother you that he's here with someone else?" It's doubtful she'll admit the truth, even to me.

Brooklyn doesn't miss a beat before answering. "Nope. Not at all."

She slicks a bright red tube of lip stain over her mouth. Where she pulled that from is a total mystery, because that bodysuit is more like a second skin. "I told you before, we're through. He can see whatever slut wants."

I smirk, unable to help myself. "I think the only slut he wants to see is you."

She snorts before sliding the tube back into a well-concealed pocket at her hip.

After a quick flush of the toilet, I wash my hands. Instead of arguing with her, I say, "Then I'm glad you've both moved on."

She brushes off the comment. "If we're finished up here, there's a hot Kappa waiting for me."

With a smile, I roll my eyes before we head back out into the hallway where everyone is smashed together like sardines. Brooklyn nudges me and nods to the right. "Speak of the devil…"

One brow lifts as a grin curves her lips. Apparently, all thoughts of Austin are long gone.

With her attention focused on the Kappa, Brooklyn mutters from the side of her mouth, "Does my hair look okay?"

"Sexy. Just like the rest of you." Brooklyn's hair is her secret weapon—long, blonde, and lustrous with an enviable amount of wave. I'm sure there's a secret underground society of Brooklyn haters here at Western who would seriously enjoy scalping her. Hell, if she weren't my best friend, I'd be half tempted to hate her.

She straightens her shoulders as her gaze stays locked on her target. "Wish me luck, I'm going in."

I lay a hand on her shoulder as she's about to take off. "You don't need luck. You've got great tits."

One corner of her lip quirks as her glittering gaze spears mine. "Damn straight I do."

"Try not tear him apart with your teeth. It's such a mess to clean up afterward."

A chuckle bursts free from her. "I'll be as gentle as I can."

I have no doubt that he'll follow her around campus like a lost puppy dog come Monday morning.

With a swing of her hips, she strides over to the Kappa to chat him up. For a few seconds, I watch in awe because there's no way I'd have the confidence to walk up to a random guy and flirt with him.

Already the guy in question looks a little dazed and confused by her attention.

It's almost impressive how she can weave a spell around the opposite sex. The smile lighting up her face is much better than the crappy mood she's been in because of Austin. As I turn away from Brooklyn and her conquered Kappa, I slam into someone. My hands shoot out to steady the person I've knocked into.

"I'm so sorry!" I say as heat fills my face.

"It's fine," the girl says. "No damage done."

Her easy demeanor has relief flooding through me. Thankfully, this girl isn't going straight to bitch-mode because I accidently bumped into her. I've seen it happen. The drunker some of these females get, the nastier they become. Claws are unsheathed in the blink of an eye. It's a slice first, ask questions later kind of situation.

With a tilt to her head, she studies me. "I saw you earlier with a friend of mine—Cole Mathews."

Any friend of Cole's is a friend of mine. Especially since she seems so cool. "Yeah, hi. I'm Cassidy."

Her smile never falters. "Jackie."

One word. That's all it takes for my heartbeat to stutter.

Jackie.

As in Cole's ex-girlfriend, Jackie?

He hasn't exactly been very forthcoming with information about her or their previous relationship. Even though I want all the details, it would be hypocritical to call him out for keeping secrets when I refused to tell him anything about my past.

From the little I learned from Sammy, Cole's cousin and one of my hockey teammates, Jackie really messed him up. I'm sure that's why he doesn't want to talk about her.

I'm a little surprised to find her at this party, dressed as a super sexy nurse.

"Um, hi." My mind blanks.

Is it at all possible that this girl isn't Jackie-the-ex-girlfriend and is Jackie-the-friend-I've-never-heard-of-before?

Probably not.

It prompts me to ask, "How do you know Cole?"

The closed off expression that flickers across her face has my belly dropping to the tips of my toes. Even before she says a word, I know this is definitely Jackie-the-ex.

Damn.

"Cole and I grew up together."

That's all the confirmation I need to know who I'm talking to.

My gaze rakes over her with new interest, attempting to take in everything about her all at once. She's taller, towering over me by at least four inches. Unconsciously, I throw my shoulders back and straighten my spine.

It probably doesn't help.

Where my hair is long, straight, and black, she has a nutmeg-colored mane that tumbles around her shoulders in big, soft curls. Even with the dim hallway lighting, I can tell that she's beautiful. And thin. Except in the boob department. She's definitely more stacked than I am. Even with my padded bra, I feel woefully inadequate.

Her breasts practically spill out of the skimpy costume she's wearing. One deep breath and her cleavage will pop the seams.

This is the first time since arriving, I wish I'd listened to Brooklyn and put on something more flattering than these blue, shapeless scrubs.

The realization that I've come up short—literally—in comparison to Cole's ex, has me feeling churlish. If nothing else, this girl gets a zero for creativity. There must be at least a dozen, if not more, sexy/slutty/skanky nurses floating around. I almost wince at catty thoughts as they swirl through my head.

You know who's to blame for the corruption?

Brooklyn. She's such a bad influence.

Jackie nips at her lower lip before asking, "I was hoping we could go outside and talk for a minute."

My brows rise at the unexpected invitation. Even though every instinct is screaming for me to find Cole, I ignore it and give her a tight nod. Without another word, she turns down the hallway. I follow until we've woven our way through the crammed kitchen and out the backdoor into the brisk night air.

My gaze reluctantly drops to her ass. Of course, she'd have an amazing one on top of everything else.

As we step into the darkness, my eyes quickly adjust as silvery moonlight falls over us. There are a few groups of people standing around talking, laughing, and smoking cigarettes.

By the skunky scent that permeates the atmosphere, they're probably smoking other things as well.

We find a secluded spot near an old wooden garage at the back of the property line. When we're far enough away from everyone else, she turns to face me before wrapping her arms around her middle.

"I didn't think it would be so cold out here," she says with a shiver.

It's on the tip of my tongue to tell her that if she'd worn actual clothing, she wouldn't be cold. Instead, I bite back the comment. This is someone important from Cole's past that he doesn't talk about. I want to find out everything I can.

Unable to keep the words locked inside, I blurt, "I know you dated Cole."

Her eyes widen in the bright moonlight that filters down on us. "Yeah, I did." Glancing away, she shifts. "You know who I am?"

Is it my imagination or is there a hopeful note tinging her voice? "Sammy mentioned you."

"Oh." Her lips wilt at the corners. "You're friends with Sammy?"

"We play hockey together."

One brow rises as her gaze slides over me. "Sammy's kind of a bruiser. You don't look like the hockey-playing type."

My spine automatically stiffens. "What's that supposed to mean?"

She huffs out a breath before shaking her head. "It didn't mean anything. Sorry."

My eyes narrow, uncertain if I should take the apology at face value. And I'm not even going to examine why it makes me feel a little better to know that she and Sammy weren't BFF's.

"Are you sure about that?"

"Yeah. You seem so small." Her expression turns to one of bemusement. "I just bet he loves that you play."

Instead of responding to that comment, I remain silent. I don't want her knowing anything about our relationship. Only now do I wonder if coming out here with Cole's ex was a smart decision. I get the feeling that Jackie is sizing me up, trying to figure out if I'm competition. When she makes another slow sweep of my body, I know I'm right.

"Why did you drag me out here?" I'm itching to get back inside and away from her. Not only that, I want to find Cole so we can take off. I don't want him anywhere near this girl, who once upon a time meant something to him.

For a long stretch of moments, she remains silent before saying, "Maybe I wanted you to know that I still love him." There's a pause. "And I want him back."

Even though her words pierce my heart like a knife, they don't surprise me.

CASSIDY

hat I know about Jackie and Cole is that they were best friends growing up before deciding to deepen their relationship. They dated in high school and were still together when they both left for college last fall. Sometime during the course of their freshman year, they broke up.

From the little Cole and Sammy have mentioned, I have my suspicions as to what might have happened.

Needing confirmation, I ask, "If you'd loved him so much, why did you cheat?"

If my blunt question surprises her, it doesn't show in her expression. Her gaze shifts to the surrounding darkness as a cold wind whips through the trees. I tighten my arms around myself as the leafless branches above us shake.

Just when I begin to wonder if she'll give me an answer, she draws in a breath before steadily forcing it out again until she looks like she's deflating before my eyes. Whatever thoughts are swirling around in her head must weigh heavily, because her entire body slumps as if it might fold in on itself.

"I experienced all my firsts with Cole." The smile she gives me is sad around the edges. "First dance. First kiss. First date. First boyfriend."

I steel myself, knowing what will come next.

"He's the first guy I slept with." She sucks in a deep gulp of oxygen. "And my first love."

I force out a breath as this information settles over me.

"And I did love him." Her gaze flickers away before cutting back to mine. "I didn't think attending different colleges would be a big deal for us. We'd known each other for practically our entire lives, and he'd always been my best friend. We talked it all out before I packed up and left. He'd visit me once a month, and I'd come home when I could. By then, Cole and I had been together for two years and we knew that, at some point, we'd get married. I wanted to experience life before we took that next step."

To hear her speak about the future she and Cole had mapped out together has my insides twisting into a painful knot. A year or two ago, he wanted to marry this girl.

"If he meant so much to you, why'd you throw away your future with him?" I don't realize the words have shot from my mouth until it's too late.

Her body stiffens as she holds my hard gaze for a tense moment before tilting her head back and staring into the bright, star-littered sky.

"I met someone a few weeks into the fall semester. We started out as friends, and I told him right away that I had a serious boyfriend. We had two classes together, so we saw each other all the time. Before I knew it, we were spending a lot of time together. Studying, eating lunch or dinner together, just hanging out. After about a month, my feelings for him started to grow and change." There's a pause. "I stopped thinking about Cole and all the plans we'd made, and started thinking about Drew. I got caught up in the guy who was with me every day." Her shoulders slump under the weight of her admittance. "I'd thought I loved him."

"Is that when you and Cole broke up?"

Slowly she shakes her head. "No."

My mind spins, trying to piece everything together. "You let him believe you were being faithful when you were actually seeing someone else?"

Her face falls as she jerks her head into a nod. "After a few weeks, I realized Drew wasn't the guy I thought he was and broke it off." She chews her bottom lip as her eyes take on a faraway look. "I'd thought about telling Cole but was scared. I convinced myself that telling him would only hurt him, and I didn't want to do that. It was easier to pretend that it had never happened. By then, I'd realized it had been a mistake and we were no longer seeing each other."

We fall into an uncomfortable silence before she whispers, "But then I found out I was pregnant."

My eyes widen as the breath catches at the back of my throat.

Pregnant.

I shudder. That could have easily happened to me last year. I was hooking up while drunk, and wasn't taking precautions the way I should have.

"I had to tell him that I'd been with someone else because the baby wasn't his."

Nausea grows in the pit of my belly.

Poor Cole.

My gaze unconsciously falls to her waistline. In the skimpy nurse's outfit she's wearing, there's no indication she just gave birth to a baby.

It's as if she knows what I'm thinking.

"I lost it," she mumbles, sadness threading its way through her voice.

Even though this wasn't a planned pregnancy, it's obvious she still mourns the loss.

"I'm sorry." Sympathy rushes through me. For a moment, I consider reaching out and tugging her into my arms. I can't imagine what that must have been like for her.

"The only way for me to look at it is to tell myself that it wasn't meant to be. After that, I decided it would be best to move back home and attend Western until I can get my life figured out." The soft laugh that escapes from her is filled with bitterness. "I went from having everything planned out, to it all falling apart."

I nod, knowing exactly what that feels like. It's weird to think Jackie and I have something other than our love for Cole in common. I really wish I could hate this girl. Instead, my heart goes out to her. I know what it's like to fuck up and want to make amends. Even though she doesn't realize it, we're both trying to find our way back from the darkness.

As my mind grapples over our shared situation, I realize she's not just here to find her feet. "You also came back, hoping to work things out with Cole."

"Yes, I did."

I take another guess. "You knew we were seeing each other."

Her bottom lip finds its way between her teeth before she nibbles on it. "I met up with Cole's mother last week for lunch. She's the one who told me that he was involved with someone at school. Although, she wasn't sure if it was serious."

Even though I haven't met Cole's mother yet, her sharing information with his ex-girlfriend about our relationship stings like a slap to the face.

"We are serious," I whisper. Jackie needs to understand that I'm not going to hand him over without a fight.

"I figured that out already." Her gaze sharpens. "I've seen you walking around campus together, and I can tell he really likes you."

He doesn't just like me, he loves me.

The words are on the tip of my tongue, but I keep them buried inside. They aren't for her.

"But you're still going to try and get him back." It's not a question. We both know the answer without her confirming it.

She holds my gaze steadily. There's nothing malicious about her demeanor. "Wouldn't you? Wouldn't you do anything to get him back?"

The word rolls off my tongue before I can think about it. "Yes."

"Look," she says with a sigh, "I don't have anything against you." She takes a step closer until there's no more than a foot that separates us. "For what it's worth, I'm sorry." There's a pause as emotion flickers across her expression. "But I need Cole. I've always needed him. I made a mistake and I hope he'll give me a chance to fix it."

"I won't just let him go," I whisper, my voice quivering.

She gives me a slight smile. "I wouldn't expect you to. What you need to understand is that Cole and I have a lot of history. It might take time, but eventually he's going to forgive me and take me back. We were each other's first loves. You don't just get over that."

Something inside me shrivels. She might be right about that. What makes it worse is that Cole is the first guy I've ever loved. He's the only one I've given myself to that matters. What hurts most is that he might be my first, but I'm not his.

This girl is.

For the first time in a while, it feels as if I can't suck enough oxygen into my lungs. My chest tightens as I fight for breath. Squeezing my eyes shut, I concentrate on drawing the chilly night air into my lungs. When I'm finally able to gather my scattered thoughts, I realize Jackie has disappeared and I'm standing outside alone.

7

CASSIDY

The last thing I want to do is head back inside the party, with all its noise, music, and press of bodies, but I have to find Cole. I need to reassure myself that he's still mine. Jackie might have returned, but she's part of his past.

I have no idea how long I stood outside, talking with Jackie. I also don't know how long it took to get the anxiety attempting to claw at me under control again. When I'd walked away from Cole, I told him I was going to the bathroom and then never returned. As I head inside, I pull my phone from the pocket of my blue scrubs. My heart rate settles as I realize I've missed two calls and three texts from him.

I hit redial and press the phone to my ear. After four rings, it goes straight to voicemail. Given the noise level, that's not a total surprise. I shoot him a quick message to let him know I'm looking for him, and set my ringer on vibrate so I don't miss another call or text.

It takes time to push my way into the crowded living room where we'd been dancing. It feels as if the amount of people smashed inside the house has doubled. My nerves ratchet up as I scan the darkened room. Now that I'm on my own, everyone with their costumes and painted faces has me feeling on edge. I stand on my tiptoes, hoping to see over the mass of writhing bodies, but I'm not tall enough. My breath hitches, and although I'm not claustrophobic, my chest tightens all over again.

I'd be overjoyed to spot Austin or Alex at this point. I need to find one familiar face in this crowd of strangers. Right now, there aren't any. Every second that ticks by has me growing more agitated.

As I'm about turn away, I see a head of dark, artfully mussed hair, and I know it's Cole. Everything in me loosens as I shove my way toward him. He's standing at the bottom of the staircase that leads to the second floor.

Even though I know it's a long shot, I cup my hands around my mouth and shout his name. I'm disappointed but not surprised when he doesn't turn around.

If Jackie thinks she can waltz in here and steal him, she's wrong. I know how much Cole loves me, and it won't take her long to figure it out, either. For the first time since stepping outside with Jackie, I feel as if the pit sitting at the bottom of my belly has dissolved.

Once I'm close enough, I open my mouth to yell his name for a second time.

Wait a minute…what's he doing?

Why is he heading up the staircase?

That's when I realize he isn't alone.

Everything inside me stills as Jackie trails behind him before disappearing up to the second floor. Even after they vanish from sight, I can only stare as all the insecurities Jackie breathed life into a handful of minutes ago flood through me, threatening to suck me under.

And then I do the only thing I can.

I fight for breath.

"Cassidy?"

I flinch when a gentle hand settles on my shoulder before spinning around. Even though I've spent almost a year working on my issues in therapy, it still bothers me to be touched by a stranger, or even be startled by someone I know.

With my hands balled at my sides, I stare into familiar blue-gray depths. His gaze narrows before sliding over me, lingering on my tightened hands.

"Are you okay?"

I shake of my head.

"Too many people?" A crush of costumed students surrounds us, pushing in from all sides.

There's no room to breathe in here.

My fingers rise to claw at my throat.

"I need to get out of here," I gasp.

Before I lose it.

With a nod, his fingers wrap around mine before towing me toward the front door. "Let's get some fresh air. That'll make you feel better."

Luke doesn't wait for an answer.

Standing at six feet with broad shoulders, he's a force to be reckoned with, and easily clears a path for us. He's a defenseman and is used to pushing people around on the ice.

Unlike everyone else who has shown up tonight, Luke isn't wearing a costume. With the flickering lights, loud music, and unrecognizable people, it's a relief to see a familiar face.

As soon as he pulls me through the front door, I suck in a breath, filling my lungs to capacity. The cold night air hits my cheeks, cooling me and calming my racing thoughts. He walks us down the front porch steps to a concrete path that cuts through the front yard until we end up on the sidewalk. Only then does he stop before turning me toward him. His hands settle carefully on my shoulders. I wait for the normal wave of anxiety to crash over me.

It never hits.

Even though I don't know Luke well, what I do understand is that he's safe.

He's already proven that.

He jerks his head to the house. "What happened in there?"

His gaze intensifies. Even in the darkness, his eyes brim with concern. It only makes me feel like a paranoid freak for thinking his motives were nefarious. My mind tumbles back to our conversation at the Union.

And the tentative friendship that has sprung up between us.

But…

He also implied that he wants more than just friendship. I'm not sure I should tell him about Cole disappearing upstairs with his ex-girlfriend. Even thinking about it makes me sick to my stomach.

I draw in another deep breath before gradually releasing it. "I was feeling a little claustrophobic. It's not a big deal. I'm fine now." I lift the corners of my lips into a slight smile. "Really."

His eyes probe mine as if he knows I'm not being truthful with him. "They let way too many people in there. You can barely move."

My muscles relax. Discussing the crowd feels safer than revealing the real reason I had to leave. "Yeah, it's ridiculous."

He clears his throat and shifts his stance. "Where's Cole? I'm surprised he'd leave you alone." His voice drops, becoming lower. "Especially in that crowd."

I hesitate before giving him a partial truth. "I went to the bathroom and when I came back, I couldn't find him."

But I did find him.

I found him climbing the stairs with his ex in tow, and that knowledge is eating away at my insides. Are they still upstairs together?

He pushes his hands into the pockets of his jeans. "Did you try texting him?"

"Yeah."

"And he didn't respond?" Surprise riddles his voice.

It makes me feel as if I need to rush to Cole's defense.

"He texted and called but I didn't hear it. It's so loud inside the house that you can barely hear yourself think."

A thoughtful expression flickers across his face. "If you're feeling up to it, we can head back inside and look for him."

I suck the corner of my lower lip into my mouth before chewing it as questions swim around inside my head.

What if he's still upstairs with Jackie?

What if they're working things out?

Is she telling him how much she still loves him?

Or begging for his forgiveness?

Even though my mind shies away from the idea, I can't help but wonder if they're doing more than that.

No. I can't go back in there right now.

I clear my throat and glance away. "I'm going to head back to the dorms. It's a little too crazy in there for me."

"All right, my truck is parked down the street. I'll give you a ride back. You shouldn't be walking around here alone at night."

I know he's right.

Maybe I should just go inside and find Cole. Even though I know my phone hasn't vibrated, I slide it from my pocket before checking for new messages.

There aren't any.

I stare at the slim device, willing it to ring. What I need most is to hear the sound of his voice. After a handful of seconds tick by, I realize that it won't.

"Okay."

Luke slips his arm around my shoulders as we walk down the sidewalk. A slight shiver works its way through my body at the contact. My proximity to Luke feels different than being close to Cole. I can't help but silently catalogue the subtle contrasts.

With a frown, he glances down at me. "Cold?"

Since I can't tell him the truth, I lie. "A little bit."

The temperature has dropped since we left the dorms earlier tonight. If I'm being honest with myself, that's not the reason for the tremor that slides through me. Luke tugs me closer as we continue walking so that the heat of his body can warm mine. It only takes a few minutes before we reach his truck. He clicks the lock and opens the door for me. I slip inside before settling onto the leather seat as he closes me inside the space. He jogs around the hood before sliding next to me and starting the engine.

"Are you hungry?" His gaze flicks toward mine before returning to the ribbon of road beyond the windshield. "Do you want to grab something to eat before I drop you off?"

All I can think about is Cole disappearing up the stairs with his ex-girlfriend. "I don't think so." Those twenty seconds play on a continuous loop inside my head, and I can't make it stop.

"It seems like something is bothering you. Are you sure you don't want to sit down and talk?" His voice dips, taking on a serious tone. "I'm a good listener."

Surprised he can read me so easily, I glance at him.

His gaze pins me in place before he says, "We both saw Cole head upstairs with that girl."

Air clogs my throat as tears prick my eyes. When he reaches over and lays his hand over mine, all the emotions I'm trying to keep locked deep inside come pouring out in a torrent.

8

———

COLE

*E*xactly how long does it take for two girls to use the bathroom?

It's been at least twenty minutes since Cassidy and Brooklyn took off. During that time, at least a hundred more people have piled their way through the front door of the house. This party was already jam-packed when we arrived.

I'm torn between staying here where she left me or heading toward the bathroom to see if they're caught up in a line. I contemplate my options for a couple of seconds before heading down the hallway. Long blonde hair catches the corner of my eye and my head swivels in that direction before landing on Brooklyn.

Relief rushes through me. She's standing with a tall, buff dude. I recognize him from around campus, but have no idea who he is. It takes a moment to realize that Cassidy isn't with them.

"Brooklyn," I shout.

It's no surprise that she doesn't hear me with the blaring music and insane amount of people. I continue to shove my way toward her before tapping her shoulder and yelling her name.

This time, both her and the guy she's with swivel toward me. The dude stiffens before stepping closer and throwing an arm around her shoulders. It's tempting to roll my eyes at the possessive heat flaring in his narrowed gaze. Normally, I'd find this guy's behavior hilarious, but I'm not in the mood for it. I need to find Cassidy.

Where the hell is she?

How did she get separated from Brooklyn?

"Chill," I mutter. "I'm looking for her friend."

Even though he remains silent, his muscles relax. Although, he still doesn't step back to give us some breathing room.

"I thought Cassidy was with you?"

Her brows pinch together as her red slicked lips settle into a concerned line. "We split up after using the bathroom."

I shake my head. It's obvious this douchebag is the reason for their split.

My knowing look isn't lost on Brooklyn as her lips lift in humor. "The last time I saw her, she was heading back to find you."

Great.

At this point, all I want to do is find her and get the hell out of here. I've had enough of this madness. I want to go home and hit the sheets.

With Cassidy.

Preferably naked.

"How long ago was that?"

Her face scrunches in thought. "Maybe about ten or fifteen minutes ago."

I run a hand through my hair before pulling my cell from my back pocket and calling her. When she doesn't answer, I fire off a couple messages and try again.

There's still no answer.

I glance over the sea of students. She's got to be here somewhere. Even if I have to wade through every damn room in this house, I'm going to find her.

"If you see Cassidy, tell her to call me."

She nods before her attention returns to the dude who is hovering over her as if someone might try to swipe the tasty bone he plans on sinking his teeth into later tonight. For a moment, I feel bad for Austin. Even though he came here tonight with another girl, he's still hung up on Brooklyn. He's been messed up ever since they broke up.

It's not that I don't sympathize, but his freaking mental state is beginning to affect his ability on the ice. The guy needs to pull it together and move on.

Instead of dwelling on those thoughts, I push my way back into the living room. My gaze roves over the crowd, searching every shadowed corner for Cassidy's blue scrubs. The continuous strobe light effect doesn't help matters.

Is it possible she went upstairs?

I have to shove more than one person out of my way to reach the staircase. When I'm on the landing, I turn, surveying the surging mob. The flickering lights make it impossible. I decide there's no harm in checking the second floor.

As much as I love a good party, this is just obnoxious. And I'm over it.

When fingers tug at my hand, relief washes over me and I spin around, reaching out to grab a hold of them. It takes a moment to realize that it's not Cassidy. Instead, I fine the last person I was expecting to see at Western.

Jackie.

I blink. It's tempting to rub my eyes until the apparition in front of me disappears.

Jackie fucking Carlton.

Here in the flesh.

As much as I try to convince myself that it's a simple case of mistaken identity, I know the truth. This girl was my best friend for over a decade. She owned my heart for two years before smashing it to pieces.

I drop her fingers as if they've burned my flesh before retreating a step.

"Hi, Cole," she murmurs.

Even though she says the words softly, I still hear them. It's like the party around us has become muted and she's all I'm aware of.

My jaw clenches until I feel the ticking of the muscle. "What are you doing here?"

She takes a tentative step toward me as her gaze searches mine. "I transferred to Western for the fall semester."

My mind spins.

"I haven't seen you around at all," I grunt.

She shrugs before glancing away. "I'm only part-time. I'm taking two classes one day a week and living at home, so I'm not on campus very much. I'll be moving into a house with Amy and Danica before spring semester starts, and then I'll take a full load."

Which means I'll probably run into her more often. The idea leaves a sick feeling in the pit of my belly. This night just took a massive nosedive.

I clear my throat, only wanting to get away from her. "I hope it all works out for you."

The need to find Cassidy and get the hell out of here feels imperative. I don't want my ex anywhere near her.

The fact that Jackie now attends Western means I'll have to open up and tell Cassidy what happened with my ex. With her living out-of-state, I never worried about running into her. It was so much easier to push her out of my mind and pretend the past didn't exist. That's no longer possible.

"Cole."

My gaze jerks unwillingly to hers.

Her tongue darts out to moisten her lips. "Can we go somewhere and talk?" When I remain silent, her voice turn pleading. "Please? Just for a few minutes?"

No way.

Maybe she feels we have a lot to talk about, but I don't.

I have nothing to say to this girl.

Which is sad. For a long time, she was my best friend, and we spent every waking moment together. Now I can't even stand to be in the same room with her.

"No, sorry, I've got to go. I was looking for someone when I came up here. I need to get back downstairs."

Before I'm able to turn my back on her, she raises her voice. "I met Cassidy."

My heart stutters as I whirl around to face her. Even though I would never hit a girl, I realize my hands are bunched like I might throw a punch. It takes effort to unlock my tense muscles.

When I'm able to keep my voice level, I growl, "Stay the fuck away from Cassidy. What you and I had is over. *You*," I emphasis by jabbing a finger at her, "destroyed everything I felt for you."

Even though there must be people milling around us, I'm not aware of anyone but her. My eyes stay locked on her wide brown ones.

She's the one who threw away our relationship, not me. The longer I hold her gaze, the more I realize that I feel nothing but anger for her. The love that had previously been there is gone.

This is the first time we've seen one another since she called me right before Thanksgiving last year to tell me that she was knocked up. At the time, I wasn't sure which hurt more. The fact she'd thought she loved another dude, or that she'd been screwing him behind my back and ended up pregnant.

She takes another hesitant step toward me. "I introduced myself. That's it." The edges of her lips slide up nervously. "She seems really nice." Her voice dips. "For what it's worth, I'm sorry about what happened between us. I really am."

The last thing I'm interested in is rehashing the past or listening to her lame apologies. The knowledge that my ex took it upon herself to speak with Cassidy makes it even more crucial I locate her.

The idea of them having a private conversation makes me cringe.

"Look, I've really got to go." Now that I know that they spoke, I'd bet my ass that Jackie has something to do with Cassidy's sudden disappearance.

Fuck.

As I try to stalk past, she blocks me. Even though I could easily push past her, I don't. I have no desire to touch her at all. That small irony isn't lost on me. When I was younger, I couldn't keep my hands off her.

"Cole?"

Impatience radiates off me in heavy waves.

Can she feel it?

I'm over this conversation. I need to get away from her and the memories that are eating me alive. What sucks most is that this girl is tied to almost all my childhood memories, not just the ones we spent dating.

I grit my teeth, more aggravated than a few minutes ago. "Yeah?"

She bites down on her lower lip. When we were together, it used to drive me crazy. Now it does nothing for me. Uncertainty fills her dark gaze. I really hate that I still know all her looks and what they mean.

"I get that now isn't a good time, but do you think we could sit down and talk at some point?" She gulps before adding, "Maybe it's not possible to be what we once were to each other, but could we be friends?"

Is this girl joking?

Hell no, we can't be friends.

Her betrayal cut to the bone and killed everything I once felt for her. I didn't just lose a girlfriend, I lost my best friend.

My lips thin as I shake my head.

"Please?" she whispers. "I miss you. We've been friends since we were seven years old. I hate that you're no longer a part of my life. Can you just think about it?" There's a pause. "Please?"

I gape at her as if she's grown a horn on her head. "You forfeited my friendship the moment you decided to screw around behind my back."

As soon as I let those words loose, tears spring to her eyes. "I'm so sorry. Can't you understand that I made a mistake? I'd do anything to go back and fix it."

I snort before taking a step and closing the distance that separates us. "I was faithful to you, and I trusted that you were doing the same because you loved me. Instead, you shit all over our relationship. So no, I can't forgive you for that."

Unable to stomach another word of this conversation, I push past her, stomping my way down the staircase. Memories are roaring through my head like a locomotive. Us as kids playing in the tree house my dad built. Working on homework or playing video games in middle school. We'd hang at each other's houses or go to the movies when we were in high school.

She never missed a hockey game. She was always in the stands cheering me on. I remember the day I realized I wanted her to be my girlfriend, but was too chickenshit to push the words out. I was afraid she didn't feel the same way about me and that it would change our friendship. When I finally worked up the courage to tell her, she beat me to the punch. It all rushes through my head as I shove my way into the living room.

I plow a hand through my hair before sliding my phone from my back pocket only to realize the damn thing is dead.

Fuck!

I have to find Cassidy and I have to find her now.

9

LUKE

"What if they get back together?" she asks. "Cole and I haven't been together for that long. And they have this long history. They didn't just go out, they were friends. Best friends." She worries the napkin between her fingers.

I don't think she realizes that she's shredding the paper into tiny pieces.

"We're talking childhood friends," she adds as if I haven't grasped the gravity of the situation.

Instead of taking her back to the dorms, we're sitting at a diner located a few streets over from campus. Cassidy just described how she was ambushed by Cole Mathews' ex-girlfriend. The very same one who now attends Western. Apparently, they were an item for two years before she screwed around on him and got knocked up.

What a mess.

Unfortunately, Cassidy is caught smack in the middle of all this crazy drama. I'm well aware that she loves him. Hell, she's been more than upfront about her feelings with me. Obviously, this new development is a potential game changer.

It's not out of the realm of possibility that Cole could break up with his new girlfriend and get back together with his ex. They do—as Cassidy pointed out—have a long history.

What sucks is how this situation is affecting Cassidy. I can barely stand all the pain and uncertainty swimming around in her beautiful blue eyes. This is one girl who deserves a man who will worship the very ground she walks on.

Clearly that guy isn't Cole.

I, on the other hand, would treat her like a queen. If she'd give me a chance, I'd be more than happy to prove it to her.

If he's boneheaded enough to take up with his ex, then I'll be right here at Cassidy's side, ready to help her pick up the pieces and move on.

The fact that Cole and I are teammates makes this situation more complicated, but that doesn't matter to me. As far as I'm concerned, there's no bro code involved. I met Cassidy last year and haven't been able to get her out of my mind since that night. She's been like a specter haunting me.

I still can't believe that she's here, attending Western.

What are the fucking odds?

I shake my head.

It's like fate or some bullshit like that.

More proof that we belong together.

It's not like I'm going to break them up. As much as I want her, this is about the long game, and I can be patient. When I realized she was dating Cole, I figured it might take a few months for their relationship to fizzle out. Maybe even a little longer. Imagine my surprise when I caught sight of Cole walking upstairs with that slutty nurse panting after him. And Cassidy watching the entire thing with a heartsick expression on her face.

All I wanted to do was wrap my arms around her and shield her from the hurt that was being inflicted.

Cole doesn't deserve her.

He can have his trashy ex.

You know what I like about Cassidy?

That she didn't use Halloween as an excuse to dress up in a barely-there costume. It's not like I can't appreciate the skimpy costumes some of these chicks wear. Hey, if they want to show off their tits and ass, I'm more than happy to look.

I blink back to our conversation when she falls silent. "What are you going to do?"

Her misery-filled eyes fasten onto mine. It takes every ounce of self-control not to yank her into my arms and soothe away all the hurt pumping through her veins.

Although, I'm smart enough to know that if I make one move toward her, she'll bolt. Cassidy reminds me of a frightened animal that spooks easily. She's someone you have to take your time with. And I'm more than willing to do that. At the end of the day, I know she's well worth the effort.

She chews her lower lip, looking conflicted. "I don't know."

Like I said before—I'm not looking to break them up. That's not the way I want us getting together. Whatever she has with Cole needs to run its course before she'll be able to move on with me.

"Just because she wants to get back together with him doesn't mean he's interested."

Her mouth lifts fractionally as she silently considers my words. Trust me, I'd like nothing better than to tell her to dump his stupid ass, but that's not the way to handle this situation.

"I know. It's just that…" Her words trail off as her eyes drop to the untouched coffee sitting in front of her.

When she doesn't finish her thought, I prompt softly, "It's just *what?*"

Her eyes are luminous as they lift to mine. Sometimes it feels like I could drown in their deep depths. "I wish I could hate her for wanting him, but I can't. I totally get it."

That's not what I was expecting her to say.

I almost snort.

This girl is seriously killing me. She's way too kindhearted.

Again, I want to tug her into my arms and hold her close. "Of course, you can hate her. It would be easy to do." My lips lift into a smile. "She's totally hate-able."

When the edges of her mouth slowly curl into something that almost resembles a smile, my heart actually constricts. "No, I can't. She made a mistake." Her gaze holds mine. "Maybe a lot of them. Just like me. I threw away all my hopes and dreams last year and so did she. When you think about it, we're really not all that different."

The fact that she's even comparing their situations is ridiculous. Cassidy and this girl couldn't be more different. I might not know Cassidy well, but she would never disrespect someone she supposedly loved by cheating on them. That's not the kind of person she is. The mistakes she made were different.

I see that even if she can't.

"You were overwhelmed by the stress and pressure of playing hockey at a Division I college while taking a rigorous course load. That girl decided to fuck around on her boyfriend of two years because she was bored and fell," I use air quotes to drive home the point, "*in love* with some other dude. That's hardly the same thing. Don't even put yourself in her category."

The fact that she's doing it actually pisses me off.

I wish she could see herself the way everyone around her does. Cassidy might have stumbled last year, but her core is still the same.

When she jerks her shoulders, I realize that she doesn't believe me.

Unable to help myself, I reach out and tentatively cover her fingers with mine as her wide gaze flies to mine. I'm aware of how Cassidy feels about being touched and I understand the reason behind it. After all, I was there the night she was almost raped by those three douche bags. I would have fucking killed each one of them with my bare hands, but it was more important to get her out of the situation than beat the shit out of them.

That's not to say I didn't give each one what they deserved at a later date. You bet your damn ass I did. I didn't want any of them getting away with what they had been intent on doing. After a week or so, it became obvious that Cassidy never filed a police report since nothing happened to those little pricks.

So, I mete out my own brand of justice, and you know what?

It felt pretty damn good bloodying my knuckles against their faces.

"Cassidy," I say quietly, "you and this girl have absolutely nothing in common, and you don't have to hate her or feel bad for her, either. She made her own choices. I think you and Cole need to talk about the fact that his ex-girlfriend is here, and figure out what it means. Which honestly, could be nothing."

With her smaller hand still ensconced in mine, she smiles softly, looking almost relieved by my comments. "You're right, I'm probably overreacting. Just because they had a conversation tonight doesn't mean they're getting back together."

Nodding, I add, "You need to talk with Cole and get things figured out instead of jumping to conclusions. Okay?" That's the best advice I can give her. In the end, I want what's best for her. I just don't think Cole Mathews is what's best for her. But she needs to arrive at that conclusion on her own.

"Yeah." When she gives me another tentative smile, something in my gut clenches. "Thank you, Luke. I really appreciate you taking the time to talk to me about this." She stares down at her untouched cup of coffee for a long moment before quietly admitting, "There aren't many people I can confide in." Her eyes lift, skewering mine with heartfelt intensity. "I'm really glad we've become friends."

Fuck.

She wouldn't be saying that if she knew how much I want her. But until she and Mathews are completely over, friends are all we'll ever be. As much as it sucks—as much as I want more—I'll be that strong shoulder she can lean on.

And when she's finally ready, I'll be more.

I'll be her everything.

10

CASSIDY

I'm about to climb into bed when there's a knock on my dorm room door.

I nearly jump out of my skin before a deep voice says from the other side, "Cassidy? Are you in there?"

That's all it takes for me to fly to the door and yank it open. "Cole!"

Before he can open his mouth, I hurtle myself into his outstretched arms. After everything that happened tonight at the party, I just want to burrow against his chest and stay there forever. I don't want him to ever let me go. We hold each other for a handful of silent moments before he pulls away just enough to search my eyes in the darkness.

"What happened to you? Where did you disappear to?" He barely sucks in a breath before rapid-firing another question at me. "Do you have any idea how worried I was when I couldn't find you?" The relief of moments ago gives way to anger. It brims in his whiskey-colored eyes. "I looked everywhere. And Brooklyn didn't know what happened to you, either."

He holds me at arm's length as his gaze slides down the length of me as if checking to make sure I'm still in one piece before backing me up into the room and slamming the door shut behind him. Only then does he pull me back into his embrace. I can't help but sink into his warmth.

"Cassidy?" This time, when he murmurs my name, he does it quietly. The sharpest part of his anger already receding. "I was worried when I couldn't find you." He squeezes me to him before adding, "I called but you didn't pick up."

"I didn't hear it," I murmur. "I tried calling back after I saw the messages. You didn't answer."

He pulls away just enough to lean his forehead against mine. "My phone sucks. It died on me."

I let out a shaky little laugh. "Your phone does suck."

"I scoured the party tried to find you."

"There were way too many people." My gaze stays locked on his. "I looked for you, too." I bite down on my lower lip, unsure if I want to add that I saw him walking up the staircase with his ex. There's a part of me that just wants to enjoy this quiet moment with him.

Cole angles his face until his lips can sweep across mine. He continues to brush them over mine until my breath hitches with expectation and longing.

"Did I mention how worried I was when I couldn't find you?" he whispers against my mouth until I'm breathless with need.

"It's been noted."

Bringing up Jackie now seems so stupid. Especially since he's here with me. If Cole wanted to be with her, that's exactly where he'd be. The last thing I want is for him to think I don't trust him, because I do.

I trust him with all my heart.

In this moment, with his lips coasting over mine, his ex doesn't mean a damn thing. She might want him, but that doesn't mean he has any interest in her. Honestly, now that I'm wrapped up in his arms, I feel foolish for thinking she could come between us.

He breaks our kiss and pulls away just enough for his gaze to skim down my body. "Lost the scrubs, huh? That's a bummer."

Rising on the tips of my toes, I suck his lower lip into my mouth before biting down on the plump flesh. "I'm game to give you a physical if that's what you want, Mr. Mathews."

A sexy smile curves across his face before his voice dips. "I was so hoping you were going to say that."

Without another word, I pull the T-shirt and hockey jersey over his head. Somewhere along the way, he lost his shoulder pads. Just like always, my breath hitches at the sight of him standing before me in nothing more than a pair of low-slung jeans. No matter how many times I catch sight of him, his chiseled musculature always sends a punch of arousal straight to my core.

Unable to resist the temptation, my hands glide over the broad set of his shoulders before drifting to the rippling muscles of his biceps. My knees weaken as I continue stroking my fingers over his cut body. Stepping closer, I press my mouth against the firm solidness of his chest before slowly licking my way down the sinewy muscles of his six-pack.

He tenses when I nip at him with sharp teeth. Maybe I get carried away, biting down a little too hard. When I pull away, there's the barest hint of indentations marring his taut flesh. The low groan that leaves his lips sends a hot wave of need straight through me.

The tips of my fingers drift over the ink that brands his skin. It begins on the right side of his ribcage before wrapping around his back. The shield is divided into four sections of red and black color. A large golden lion stands on its hind legs in the middle. On top of the shield sits a golden crown. The detail is gorgeous and intricate.

What I've learned is that Cole's father's family is Scottish, and this is the Mathews family coat of arms. Under the shield is his dad's name, written in beautiful script, along with the dates of his birth and death. He inked it onto his skin when he turned eighteen in memory of his father who was killed a decade ago by a drunk driver.

"I love the way you touch me," he growls.

"Not half as much as I love touching you," I whisper against his warm flesh. I could do this all night long and never grow tired of it.

His hands wrap around my ribcage, the thumbs brushing the undersides of my breasts through the thin fabric of my tank top.

Another ripple of pleasure shoots through me as his fingers drift to the frayed hem before slipping the tank top over my head.

A heartbeat later and I'm just as bare-chested as he is.

Not so long ago, it would have embarrassed me to stand in front of him like this, especially since I can feel the heat of his gaze licking over my upper body. Now, however, I love it. I love the worshipful way his eyes eat me up. The thrill of his attention has my nipples tightening. A sexy growl escapes from deep in his throat as his hands rise to gently cup the fullness of my breast before stroking the pebbled tips.

"Do you like that?" His voice is low and gravelly as his attention stays locked on the movements of his fingers.

When I don't immediately respond, he tweaks each puckered bud.

My breath catches. Who would have ever thought pleasure could ignite from a bit of pain?

"Hmmm?" His hot gaze arrows to mine, skewering me in place.

When he pinches them again, more pleasure floods through me before settling in my core as I gasp. "Yes!"

"Good, because I love touching you." He palms a breast in each hand, lifting the softness before leaning down to sooth each tip with his tongue and lips until I'm squirming.

Just when I don't think I can bear another moment, he pulls away, and the cool air of the room wafts over my damp flesh. His hands sweep down my sides to the curve of my ass before lifting me until I can wrap my legs around his waist. My arms tangle around his neck, tugging his face to mine.

Flexing my hips, I rub my core against the taut muscles of his abdomen, wanting only to relieve some of the intensity building and swirling within me. Cole is the first guy who showed me what desire and passion could be like. The way he sets my flesh to flames is something I never dreamed existed before.

I have no idea how I'll ever get enough of him.

Each frantic buck of my hips has him hissing out a breath as he quickly crosses the room and lays me out on the twin bed. Before I can blink, he's following me down, covering my body with his muscular one. There's nothing I love more than the feel of his heavy weight settling on top of me, pressing me into the mattress. Or his thick erection nestled against my aching center.

It never fails to steal my breath away.

As his lips crash onto mine, his tongue slips inside my mouth to mingle and dance with my own. The way he kisses drives me insane. There's a mindlessness that sweeps through me as pleasure floods every cell of my being. Just as I sink into the caress, his mouth disappears. It swoops lower, trailing across my chin and then the column of my throat before licking a hot path to one breast.

He pulls back enough to mumble, "You have no idea how damn sexy you are. I just want to fuck you until I'm all you can think about. Until I'm your everything."

My gaze locks on his as the possessiveness of his words wash over me.

My lips lift as I whisper, "You *are* my everything. The way you touch me...no one else could ever make me feel the way you do."

He thrusts his hips against my core, making even more moisture flood my panties. "No one will ever make you feel the way I do." His cock strains against the V between my thighs. Hot bolts of pleasure shoot through my body as he pushes against me. "Say it. Tell me that I'm the only one you want."

"You are, Cole. I don't want to make love with anyone but you."

His hand slips between us until his fingers can slide beneath my panties and shorts. "No one but me gets to touch this."

My eyelids feather closed as I arch into his warm palm, wanting to feel his fingers slide inside me. I need him to relieve the throbbing pressure building deep within me. When he doesn't make a move, I arch, pushing against him.

"Say it, Cassidy."

"Only you," I whimper. "You're the only one who gets to fuck me."

As soon as the words escape, he slides two thick digits inside, stroking my wet heat until I'm mindless with the need he has stoked to life within me.

He swirls his finger across my slit before murmuring, "Your pussy belongs to me."

"Yes," I moan. At this point, I would agree to just about anything, and he knows it. My hips gyrate against him, seeking release.

His fingers still as he leans down and presses a kiss against my mouth. "Oh no, you don't. Not like this. When you come, I want to feel you pulsing and throbbing around me."

I groan when he drags his fingers from me.

A devilish smile spreads across his handsome face, making him look even sexier.

I love him so much.

That thought cartwheels through my mind as my gaze stays locked on his.

"I love you," I whisper, wanting him to know what's in my heart.

He stills, poised above me as emotion fills his eyes. The heated sexiness turns into something softer.

My heart expands until the fullness of it becomes almost too much to bear within the confines of my flesh.

"I love you, too. So much. So fucking much. I would do anything for you." There's a pause as the world shrinks down until it encompasses just the two of us. "You know that, right?"

Emotion wells in my throat as I jerk my head into a nod. I never thought it was possible to fall in love with someone the way I have with Cole. He was a total surprise who slammed unwantedly into my life.

He presses his lips against mine and takes us to a place where only the two of us exist.

"I think there are too many pieces of clothing separating us," I whisper.

"That's funny, because I was just thinking the very same thing."

Before I can remove my sleeping shorts and panties, Cole's lips are at my navel, licking a fiery path downward. He lowers both the panties and shorts one inch at a time. With every strip of flesh that is bared, he traces little circles across me until he's kneeling between my thighs. I widen my legs as his tongue dances over my slit, wanting to feel his mouth devouring me. The more I attempt to spread my legs, the more hampered I become by the fabric of my clothing as it stretches across my pulsing core.

"Take them off," I plead. "Please take them off." I want all the clothing standing in our way to disappear. I need to feel every ripped muscle pressed against me. I want him rocking into me, thrusting so deep inside my body that I can't think.

Only feel.

My mind empties as he slides his tongue over me. Another groan tumbles from my lips as I arch into his mouth. His tongue stabs deep inside me as his fingers find and stroke my clit. My body tightens as hot licks of pleasure swirl through me. A gasp escapes when both his fingers and his mouth disappear from my aching flesh.

I blink as his body lifts from the bed before I feel the shorts and panties being dragged from my body. He makes quick work of stripping off his jeans until they're crumpled in a pile with the rest of our clothing.

My gaze drops to his erection. It's long and thick as it juts out from the dark nest of springy curls. A tiny little thrill shoots through me at the sight of him.

He's so beautiful.

How could I ever get tired of being with him like this?

For just a heartbeat, he pauses, looming over the bed and staring down at me. "Spread your legs for me," he whispers thickly, attention glued to the apex of my thighs. "I want to see every pink inch."

Heat floods into my cheeks.

Even though I'm not a hundred percent comfortable with my body, I want to please him and give him exactly what he's asking for. The way he looks at me—almost as if he's worshipping me with his eyes—isn't something I'll ever get used to.

I love the way he makes me feel.

Slowly, I allow my thighs to fall open. Inhaling a shaky breath, I feel completely vulnerable. And yet, oddly powerful. For a long moment, he doesn't move a muscle. He's barely breathing as his gaze wanders over the part of me that only he's allowed to see.

To have.

"You're so fucking gorgeous." His possessive gaze rises to mine. "You know that, don't you?"

My lips lift just a faction as he stalks to the bed. The thin mattress dips as he kneels between my outstretched legs. I can't help but arch into his caress as his hot breath drifts over my delicate skin, igniting a fire within me. He continues to tease, never quite giving me what I need.

Argh.

I just want to feel his lips on my slick heat as his tongue thrusts deep inside me.

His fingers stroke over every part of me. With every unhurried pass, his thumbs move closer to my center until they're grazing the outer edges of my plump lips. The sensation he creates deep within my core makes me want to scream. It's tempting to claw at his shoulders until he's driving forcefully into me, releasing the tightly coiled tension he's created.

I want to come.

Right now.

I don't care if it's with his mouth or thick fingers pumping into me.

All this touching has become unbearable.

His golden gaze slices knowingly to mine. "I could play with you all night long."

"No," I whimper. I almost hate myself for the whine that threads its way through my husky voice. I'm not a whiner. But this is sweet torture. It drives me crazy. And has me doing and saying things I normally wouldn't.

I love it.

Love that he's able to tease this out of me.

On the next swipe, his fingers stretch even further until they're able to massage my heated flesh, smoothing the slickness over me. My back bows as his fingers dip inside my body.

"So wet," he growls before lowering his face and sliding his tongue across me. He laps at the cream with long strokes. "You taste so fucking good. I need to be inside you right now."

"Yes," I whimper.

There is nothing better than the feel of his thick, blunt cock sliding inside me, filling me to the brim.

He rips open a package before sheathing himself with a condom, and then he's exactly where I need him most. He looms above me as his muscular arms bracket me and his rock-hard abs press against the softness of my belly. For just a heartbeat, his thick erection remains poised at my entrance.

I sigh as he fills me in one smooth stroke before rocking against me. It doesn't take long before our bodies are moving in complete harmony. I can't imagine sharing this kind of intimacy with anyone other than Cole.

It doesn't take more than a few strokes. We're both so turned on, ready to burst with the frenetic energy we always seem to generate. His pace quickens just as the first wave of an orgasm pummels my senses. Not wanting to scream, my teeth sink into the sinewy muscle of his shoulder. As soon as I do, he grunts, his own release streaking through his powerful body.

"I love you, Cassidy," he rumbles before emptying himself inside me.

"I love you, too," I whisper. "So much."

11

CASSIDY

Once we've both spent ourselves, all that can be heard in my darkened room is the sound of our ragged breathing. He lowers his face to the delicate hollow of my neck so that his warm breath can feather across my skin. His heart pounds, racing against mine.

I press a tender kiss against the side of his face before he rolls away and grabs a Kleenex off the table beside my bed. He slides the condom off his softening length, wrapping it up, and disposing of it in the trash can by my desk. And then he's back, settling against me on the twin bed. His bigger body takes up most of the space as I drape myself across him, sifting my fingers through the dark sprinkle of hair smattered across his chest.

Have I felt this kind of contentment?

It's not a question that needs answering.

His fingers comb rhythmically through my hair.

After a handful of quiet moment, he says, "I was really worried when I couldn't find you. I hate that you left the party without me. Something could have happened to you." His fingers still. "Don't do that again, okay?"

I nip my lower lip as everything from earlier comes crashing back at me.

Jackie.

Her telling me that she wants him back.

Watching her follow Cole up the stairs.

And then leaving the party with Luke.

I draw in a deep breath and wonder what to say. I don't want to lie to Cole. I promised myself that I wouldn't keep any more secrets from him, but I also realize he won't like what I have to tell him.

"Cassidy, babe, did you hear me? It's too dangerous for you to walk home alone from a party."

I squeeze my eyes tightly shut and force out the truth before I lose my nerve. Everything feels so perfect between us. I don't want to ruin that.

"I didn't walk home alone," I murmur.

"You left with someone from the dorm?" His fingers resume their movements, but it's not enough to settle the nerves that are now dancing across my flesh.

"No." Crap. "Umm, Luke was at the party, and I ended up catching a ride home with him."

When Cole's muscles tense, nerves explode in the pit of my belly. "You went home with Luke?"

I pull myself up until our gazes lock. I need to see every emotion as it sweeps across his face in the moonlight that filters in through the large window. "Only because I couldn't find you."

But that's not altogether true. Seeing him head upstairs with his ex-girlfriend in tow had my chest tightening and left me fighting for breath. Suddenly, I'd felt claustrophobic with the press of all those bodies closing in on me. Even conjuring up the memory is enough to have my skin prickling with unease.

"Did he drive you straight back here?" His voice is whipcord tight as he fights to stay calm. After seeing Luke and me at the Union a few days ago, he doesn't want us spending time together.

I hate that my answer will only cause more problems between us.

"We stopped for coffee."

"You couldn't find me, so Luke swooped in and took you out?" There's a razor-sharp edge to his voice. One that cuts because I didn't do anything wrong. After the way we shared our bodies with one another, can't he understand that he has nothing to worry about where Luke is concerned?

Cole is the one I love.

The only one I want to be with.

Luke is nothing more than a friend. I can't help but wonder if I'm the one who has something to be concerned about. Cole hasn't bothered to mention that his ex is here at Western. Or that she was at the party tonight.

Why is he keeping it from me?

All of the good vibes from moments ago dissipate as I sit up and gather the sheet around my naked body. How is it possible that all the love and trust we've managed to forge between us have disintegrated in the blink of an eye?

My voice stays level as I attempt to explain. "I was feeling claustrophobic with the amount of people there, and he recognized that and was only trying to help. That's it."

Needing space to breathe, I pull the sheet with me as I leave the bed and collect my small pile of clothing. Even though he hasn't come right out and accused me of anything, that's the way it feels.

"Cassidy, come back here."

Just as his strong fingers wrap around my upper arm, I jerk out of his grasp.

"Don't!" Without thinking, I snap the word out before spinning away. I don't like being grabbed. Even though I know Cole would never hurt me, it still makes my heart leap and my chest tighten.

His face falls as he stares at me from the bed. I yank the tank top over my head before stepping into my shorts and sliding them over my hips.

"I'm sorry." His tone is low, almost pleading. "Please, don't get upset. It just feels like he's waiting for me to fuck up."

"It's not like that," I say. Irritation fills me.

With my back to him, I grab a rubber band before gathering up my hair in a ponytail. I need a moment to calm everything raging within me. As I squeeze my eyes closed, I take another deep breath and try to settle the chaos in my head.

There are times when it feels as if everything will be okay. When the days slip by with no incidents, and I pray I've experienced my last anxiety attack.

But then something will happen and the feeling of being out of control yanks the rug out from beneath my feet. It brings everything —all the steady progress I've been fighting for— crashing down around my head.

It makes me wonder if I'll ever be *me* again.

The me who didn't suffer from anxiety attacks.

The me who wasn't bothered by being grabbed or touched.

The me who didn't care about huge crowds.

I want to be me again…the normal one.

Sometimes it feels like that girl died an ugly death last year for being young, stupid, and making mistakes. Drinking and getting herself into a bad situation…one she almost didn't come out of unscathed.

Except I didn't escape unscathed, I remind myself. But it would have been so much worse if Luke hadn't stepped in and gotten me out of there when he did.

This me, the one that emerged from the wreckage, is more tentative. Scared. Nervous. Reserved.

Sometimes, I don't think I'll ever be whole again.

It makes me want to curl up in a tight little ball and cry for all that's been lost. All I want is to feel normal again.

Lost in the jumbled thoughts that crash around inside my head, I startle when Cole's arms gently band around me.

He presses a kiss against my shoulder before whispering, "I'm sorry. I didn't mean to upset you." He drops another soft caress against my skin. "You know I'd never hurt you."

I draw in a deep breath and do a quick self-check. No tightening in my chest. No fighting for breath. I'm okay. Everything is okay.

"You didn't," I lie, because more than anything, I want that to be the truth.

His lips settle at the delicate hollow of my neck. "I did and I'm sorry."

If I'm going to do this, it needs to be now before I lose my nerve.

"I saw you with Jackie tonight on the stairs."

When his muscles stiffen, I turn in his arms so I can read the expression in his golden-brown eyes.

An expression I'm unable to read flickers across his face. "Oh."

As I search his eyes, his are doing the same, carefully sifting through mine for answers to questions he has yet to ask. I realize with a sinking heart that we're both keeping secrets.

"She introduced herself when I was coming back from the bathroom."

He glances away before shoving his fingers through his messy hair. The urge to tug all those thick, chocolaty-colored strands into place bubbles up inside me. Instead, I keep my hands to myself.

"Did you two speak for long?" he asks tightly.

"Ten minutes or so." But it was more than enough.

"What did she say?" A muscle tics in his jaw as anger brims in his eyes.

"She said you two had grown up together and were close friends before you started going out in high school." There's a beat of silence before I add, "And that you two were serious. *Really serious.*"

"Yes," he whispers hoarsely as if hearing those words is actually painful. "Did she tell you how it ended?"

I bite down on my lower lip. "She cheated on you and...ended up pregnant."

Cole's eyes become shuttered. It's the strangest thing to watch someone who has always been so open and unguarded become devoid of expression.

"There's nothing between us, Cassidy. I haven't seen her since before we broke up. She means nothing to me."

My hand rises to stroke over his cheek. "She wants you back. Did she tell you that?"

He shakes his head as his hand rises to still my fingers so that I'm able to cup the side of his face. "No."

"She understands that she lost the best thing in her life and now wants it back. She wants *you* back." I shake my head. "I can't really blame her for that."

"Cassidy," the closed off expression dissolves before being replaced by a fierceness I've never seen before, "I love you. *Only you.* She's not going to come between us." He tugs me into his arms until we're able to hold onto one another for dear life before whispering against my hair, "And I won't let Luke come between us, either."

12

CASSIDY

I gulp down a fresh burst of nerves. "Is it too late to cancel?"

Cole squeezes my hand as his gaze darts to mine in the close confines of his Mustang.

His eyes fill with humor. "You don't have anything to worry about. They're going to love you." He gives me another squeeze as if that alone is enough to reassure me.

It's not.

"I promise," he adds.

I nibble my lower lip before blurting, "And what if they don't?"

At the moment, all I can imagine is his mom and stepdad hating me. Jackie's admittance about having lunch with Cole's mother snakes its way through my head before nesting in a place that makes it is impossible to evict it from. She's probably hoping her son will get back together with his high school girlfriend.

Are Jackie and his mother still close?

The question gnaws away at me.

Unaware of the dark thoughts swirling through my head, Cole says, "Then I'll probably end up dumping you."

My wide gaze swings to his. A smile simmers across his face and it takes a moment to realize he's joking. "That sounds about right," I mutter.

His voice drops. "You know I'm kidding, right?"

He shakes his head as if I'm making a big deal out of nothing. Here's the thing—I've never met a guy's parents before. This is a new and scary situation. Add in an ex-girlfriend who his family probably adored, and disaster feels imminent.

One of my dark brows lift. "Are you?" A drop of acid seeps into my tone. I hate that all my insecurities have a massive case of bitchiness flaring up within me.

"Of course, I am. I like you way too much to cut you loose at this point." His twinkling gaze flickers to mine before he winks. "You're mine, Cassidy Jameson. And I won't be letting you go anytime soon."

He flashes his dimples, knowing that they'll melt my heart and soften my disposition.

"You're only saying that because you're addicted to the sex," I say with a smirk.

"Hell yeah," he cuts into the whirl of my thoughts with a low rumble. "It's damn good sex. Totally hot."

I can't resist punching him in the bicep. Although, not very hard because he's right. Sex with Cole is scorching hot. If given the choice, I'd much rather be in bed with him than meeting his parents for the first time.

"Hey, I'm driving over here." He drags my hand back onto his lap where he holds it securely. "Everything will be fine. My mom has been dying to meet you for weeks now. And if I don't bring you home soon, she'll randomly pop over on a weekend morning." He arches a brow before glancing at me. "Does that really sound like a good idea to you?"

Since I've been spending most of the weekends crashing at Cole's place, it sounds like a terrible idea.

"No," I mutter. "I guess this is a better alternative." But that doesn't make me any less nervous. Even if Cole doesn't realize it, Jackie feels like a specter sitting between us.

Unaware of my thoughts, he brings my hand to his lips before brushing a soft kiss against my knuckles. "Definitely better. Plus, Mom's a great cook. No matter how the afternoon turns out, at least you'll get an awesome home-cooked meal out of it."

That doesn't necessarily make me feel better. "Super comforting. Thanks for that."

"I'm just teasing. You'll see, everything will be fine."

Unfortunately, my brain is spinning with all the ways this afternoon could go up in a burst of flames. There are so many ways…

"Maybe we need to have a code word in case I want to leave early."

A grin slides across his face. "Seriously? A code word? What are we, like twelve?" He shakes his head as if I'm crazy.

The more I turn the idea over in my head, the more I like it. It makes me feel less anxious to know that if I need an out, I have one. Kind of like an escape hatch.

"How about…Guggenheim."

He busts out laughing. "*Guggenheim*? Really?"

I slip my fingers from his to twist nervously in my lap. "It can't be something common, otherwise it could get confusing." I give him a look that says—*duh*.

"Right," he drawls. "*That's* the problem with Guggenheim. Don't you think you're overreacting just a bit?"

I scrunch my face. "No, not at all."

Before I can argue further, he holds up his hand. "You know what, Guggenheim it is."

Surprised that he's capitulating so easily, I smile. "Really?"

"Yup." He stretches out the word so that it sounds more like *yuuuuup*. "The last thing I want is for us to have a fight right before we arrive at my parents' house. If the afternoon takes a turn for the worst, all you have to do is find a way to work *Guggenheim* into the conversation. For example, you could say—Cole just made my Guggenheim feel super good. Or—would either of you like to see my Guggenheim? It's freaking gorgeous."

Even though he doesn't glance in my direction as he utters those ridiculous sentences, the edges of his mouth twitch in amusement. "Okay? Does that work for you?"

My eyes narrow until they're practically slits. "I have two questions for you. One, are you really making fun of me at a time like this?" The closer we get to his parents' house, the more jacked up my nerves become. "And two," I tilt my head before asking rather seriously, "you think my Guggenheim is gorgeous?"

He bursts out laughing before his gaze locks briefly on mine. It doesn't take long for the chuckles to die away as those golden-colored depths heat up. "*Fucking gorgeous*. Best Guggenheim I've ever seen."

The edges of my lips lift just a bit.

Well, alright then…

"And later on, I'm going to show you just how much I love your Guggenheim."

Before I can say anything more, he zips the car into a driveway.

"We're here."

I sit frozen in place, studying the house Cole grew up in. It isn't all that different from my own childhood home. A large, brick two-story with huge white pillars in front. It's a bit fancier, with maybe more square footage, but aside from that, the architectural style is very similar.

For a moment, I can almost see Cole as a nine- or ten-year-old boy, winding up and taking slap shots in the driveway. The image brings a hint of a smile to my lips. I bet he was adorable, with his mop of unruly dark hair and golden-brown eyes.

I'm so lost in thought, that it's a surprise when the passenger side door opens and Cole offers his hand for me to take a hold of.

"You'll see, it'll be fine." He smiles and his dimples flash. Even though I'm nervous, my heart squeezes at the sight of them. God, I love his dimples.

Oh, who am I kidding?

I'm completely head over heels in love with the guy.

Dimples or no dimples.

It's why I agreed to this. I want to know more about Cole and his family. Meeting them re-solidifies that we're taking our relationship to the next level.

With a quick intake of air, I place my hand in his as he helps me out of the Mustang. Unwilling to show up at his parents' house empty-handed, I grab a hold of the small bouquet of wildflowers we picked up at a grocery store on the way over.

Nerves buzz across my skin as I stand behind Cole on the front porch.

He throws open the door and calls out, "Hello?"

A second or two pass as the house remains silent. Stupid as it sounds, I send up a quick prayer that maybe his parents forgot about us getting together this afternoon and aren't around. Just as my hopes begin to rise, they burst into a ball of flames when we hear footsteps trudging up the basement steps.

"Cole?" It's a man's voice. "Is that you?"

"Yup, we just got here," he hollers back as we wait in the foyer.

My gaze darts around the entryway and the living room, which is to the right of us. All the furnishings are elegant and polished to a high shine. There's a warm, inviting quality that makes it feel like home.

Like outside, I can picture Cole kicking up his feet and watching TV on the couch or making out with his ex-girlfriend...

I shift my attention away from the room as an older man who looks to be about fifty or so, walks into the foyer. A heartfelt smile curves his lips upward, and it instantly eases my frazzled nerves as he stretches out a hand for me to shake.

"Hi, you must be Cassidy. It's nice to meet you. I'm Thomas. We're so pleased you were able to join us for dinner."

He pumps my hand so enthusiastically that I'm unable to stop the small smile from creeping its way across my face. A moment later, he turns to Cole and claps him warmly on the back.

Cole's gaze darts around before settling on his stepfather. "Where's Mom?" His brows draw together. "Is she here?"

Thomas runs a hand through his thinning gray hair. "She was called into work about thirty minutes ago. But you know your mother, she had everything prepared ahead of time or we'd be ordering a pizza. Everything is in the oven and should be ready in an hour or so. I would imagine that she'll be back by then as well." He waves us into the living room. "Come and sit down. Can I get either of you something to drink?"

Cole takes the flowers from my hand. "Sit down, Thomas. I'll put these in a vase and grab a couple of waters."

His stepdad smiles after him as Cole walks away. Once he's certain that Cole is in the kitchen, rifling around in the refrigerator, Thomas leans toward me with a mischievous grin as if we've been friends for years. Oddly enough, that's exactly the way it feels.

"Did you two come up with a signal if this dinner looks like it's heading south?"

My eyes widen as my mouth tumbles open. "Um, no." Heat gathers in my cheeks until it feels like I'll self-combust.

How could he have possibly guessed that?

No…seriously.

"Guggenheim," Cole yells from the kitchen.

I bury my face in my hands, embarrassed that he just outed me within five minutes of meeting his stepdad.

As soon as we leave, I'm going to kill him.

Thomas chuckles as Cole returns to the living room with a wide grin curving his lips and his dimples popping. It's probably the only thing that saves him from being a crime scene victim later this evening.

I give him the evil eye and mutter, "I hope you enjoy the dinner your mom made, because it's going to be your last."

His chest rumbles with barely suppressed laughter as he offers me a bottle of water. When I yank it from him, he leans over and brushes a soft kiss against my lips.

I feel the curve of his mouth pressed against mine as he whispers, "Don't be mad, I'll make it up to you later."

The guy has the audacity to wink at me.

In front of his stepdad.

Could I be more embarrassed?

Nope. Don't think so.

"You won't be able to make anything up to me later because you'll be dead," I grumble, attempting to shove him away from me.

My death glare has zero effect on Cole, because he practically plunks himself down on top of me before grabbing my hand and dragging it onto his lap as if for safekeeping.

His stepdad beams as he watches our interaction.

It takes about twenty minutes or so for me to loosen up and enjoy myself. No one is more surprised than me when the next hour flies by with lots of amusing stories about Cole growing up. It's nice to see Cole with his stepdad. You can tell by their effortless banter how much they enjoy each other's company.

Then again, Cole is so easy to get along with. He has such a chill, laid back personality. On top of that, he's a nice guy. In my limited experience, there aren't too many of those floating around.

As Cole and Thomas discuss the upcoming hockey season, I can't help but take in everything about him. From his disheveled hair and gorgeous golden-brown eyes to his lopsided smile and broad shoulders that are chiseled perfection. His chest is droolworthy, and those rock-hard abs are totally dreamy.

I should probably stop with the mental inventory because I'm kind of getting turned on, and that's not good for business.

His ex may want him back, but she isn't going to get him. She might have been foolish enough to break his heart, but I won't be making the same mistake. I understand what I have in Cole, and I plan on holding onto him with both hands.

When dinner is ready, Thomas hands us the dishes along with four sets of silverware so we can set the dining room table. We're all just settling in, passing the food around, when the front door opens before getting slammed shut. The easy camaraderie of moments ago disappears.

"Hello," a woman calls out cheerfully from the foyer.

Everything has been going so well with Thomas, I'm almost afraid to meet his mother. She's the one I need to impress, right?

Aren't mothers supposed to be overprotective and overbearing when it comes to their sons?

Especially since this is her only son.

And let's not forget that she was just out to lunch with Cole's ex whom she probably adored.

Fresh nerves ignite within me as all the food I heaped onto my plate loses its appeal.

"We're in the dining room, just sitting down to dinner. You'll be delighted to know that I haven't run Cassidy off just yet." Thomas smiles before winking at me from the far end of the table.

I give him a weak smile in return.

"Wonderful!"

As she steps into the formally appointed room, she pauses, almost as if she's in the midst of catching her breath. The friendly smile gracing her lips freezes in place as her gaze collides with mine.

Oh shit.

Shit, shit, shit.

That's the only thought racing through my head as my attention stays locked on hers. Everything in the room grinds to a screeching halt. In that moment, it feels as if a trapdoor springs open beneath my feet and I'm in a free fall. I clench the edges of the table with my fingers as I gape at her.

This can't be happening.

There's a flurry of activity as Thomas rises to his feet and places a kiss against his wife's cheek. Cole also gets up, greeting his mother with a warm hug. Instead of doing the same, I remain seated. It feels as if my feet are cemented to the floor. Unsure of what to do, I blink as Cole drags his mother over to where I'm still sitting. My legs shake as I force myself to rise. Any moment, my knees will give out and I'll fall to the wood floor.

This has turned into a nightmare.

Except, in the far recesses of my brain, I know it's real.

Unaware of the suffocating undercurrents that have sucked all of the oxygen from the room, Cole introduces us. "Mom, this is Cassidy." Even when he flashes the lopsided smile I love so much, my heart remains frozen. "Cassidy, this is my mother, Allison."

Dr. Thompson's lips curve before she thrusts out her hand. "Hello,

Cassidy. It's so wonderful to finally meet you. I'm glad you were able to join us for dinner."

Holding my gaze expectantly, she waits for me to respond.

But I can't. I'm too stunned.

After a few silent seconds tick by, I release the breath clogged in my throat and force myself to reach for her hand. My voice sounds like it is traveling through a tunnel, as if there is nothing odd about the farce playing out. "Thank you for having me, it's great to meet you, too."

My mind continues to whirl, and I can't make it stop.

After introductions are made, we all sit down. Thomas peppers his wife with a few questions about the emergency that called her away on a Sunday afternoon. Cole keeps glancing at me with concern, but I pretend not to notice as I pick at the baked chicken and roasted vegetables on my plate.

Unconsciously, my gaze flickers to Dr. Thompson. Every so often, our eyes catch before I quickly lower mine to the plate. My belly pitches and roils with nausea, making me feel sick.

Now that Cole and his mother are sitting next to one another, I'm able to see the resemblance between them. Although, it's certainly not enough for me to suspect they are mother and son. Where Cole has artfully messy, dark brown hair and golden-brown eyes, his mother has chin-length, perfectly styled blonde hair and deep brown eyes. She's smaller, more petite, whereas Cole is at least six foot two and broad in the shoulders.

I'm going with the assumption that Cole resembles his father.

Laughter gurgles up in my throat. I suppose we have that in common. In the looks department, I resemble my father, but have my mother's smaller build. Whereas my dad is strapping—built for defense—I'm smaller and sleeker, better suited to play a forward position.

Cole snags my distracted attention before giving me yet another reassuring smile. I return it, but even I realize that it's a feeble attempt. He knows me well enough by now to understand that something isn't right.

And really, what am I supposed to tell him?

That his mother is my shrink and knows all my dirty little secrets?

I almost blanche, remembering that I told his mother the last time I saw her that I was sexually attracted to someone other than her son.

Kill me now.

Just pull the freaking trigger and get it over with.

Throughout the rest of the meal, I fidget nervously, waiting for her to out me.

Oh god, she knows I've been having sex with her son because I told her.

I want to bash my forehead against the dining room table until I knock myself out.

She also knows we've been using condoms and that I'm looking to go on the pill.

A fresh wave of humiliation crashes over me.

Unable to sit still for another second, I shoot out of my seat. The conversation screeches to an abrupt halt as three startled gazes settle on me.

It takes effort to pull my lips into an anemic-looking smile. "I, ah, need to use the bathroom."

"It's through the kitchen and to the right," Thomas directs.

I force myself to take deep, calming breaths before releasing them back into the atmosphere.

A mirthless laugh gurgles up inside, because here I am, using Dr. Thompson's breathing techniques in her own house.

It's just too much.

Finding the bathroom, I lock the door and rush to the sink before running the tap and splashing a handful of cold water onto my face. I squeeze my eyes tightly shut, all the while continuing to inhale and exhale.

This is crazy.

And when I say *crazy* what I really mean is *totally fucked up*.

How can I possibly continue seeing Cole when his mother knows every ugly detail about my life? She knows how I fell apart under the pressure and strain during my freshman year. I swallow thickly as the next thought pops into my head.

How I used sex as an escape…

Guilt and shame crash over me, threatening to drag me to the bottom of the ocean. There's no way in hell I'll ever be good enough for Cole. And she knows it.

I'm the girl who failed out of school. Got kicked off the hockey team. Threw away all her hopes and dreams—everything she spent her entire life working toward.

My own family didn't want to deal with me, so they shipped me off.

Who would want their son dating someone like that?

Umm…no one.

That's who.

Cole is probably the most put-together person I've ever met. He knows exactly who he is and what direction he's moving in. He deserves a girl who already has her shit together, and maybe I'm getting there, but I'm not there yet.

I honestly don't know how I'm going to gather enough courage to go back out there and face Dr. Thompson again. A light knock on the bathroom door has me freezing like a deer in headlights.

Please don't let it be her.

Please don't let it be her.

"Cassidy? Are you all right?"

Air rushes from my lungs. My shoulders collapse as I hang onto the sides of the sink for dear life.

Cole.

I clear my throat. "Yeah. Sorry for taking so long. I'm not feeling so well."

"Guggenheim?" he says softly from the other side of the door.

A slight smile tugs at the edges of my lips as I squeeze my eyes tightly shut again. "No, no. Not at all." Lie. Big, huge lie. "My, um, stomach is upset. I hate to ask you this, but would you mind taking me back to the dorms?"

I need to get out of here before I totally freak out. The anxiety is building, swirling its way through me. The perfect topper to this afternoon would be a full-on anxiety attack.

Thanks, but I think I'll pass on that spectacle.

"Sure, no problem." Even though he doesn't say anything more, I hear the disappointment threading its way through his voice. It only makes me feel worse than I already do. I know how close Cole and his mom are. After his dad died, all they had was each other. He was really looking forward to introducing us.

With one last deep breath, I open the door and find Cole standing on the other side. His hands are jammed into the pockets of his khakis as his gaze fastens onto mine.

"I'm so sorry about this," I whisper.

I'd been so wound up about meeting his family. I just wanted them to like me. And now...

Well, that certainly isn't going to happen.

I realize it, even if he doesn't.

His lips lift but the smile doesn't quite reach his eyes. "Don't worry about it. I'm just sorry you don't feel well."

"Me, too," I say honestly.

He searches through all the lies that are swimming around in my eyes before gently wrapping one arm around my shoulders and tugging me close.

He whispers against my hair, "They like you, Cassidy. Just like I knew they would. No worries, okay?"

Not believing him for a second, I rein in the snort that threatens to escape. There is absolutely no way that Dr. Thompson wants me anywhere near her son. Of that, I am positive.

I paste a smile on my face as Cole steers me into the dining room.

"Cassidy isn't feeling well, so we're going to take off."

Concern flickers across Dr. Thompson's face as her gaze fastens onto mine and she swiftly rises from her chair. "I'm sorry to hear that. Let me pack something up for your roommates, and then you two can be on your way."

His mom and stepdad begin clearing away the dishes from the table.

"Thanks, they'll appreciate it." Even though he's speaking to his mother, his gaze keeps flitting to mine as if he's trying to figure out what's really going on. I'm pretty sure he knows I'm lying through my teeth.

Within five minutes, Cole is handed a grocery bag overflowing with food. Every time his mom's gaze drifts to me, she smiles warmly, just like she always does when I'm in her office. "It was a real pleasure to meet you, Cassidy. I hope we'll see you soon."

Again, I want to snort.

Instead, I give her a polite smile, knowing that within a few moments, this nightmare will be over, and I'll be able to breathe again. "Thank you so much for having me. It was wonderful to meet both of you."

As soon as we hit the sidewalk outside the house, I gulp in a big breath of air before hightailing it to his car and sliding into the front seat as Cole loads the food into the back of his Mustang. With shaking fingers, I fasten my seatbelt.

The drive back to campus is made in silence as I stare out the passenger side window. I had thought everything was a mess when Cole hadn't known the truth about my past. It had taken a while, but I finally worked up the courage to come clean. Now, it seems like more secrets have sprouted up between us.

As my mind cartwheels, I realize that Cole isn't aware I've been meeting regularly with a psychologist at the school. He knows I was in therapy before I came to Western, but I never mentioned that I was still seeing someone. Although, that's over with. There is no way I can go back and see Dr. Thompson now that she knows I've been dating her son.

I blink back to awareness when Cole reaches out and grabs a hold of my fingers before pressing a kiss against my knuckles. "Are you okay? Do you still want me to drop you off at the dorms?"

I get the feeling that he hopes I've changed my mind.

I haven't.

It's on the tip of my tongue to tell him that I need some time to myself, to think about what I'm going to do, but I stop myself before the words can spill from my mouth.

Instead, I whisper, "I just need to lie down for a while." There's a pause before I add, "I'm really sorry about dinner. I didn't mean to ruin it."

He glances over and gives me a small smile. I can't help but notice that it's strained around the edges, as if he suspects I'm not being truthful with him.

"Don't worry about it. There will be plenty more."

Yeah…I don't see that happening any time soon.

How would I even begin to explain that his mother and I are already well-acquainted? That I've known her since mid-August.

No, I'm definitely not ready to spill that secret.

Instead of responding, I turn away and stare out the window.

13

CASSIDY

y feet stutter to a stop as my breath catches at the back of my throat. My heart thumps a painful beat as I watch my dad stare down at his phone. He must be texting, or emailing, or something. Even though I've arrived at the restaurant early, he beat me here and is already seated at a table.

I've been a nervous wreck all day in anticipation of this dinner. This is the first time since failing out of school last year that my dad and I are going to sit down to talk. And I failed out last December. It's now November.

That's eleven months of radio silence.

Apparently, when I failed out, I not only destroyed my own aspirations and dreams, but my father's as well. He always wanted me to play Division I hockey at a prestigious East Coast college. I had been poised to make both of our dreams come true until the pressure, stress, and rigorousness of my course load, coupled with the intense level of play, had been too much for me to handle.

And I cracked.

More like shattered.

I've spoken with my father twice in all that time. The first was when Cole and I had sneaked into my parents' house to grab my old hockey gear. Dad, unfortunately, came home and found us in the basement. The memory still has the power to make me wince when I think about the ugly words he'd hurled at me.

And the second time was when Cole reached out after I made the Western women's intramural hockey team and invited him to my first scrimmage. That's when it seemed like we might actually be able to bridge the gap separating us.

It's the reason I'm here to meet with my father for dinner.

"Miss?"

The hostess smiles as I shake off the cobwebs from my past. I remind myself to smile. Even though I'm nervous as hell, I'm thankful my dad reached out, wanting to sit down and hash out our issues. I've missed my family over the past year and want them back in my life. While nothing will ever be the same between any of us, maybe it can be different.

Better.

My dad ruled my life while growing up. He set schedules for hockey practice, extra workouts, and studying. Even thinking about how he'd structured my childhood has my chest constricting with thick tendrils of anxiety. Refocusing my attention, I breathe in slowly before forcing it out again.

"Sorry," I murmur. "Lead the way."

As we get closer to the table, Dad glances up from his phone. A tentative smile lifts the corners of his lips as he rises to his feet. For just a sliver of a second, we stare at each other. Awkwardness descends and I wonder if coming here was a mistake. That's all it takes for my expectations to nosedive.

What sucks most is that my dad and I used to be so close.

Before I can decide how to handle the situation, he swallows up the distance between us and wraps his arms around me. I can't help but burrow against his wide chest as his arms tighten. We cling to each other in the middle of the restaurant for at least a minute, maybe two.

And it feels good.

So good that moisture gathers in my eyes. When we finally break apart, the uncomfortable tension crackling in the air around us dissolves as if it had been a figment of my imagination.

Once we're seated, his gaze sweeps over me. "You look good, Cassidy," he says before adding approvingly, "healthy."

My lips lift at the compliment. "Thank you, I feel good. I've been running three times a week, and I'm practicing with the team a couple of times a week. Sometimes, Cole and I skate in the mornings before school."

That being said, there's no way I'll ever be as sleek and muscular as I was in high school. I adhered to a strict diet and workout regimen to maintain a peak physical condition. I have no desire to ever live such a regimented or restrictive lifestyle again.

After I'd failed out of school last year, I stopped working out and hadn't wanted to go anywhere near an ice rink. But all that changed when I met Cole. He introduced me to his cousin, Sammy, the captain of the Western Timber Wolves women's team, and I was able to join even though the season had already started.

It's Cole I have to thank for pushing me to skate with the team and giving me back something I truly love. He's the one I have to thank for reaching out to my father and inviting him to watch my first scrimmage. Without him doing that, my dad and I wouldn't be sitting here, working on our relationship.

It doesn't escape me just how wonderful Cole is.

Or how lucky I am to have him in my life.

My dad nods. "I'm glad you're skating again."

The waitress brings us both glasses of water and I take a drink before responding. Just because I'm happy to be here, and bridging the yawning expanse that separates us, doesn't mean it's easy. Hockey now feels like a minefield between us.

It was what we'd bonded over during my childhood. It had always been our thing. My two younger sisters danced and didn't want anything to do with skating. My dad had always been into hockey. I'm sure he'd secretly hoped for a boy but got stuck with three girls instead. Me getting kicked off the team last year had devastated him.

It was an abrupt end to all the goals and dreams we'd spent years working toward.

I clear my throat and stare at the menu. Only then do I realize how tightly I'm gripping the plastic. One by one, I pry my fingers loose. It takes effort to consciously relax my muscles.

"Me, too. But I'd needed a break."

That comment has the conversation stalling as we study our menus in silence. The waitress returns and we both order burgers. In a small way, being out to eat with my dad feels normal. When we traveled for games and tournaments, it was always just the two of us. We'd go out to eat, sleep in hotels, take in some of the local sights, and sometimes, if we were lucky, catch a classic car show. I loved spending a few hours between tournament games checking out muscle cars and old roadsters.

Not only did my dad give me a love for hockey, but an appreciation for classic cars, too.

It makes perfect sense that we ended up being so close. We spent a lot of time together. It's just as understandable that it hurt like hell when he turned his back on me. It takes a moment to realize that I'm not ready to forgive him for that. Like everything else in life, it's going to take time.

My eyes lift and our gazes collide. Dad's eyes are a deep ocean-blue, like mine. We also share a headful of inky-black hair. Although, his has a good amount of silver shooting through it. There are more lines bracketing his eyes, and deeper grooves marring his forehead.

It makes me wonder if the last year was as hard on him as it was on me.

Before I realize it, the emotion-filled words are slipping from my mouth. "I'm sorry, Dad. Sorry for screwing everything up."

I spent my entire life trying to please this man. Will I ever get to a point in my life when his approval doesn't matter?

His guarded expression crumbles as he sucks in a quick breath before saying in a rush, "I know you are. And for what it's worth, I'm sorry for how I handled the situation." With a shrug, he glances away. "Maybe I pushed you too hard. Or pushed you into playing a sport you didn't want to. I just don't know anymore…" A hint of a smile lifts his lips. "I used to think I had all the answers, now I realize that I don't have any of them. Raising children is a humbling experience."

A thick sheen of tears fills my eyes as I shake my head. "No, Dad. I wanted to play hockey. I loved playing." I loved being out on the ice. I felt at home in a freezing cold rink. I still do. So many of my childhood memories are centered around the ice. Hard-fought wins. Crushing defeats. Time spent with my dad. I wouldn't trade any of those memories. They mean too much to me.

My experience growing up wasn't a perfect one, but it's mine. And it's what shaped me into who I am today.

And maybe that person isn't so bad, after all.

Dad's gaze locks onto mine from across the small table that separates us. "Sometimes I wonder if I wanted your success more than you wanted it for yourself."

This time, I'm the one inhaling a deep breath, trying to steady all the raging emotions that are roiling through me. I hadn't expected to delve headfirst into this conversation before our food was even served.

Part of me wondered if we were going to sweep everything neatly under the rug and pretend that last year didn't happen. I'm kind of shocked that my father is talking about all this so openly and easily. Well, maybe not easily, because I can see that the past is as painful and tender for him as it is for me.

But you know what?

We're doing it and we're getting through it.

It's what makes me realize that if I want our relationship to heal, I need to be honest with him. I can't just tell him what he wants to hear. That won't help the situation. If this past year of therapy has taught me anything, it's that you need to be open and honest about what you're feeling and not just gloss over it because it's the easiest thing to do. Or makes the people around you more comfortable.

"In the beginning, I played hockey because you loved it so much and I enjoyed when we spent time together…just the two of us."

Anguish flickers across his face as he runs a hand through his hair.

"You played all these years because of me?"

I shake my head. "No, I played because I fell in love with the game, but I also liked that it was something we had in common. I liked when we were off on our own." Years of tournament weekends roll through my head. The muscle car shows we were able to drop in on. Spending time out on the ice with him. Having him coach my teams when I was younger. My dad was always tough but fair, and he pushed me to be my best. To give one hundred percent. Again, it hits me that I wouldn't be the person I am today without this man pushing me to excel.

He expected excellence and I gave it to him until I left for college. Then, unable to hold it together, I cracked under the pressure and fell apart. In the end, all my dad had wanted was the best for me. And I had wanted the best for myself as well. I guess neither of us realized that funneling every ounce of energy into hockey wasn't the way to achieve it.

"Maybe I pushed too hard with all the dryland practices and private skating lessons." His eyes search mine for answers.

The question has my shoulders slumping because there's no other way to answer but truthfully. I take another deep breath as I attempt to word my response just right. I want him to understand how I feel, but don't need to bash him over the head with it.

"My life revolved around hockey to the exclusion of everything else." When his facial expression doesn't change, I continue. "I didn't realize what I was giving up until it was too late. I wish there'd been more of a balance. Friends, other activities, parties. A social life. Sometimes it feels like I missed out on all the normal kid stuff because I'd been too wrapped up in hockey."

When I finally run out of steam, I realize that the air has become clogged in my throat as I wait for his reaction. Instead of getting angry, he surprises me by agreeing with everything I've said.

"I suppose I'd wanted you to succeed where I had failed. You were so good at such a young age. It was obvious to everyone that you were talented, with unlimited potential." He jerks his shoulders. "I'd wanted you to have it all. Every advantage. It never occurred to me that you were missing out on growing up. I'm sorry for that. And for pushing you so hard." There's a beat of silence before he adds, "For what it's worth, I enjoyed spending time with you, too."

As I open my mouth to respond, our waitress arrives with our food. After she disappears, all I can do is stare at the burger and fries on my plate as his words churn in my head. Never in my wildest dreams did I expect for us to have such a candid conversation about the past. But here we are, doing exactly that. And it feels good.

My mind tumbles back through the years, looking at all the mistakes I made and what I could have done differently. The thing is, if that had happened, I wouldn't be where I am right now.

At Western.

With Cole.

Any other decision would have altered the course of my life.

There's nothing I can say to argue those words in my head.

In a twisted way, my failure brought me to Cole. No matter how difficult everything was to get through, I can't bring myself to regret it. If I hadn't failed out of Dartmouth, I never would have decided to attend Western.

When I'm halfway through my burger, I say, "What's done is done. No matter how much I wish I could go back and make different decisions, I can't. I have to live with what happened and move on the best I can. And that's exactly what I've been trying to do." Dr. Thompson's words echo throughout my head, and I can't help but repeat them. "What I've tried to do is learn from my mistakes. I'm happy to be playing on an intramural team." Quietly, I admit, "It's nice not having the pressure of a Division I program hanging over my head. Hockey has become fun again."

He nods. "I want you to know that you don't have to play if you don't want to." He shifts on his seat before adding, "I love you for *you*, not because you play hockey like I did."

The first genuine smile of the evening flits across my face. "I'm playing for me right now, and I'm enjoying it. I like the girls on my team, and I don't want to quit."

His expression matches mine. "Good." There's a pause before he asks, "You wouldn't mind if I catch a few more games this season, would you?"

I beam. I've always enjoyed having my dad in the stands cheering me on. "I would really love that."

14

———

CASSIDY

I trudge through the dorm hallway and am about to slide my key in the lock when I hear shouting from the other side of the door. I lean a bit closer, trying to hear what's going on, because honestly, I'm not in the mood to stumble into some huge ass drama.

Just as I consider backing away, the door is ripped open, and I come face-to-face with Austin. With a scowl, he grunts something that might be a *hey* or *hi* before stalking past me. I watch him retreat down the hall before my wide gaze swings to Brooklyn, who wears a similar expression.

Kind of like his and hers matching sweaters.

Except scowls.

Tentatively, I step inside the room. "Do I even want to know what that was all about?" My guess is that I don't. I didn't even know they were on speaking terms. Brooklyn has been icing Austin out for weeks now. I had assumed everything was still status quo in that department.

She shrugs before flopping onto her bed with a groan.

Without any preamble whatsoever, she says, "We sort of slept together."

I'm in the process of unbuttoning my red wool coat when she

throws out that little tidbit of information. It's like a fishing lure I can't resist swallowing down whole. With my fingers still hovering over a large, black button, my eyes widen. *"Sort of?"* There's a pause. "You're joking, right?"

Instead of meeting my inquisitive gaze, Brooklyn stares up at the ceiling as if it's the most fascinating thing in the world. Which it's not. Okay, maybe that's not altogether true. She does have a huge poster of a practically naked guy taped up there.

"Do I look like I'm kidding? Would I joke about having sex with Austin?" Her voice drops. *"Again."*

I peel off my jacket and throw it over my desk chair before dropping down across from her on my bed and holding up a hand. "Whoa, whoa, whoa. Back this train up. What do you mean by *again?"*

Very slowly, as if it's painful, she turns her head until her gaze collides with mine. "All you need to know is that each and every time it occurred was during moments of great weakness."

"All?" My mouth tumbles open.

Her dark blonde brows pinch together as she grumbles, "Would you please stop looking at me like that. I had sex with someone. I didn't murder a family of four in their sleep."

It takes effort to smooth out my facial features. "So, exactly how many moments of weakness have you experienced of late?"

Brooklyn ticks off the number on her fingers. When she needs to use her other hand to count, I think that incredulous look sneaks back onto my face again.

She doesn't bat an eyelash in my direction before saying with enough heat to chastise, "You're doing it again."

"Sorry." I shake my head. "I don't understand why you've been sleeping with the guy who was practically stalking you after you broke up with him. I'm not bent out of shape that you're having sex… just that you're having sex with Austin." I lower my voice, trying to gentle my tone. Even though I don't particularly want to think about Dr. Thompson, I try to channel her for this conversation.

What kind of thought-provoking questions would she ask?

"So, ah, do you think that's the best idea?"

Brooklyn gives me an exaggerated eye roll. "Of course not! In fact, it's probably one of the stupider things I've done."

"Then why are you doing it?"

This situation clearly has disaster written all over it. Can't Brooklyn see that?

I mean…I just walked in on them shouting at one another.

Her face scrunches. "Remember those conversations we had about the rather impressive things he can do with his tongue?"

I wince, not wanting another visual to go along with that comment. It took a really long time to eradicate it from my brain the first time. "Umm, yes…I do."

She gives me a penetrating look. "Need I say more?"

"I'm begging you not to."

Her body deflates before she admits, "For some reason, that guy is my kryptonite. I wish he wasn't, but he is." She stares glumly up at her hot guy poster, which is a first. He is, after all, sporting a rather impressive boner. It's like her very own happy place.

"Kind of sounds like a mess."

Inhaling a deep breath, she agrees softly, "You have no idea just what a clusterfuck it is."

Unfortunately, I'm no stranger to the concept of a clusterfuck. I'm living it right now. Instead of telling her about my own situation, I decide to keep it to myself. I don't want to turn the focus away from Brooklyn and the issues she's struggling with. There'll be more than enough time for me to dump all my crap on her later.

Today is for Brooklyn.

And her big pile of crap.

"Are you thinking about getting back together with him?"

Why else would she be having sex with him…tongue thing excluded, of course. There have to be other reasons she keeps hooking up with him.

At least I hope there are.

"No. I don't want to fall for him any harder than I already have." There's a pause as she squeezes her eyes closed. "I just wish I could get him out of my system. I don't understand why he's so different from the others."

Even back in high school, Brooklyn was a serial dater. Austin is the first guy to ever force his way into her heart. Even if she doesn't necessarily want him there.

"Maybe the reason you can't get over Austin is because you actually have feelings for him. Have you considered giving him another chance to prove that he can be the guy you need him to be?"

She stares at me like I just told her to drown a bag of kittens. "But that's the problem. I don't want to feel anything for him. Relationships are so much easier when emotions aren't involved."

"Isn't it a little late for that?" I shake my head. "How are you going to kill the feelings you already have for him?"

With a straight face she asks, "Why do you think I'm trying to fuck him out of my system?"

I roll my eyes. "How's that been working for you?"

"Not well." A thoughtful expression crosses her face. "Is it possible we aren't having enough sex?"

"Let me get this straight," I say drily, "your plan is to screw around with him in hopes that you can *lessen* your feelings for him?"

Total.

Disaster.

And I certainly don't want to be around when it backfires in her face.

Brooklyn snorts before throwing an arm over her eyes. "When you put it like that, it just sounds ridiculous."

A burst of laughter escapes from me. "That's because it *is* ridiculous."

"Then tell me what to do," she groans, "because I don't want to keep thinking about him. I can't keep hooking up with him in hopes that it'll finally be enough."

Understanding dawns, albeit a little late. "That's why he was here, wasn't it?"

She lifts the arm from her face before rolling onto her side and blinking the harsh sunlight filtering in through the window out of her eyes. "Yup. Booty call. In the middle of a Wednesday afternoon. So sad."

"Why were you two yelling at each other if it's just sex?"

"You heard that, huh?"

"Just the voices, not the actual words."

"Believe it or not, he's tired of hooking up and gave me an ultimatum. We either make this legit and stop sneaking around, or he's moving on." Brooklyn plows both hands through her hair as if she might yank the strands out of her head. "Riddle me this—if guys prefer no-strings arrangements, why is he pressuring me into a relationship? You'd think that what we're doing would be an ideal situation."

I'm not a relationship expert, but I think Austin has developed feelings for Brooklyn and he's not afraid to do something about them.

"So…what you're telling me is that you don't want to go out with him, and he won't continue hooking up with you."

"Yup, that just about sums up our situation. Do you have any words of wisdom to impart upon me?"

Oh.

Hell.

No.

I refuse to touch this problem with a ten-foot pole.

"Sorry, I don't."

I'm the last person who should be doling out relationship advice. This is the first time I've actually found myself in one and it's turning out to be riddled with issues.

Ones I don't know how to solve.

It occurs to me, as I stare at my friend, that I'm not alone.

15

CASSIDY

*N*inety minutes.

That's how much time I have to hit the books before I'm supposed to meet Cole for a quick dinner. He has a hockey scrimmage tonight, and Brooklyn and I are planning on being there to support the team.

I still haven't worked up the courage to tell him that his mother is my psychologist. I keep putting it off. How familiar does that sound?

Unfortunately, all too familiar.

And here I thought telling him about all the meaningless hookups and failing out of school would be the hard part. I'd really thought we were past all the secrets, lies, and omissions.

Turns out, we're not.

With one last glance at my phone, I turn off the ringer before shoving it back into my messenger bag. Then I head up to the second floor. There's a quiet area buried behind the stacks. I always gravitate there because no one else ever uses the space.

Imagine my surprise when I find someone camped out at the table I usually park myself at. Annoyance flares within me because I'm a creature of habit, and I like sitting at what I consider to be *my* table.

And no…there's nothing weird about that.

Just as I'm about to stalk away, the encroacher glances up and skewers me in place with his eyes.

Luke.

As soon as our gazes lock, a smile curves his lips. "Hey, Cassidy!" He waves me over.

Something unwanted tightens in my belly as I hesitantly step toward him and lift my hand in an awkward wave. "Hey."

He takes in the bag hanging off my shoulder. "You need a place to work?"

I look around for an alternative, but there isn't one. There are only a few tables scattered around the space and they're filled with students. "Yeah."

He clears off part of the table closest to me. "You can work here if you want."

For a moment or two, I shift uneasily, knowing in the back of my mind that Cole wouldn't like the idea of us spending time together. If I'm being completely truthful, the feelings I have for Luke make me uneasy. I'm beginning to suspect they aren't one hundred percent friendship. My life is already complicated enough without adding these unwanted feelings into the mix.

Deep down, I know the best thing to do is stay away from Luke until I have a better handle on my emotions where he's concerned. I glance around, scanning the area for an open table.

Any open table.

Just one open table.

But there aren't any.

"Cassidy?"

I gnaw my lip, unsure of what to do.

Am I making too big of a deal out of this?

It's just studying. We probably won't even talk. Like at all. After a moment of internal struggle, I decide there's no real harm in sitting at the same table with Luke for an hour and a half.

"Okay." I give him a small smile before dropping my bag on the table and pulling out my economics book. Luke returns the expression but doesn't say another word as he gets back to work. I reassure myself again that what I'm doing is fine and crack open my book to chapter thirteen before reading, highlighting, and jotting down a few notes.

After a while, I realize my shoulders ache from my body being hunched over my book. With a stretch, I pull out my phone to check the time and realize that an entire hour has slipped by. Crap. I didn't even get through everything I wanted to. I peek over at Luke and notice he's still typing away on his laptop. He hasn't said one word to me since I sat down.

Relief floods through me.

See?

I knew studying together would be fine.

Why did I even think it would be such a problem?

All of my previous concerns seem ridiculous.

I have roughly thirty minutes left to study before meeting Cole for dinner. Just as I'm about to get back to it, Luke straightens in his chair and stretches. He arches his back, reaching his arms toward the ceiling as he rotates one shoulder and then the other. Even though I shouldn't notice how the soft fabric of his T-shirt plays across the broad expanse of his chest, that's exactly what's happening. It feels as if my gaze is glued to the way his short sleeves mold to the thickly-corded muscles of his arms and shoulders.

Nope. I definitely shouldn't be staring.

Look away!

I can't. Objectively speaking, Luke is gorgeous. With his handsome face, sculpted shoulders, powerfully built chest, and massive biceps, he's catnip to the female species.

Just as those unwelcome thoughts crash through my head, I realize I'm totally checking him out. The last thing I should be doing is checking Luke out. Heat fills my cheeks as I rip my gaze away from him and force myself to look at the book splayed open in front of me.

How embarrassing. I really hope he didn't see the way I was staring.

Luke is my friend.

Nothing more.

Nothing.

More.

"Do you have a lot of reading to finish up?"

I force my gaze to meet his before carefully searching it. Thankfully, there isn't any kind of smirk or knowing light filling it. If there were, I'd have to pack up my books and hightail it out of the library. For all intents and purposes, he's unaware of my previous scrutiny.

I wish I could be as oblivious.

It takes effort to clear my throat along with those thoughts. "A little bit more. I wanted to get through as much as I could before the game tonight."

He smiles, stretching again, as he holds my unwavering gaze. This time, I don't allow my stare to deviate from his. "You'll be there?"

"Yup. Brooklyn and I are planning on it."

"I've spent time going over film and it should be a tight game. We've got a faster defense and more talent upfront, so I think we'll be able to pull it off." His fingers rise to rub his chin. "But their goalie is solid."

I don't mention that Cole pretty much said the same thing. "It should be a good game."

He leans back in his chair and tilts his head. I can almost feel the intensity of his gaze licking over me.

What I can't decide is if I like it or not.

When it comes down to it, I shouldn't like his perusal at all.

And I definitely shouldn't feel awareness prickling at the bottom of my belly.

"Is everything okay, Cassidy?"

Surprised by the question, I say, "Yeah, everything's fine. Why do you ask?"

For a long moment, he watches me. It's almost as if he's silently combing through all my thoughts and emotions.

It's a disconcerting sensation and yet...

I don't know.

For some unknown reason, one I don't have a grasp on—or maybe I do, maybe it all stems to what happened last year—I feel like I can talk to Luke. Like I can drop all the pretenses and be honest with him. There aren't many people I feel that way with.

My teeth sink into my lower lip as indecision floods through me. It would feel so good to talk to someone about everything that's going on in my life. It's not like I can pop into Dr. Thompson's office. I never realized how much I'd come to depend on her until I started to avoid the counseling center. I miss her objective opinions and thought-provoking questions.

I've spent the last ten and a half months working with a psychologist. This is the first time I haven't had someone to sit down and unload on. I could always talk with Brooklyn, but she has her own issues she's trying to navigate through. The last thing she needs is to get mired down in my drama.

"It seems like there's something on your mind." He gives me a half-smile before adding, "We're friends, right?" He waits for me to signal my agreement before continuing. "If you need help with something, I've got a strong shoulder to lean on. You can always talk to me."

His words crash around inside my head before my muscles gradually loosen. He's right. We *are* friends.

I suck in a breath before deciding that I can't keep all this to myself. It feels like I'm going to explode. Once I turn on the spigot, the floodgates open and everything comes pouring out in a torrent.

After I've told him the story, my shoulders slump as his dark blond brows shoot up across his forehead and he releases a low whistle.

I can't help but wince.

Apparently, this situation *is* just as bad as I suspected it was.

Perfect.

"And you haven't told Cole yet?"

I shake my head.

"Yikes."

When a smile trembles around the corners of his lips, I crumple up a piece of notebook paper and throw it at him. For a moment, he looks stunned, as the wadded-up ball of paper hits him square in the chest, before he bursts out laughing. A few of the students working close by glare in our direction.

As my attention returns to him, he stifles his laughter before angling his body forward and resting his elbows on the table. "Sorry. That is a completely serious and jacked up problem. Please continue."

I narrow my eyes and continue to scowl. He isn't telling me anything I don't already know. Had I realized he would find humor in this situation, I wouldn't have bothered to share it with him.

"Just so you know, I'm two seconds away from packing up and leaving."

His expression becomes serious. "All right. The obvious answer is that you need to tell Cole. Honestly, it's not that big of a deal."

How can he say that?

It feels massive.

I glance away before admitting, "I've told her intimate details about our relationship."

His brows slide upward, but this time, he's smart enough not to chuckle. Or he'd find himself alone.

"The way I see it, whether or not you told her about what you guys do, she probably would have suspected it anyway. I mean, come on, you're in college. You're making a big deal out of nothing."

Hope fills me. "You really think so?"

"I do." He leans even closer before adding, "You went through a difficult time last year and Cole accepts that. Whether he realizes it or not, you've had a lot of shit to work out in your head. And you were seeing her before you even met or got involved with him. Her being your psychologist doesn't mean anything in the grand scheme of things. You just need to get it all out in the open and then, I promise, you'll feel better."

"Yeah, I guess that's true."

He reaches out and takes my hand with his own before gently squeezing it. "If Cole loves you as much as you think he does, he'll understand. It's that simple."

Silently, I turn his words over in my head.

Maybe Luke is right, and it isn't that big of a deal.

A tentative smile lifts my lips.

Luke's perspective has made me feel so much better about the situation. "You're right. I'm going to talk to him about it." The sooner I can get this out in the open, the better off I'll feel. Maybe then I can even stop in and see Dr. Thompson.

At least say goodbye to her.

Finally, I have a plan. It's like a huge weight has been lifted from my chest and I can breathe again.

He smiles in return before releasing my hand and grabbing his phone. "I wish there was more time to talk but I've got to get going, it's almost six. I still have to eat and get over to the arena."

Wait…what?

Six?

It can't be that late already!

I gasp and search my bag for my phone. Once I've found it, I hit the screen only to see that Luke is right. It's six o'clock. All those good feelings surging through me dissolve, leaving panic and dread to fill their place.

Crap!

I was supposed to meet Cole at the Union at five-thirty. I remember glancing at my phone, and it was only five o'clock. How did a whole hour slide by? It doesn't even feel like Luke and I were talking for that long.

A groan escapes from me when I realize there are three missed calls and a slew of unanswered text messages. I didn't hear any of them because I'd silenced the ringer. I jerk to my feet and shove everything into my bag.

"Cassidy?"

I glance up only to find that Luke has already risen to his feet. His brows are drawn together, and concern fills his eyes.

"I was supposed to meet Cole for dinner at five-thirty and I completely lost track of time."

"Okay," he says calmly. "I'm sure he'll understand. It happens."

I pause before taking a deep breath.

He's probably right.

At least, I hope he is.

I feel terrible about getting so wrapped up in our conversation that

I missed my dinner date with Cole. As much as I hate to admit it—even privately—Cole and I are a little out of sync right now and I don't understand why.

Or maybe I do.

There are a lot of obstacles that have cropped up.

And Luke is right.

Cole and I need to sit down and talk. As much as I want to clear the air right now, there's no time. This isn't the kind of conversation I want to have with him before he goes out on the ice for a game.

With a quick nod, I give Luke a hasty wave before literally running off. As I'm racing down a flight of stairs, I call Cole, praying that he answers and isn't pissed that I accidently blew him off. We've both been so busy lately. Him with classes and his hockey schedule, and me with classes, hockey, and working at the tutoring center. It's becoming more of a challenge to carve out time for one another, and when we do, I end up missing it.

"Cassidy?" Cole's tone is full of concern when he picks up the phone. "Where are you? Is everything okay?"

The worry pricking his voice makes me feel like crap.

"I'm so sorry about flaking on you. I was at the library studying and turned off the ringer on my phone."

"Are you still there?" The fear that had filled his voice drains away.

"I'm leaving right now." I'm huffing and puffing as I reach the glass doors that lead outside. "I can meet you at the Union, if you're still there. It'll only take me a few minutes to get across campus." I'll have to run, but so what. Spending a few minutes with him before the game is worth it.

"No, I had to grab something without you. I need to head over to the arena and get ready. I'm already in the car. Stay where you are. I'll pick you up and take you back to the dorms on my way."

Disconnecting from the call, I shove my cell back inside my bag. A few moments later, Cole rolls up and I dash over to his electric blue Mustang, yanking open the passenger side door and sliding in next to him. Instead of pulling away from the curb, he allows the car to idle as he leans over and presses a kiss against my lips.

And just like that, a little piece of normal falls into place between us.

Once we break apart, I whisper, "I'm so sorry about missing dinner. I was working on econ and completely lost track of time."

When his lips quirk into a lopsided smile, my heart melts. "Wow... thrown aside for economics." His eyes crinkle at the corners. "Talk about a blow to my ego."

A lighthearted smile springs to my lips as I give him a heavy-lidded look. "Well, economics *is* pretty damn sexy."

Before I can say anything else, he nips at my neck, and I squeal before giggling. "I'm kidding! You're way sexier than arbitrage, fiscal drag, and monetary policy."

"It would be sad if I weren't." With a grin still hovering around the corners of his mouth, he kisses me until I can barely think.

His tongue slips inside my mouth, rubbing against mine, slowly exploring every part of me until I have no idea where I end, and he begins. A whimper of need slips free.

If only it were possible to go back to his place.

When he finally pulls away, I see the desire that has flared to life in his eyes, and it turns me on even more.

"Are you still planning to come to the game, or do you have too much work?"

"I was able to get most of it done at the library." There's no way I'd miss one of his games. Since we became friends, and then more, he's always done everything he could to support me. "I'll be in the stands, cheering you on. Promise."

His dimples flash, and that's all it takes for my pulse to kick into overdrive.

"Good."

Just as he's leaning toward me again, there's a knock on the passenger side window. Startled by the unexpected noise, we jump apart. Something uncomfortable twists in the pit of my belly when I see Luke standing on the other side of the glass staring at us.

"What the hell does he want?"

Even though Cole mutters the words, I still hear them. Instead of letting me go, his arms stay wrapped around me.

It takes Cole a couple of seconds to hit the button and unroll the window. Luke leans down, resting his forearms against the car so that his face is level with ours. His gaze touches mine before bouncing to Cole, who sits tensely beside me.

"Hey."

Cole jerks his chin. "What's up?"

Luke's gaze arrows back to mine. "You forgot your econ notebook. I wasn't sure if you needed it tonight." He holds out the notebook for me to take. As my fingers wrap around the edge, I realize they're trembling. "You took off like a bat out of hell."

"Thanks," I whisper.

I don't understand why it feels as if I'm locked between these two men. There isn't a choice to be made.

I'm with Cole.

Not Luke.

The thick tension permeating the air is almost enough to suffocate all of us.

Luke nods before straightening to his full height and taking a step away. "I gotta get going." His attention flickers to Cole. "Catch you later."

Cole remains silent. I have no idea if he acknowledges the comment.

Relief rushes from my lungs when Luke swings away, striding toward the library. It's short-lived when Cole jerks his arms from around me and throws the car into gear before peeling away from the curb. I fumble with the seatbelt before finally snapping it into place, and glance at Cole to silently assess the damage.

My heart clenches almost painfully at the anger radiating off him. His lips are compressed in a tight line, and his eyes are fixated on the ribbon of road stretched out before him as he white-knuckles the steering wheel.

I gulp, unsure of how to make what just happened better.

But what *exactly* am I trying to make better?

I haven't done anything wrong.

Not really...

I studied at the library with a friend. It wasn't planned. Luke being there was a coincidence. It's not like we're sneaking around behind Cole's back.

My tongue darts out to moisten my lips. "Cole?"

I shouldn't have to apologize for studying with Luke, but that's the way it feels. The words sit perched on the tip of my tongue. All I have to do is push them out. My fingers tangle together in my lap as I chew my lower lip with indecision.

Cole continues to stare straight ahead. "You weren't going to tell me, were you?"

It's a question.

And yet it's not.

My heart races, pounding painfully under my breast as my gaze darts to him before staring straight ahead.

Was I going to tell him?

I...don't know.

Deep down, I knew spending time alone with Luke—even though we were in a public space—would bother him. It's why I hesitated in the first place.

"Cassidy?"

My attention snaps to him again. "I don't know," I admit. "We were just studying. It wasn't planned. He was just there and," I shrug helplessly, "asked me to sit with him. That's it. It wasn't a big deal."

When he finally glances at me, I can't help but notice all the hurt and distrust swimming around within his eyes. After coming clean about everything that happened last year, I told myself that I wouldn't keep any other secrets from him.

If ten months of therapy have taught me anything, it's that you can't build a healthy relationship on lies and omission. And yet, I'm keeping secrets from Cole.

Already I can see the damage it's inflicting.

His brows knit together. "If it wasn't a big deal, then why didn't you tell me?"

I release a pent-up breath and shake my head at my own stupidity. All I've done is give him a reason to distrust me.

"I know you don't want me spending time with Luke, and I didn't want you to worry."

An uncomfortable silence stretches between us before he murmurs, "Then why does it feel like I should be worried?"

16

———

CASSIDY

"Are you going to tell me what's wrong? You've been all mopey since you came back from the library," Brooklyn asks as we sit in the bleachers, waiting for the game to get under way.

Unable to stand the way she continues to eyeball me, I mutter, "No." I keep my gaze trained on the Zamboni as it slowly sweeps water over the ice to smooth out all the rough patches while my mind tumbles back to the ride home with Cole.

None of this would be happening if I'd found my own table to work at. I wouldn't be sitting here in the stands with a pit the size of Texas at the bottom of my belly, feeling as if Cole and I are on the precipice of something terrible.

Brooklyn refuses to take the hint. "No, there's nothing wrong? Or no, you're going to keep it all to yourself and not tell me what's going on?"

"I'll go with what's behind door number two, please."

Before she can respond, the Zamboni disappears into a garage-type door at the far end of the rink, and both teams jump onto the ice for warm-ups. My gaze fastens onto Cole as he stretches, making wide circles. There must be something in my eyes that clues Brooklyn in on what's happening.

"I should have known this had something to do with Cole."

My shoulders collapse in defeat. "I don't want to talk about it. There's too much going on, and I just need some time to figure out what I'm going to do."

She throws her hands up like I'm the one who's breaking some kind of friendship code by not spilling my guts. Does that really make me a lousy friend?

I have no idea.

Maybe it does.

"Far be it from me to try and help," she grumbles.

For the first time, my gaze flickers toward her as I reach out and grab a hold of her hand. "I'm sorry." I huff out a breath. "You and I are quite the pair, aren't we?"

Her attention is drawn to Austin as he circles the ice with the team. A small frown tugs at the corners of her lips as she watches him. "I suppose we are."

We fall into silence for a long stretch of minutes before she nudges my shoulder and whispers, "Why is that couple over there scoping you out? It's kind of weird."

I glance down a few rows only for my gaze to collide with Dr. Thompson's. I shouldn't be surprised to find her and Thomas here.

For some reason, it never occurred to me that I would run into them again.

I shift on the hard bench and try to keep my tone nonchalant. "That's Cole's parents."

The longer I stare, the more my throat feels as if it's closing, and my heart beats an uncomfortable tattoo against my chest.

"Who's the girl with them? Is that his sister?" With a frown, she pauses. "Does he have a sister?"

I rip my gaze away from Dr. Thompson only to have it land on Jackie. Thankfully, she's oblivious to my presence. Instead, there's a smile on her face as she talks with Thomas as if they've known each other forever.

Now that I think about it, they probably have.

For some reason, the fact that Jackie is sitting with his parents has a giant lump settling in the middle of my throat. Not only did she and Cole date for two years, but they were best friends for more than a decade.

As I stare at the three of them, it occurs to me that I'll never have that kind of history with Cole. I'll never feel like I'm part of his family the way Jackie apparently does. There are too many obstacles standing in our way. That realization slams into me like a ton of bricks, knocking the air from my lungs until it feels like I can't breathe.

"That's Cole's ex-girlfriend." My voice sounds thin and reedy, as if it's traveling from a great distance.

Brooklyn's widened gaze darts to me before resettling on Jackie again.

"If she's the ex, then why is she sitting with them?"

It takes effort to force the words from my lips. "She and Cole grew up together. She's more like a family friend." It's yet another reminder that I don't belong.

Did Cole invite her to the game?

That thought is enough to have my stomach twisting into tiny knots.

He wouldn't do something like that, would he?

"Hmmm." Brooklyn doesn't say anything more than that.

And really, what else is there to say?

Knocking into her arm, I pull her distracted attention back to the ice by pointing to the players who are now moving through passing and shooting drills. With a glance at the clock, it's a relief to see that the game will start in less than five minutes. I just want to get this over with.

What sucks is that before the library incident, I'd been looking forward to watching Cole play tonight. Now, I have no idea where Cole and I even stand. After he dropped me off, I couldn't help but feel as if there'd been so much left unsaid between us, and not enough time to sort it out.

My gaze drifts back to Cole's mother and stepfather. A thick jolt slices through me when I realize that Jackie is scrutinizing me in much the same way I'd been staring at her a handful of minutes ago.

Brooklyn nudges my shoulder to reclaim my attention. "Someone sure knows who you are."

A soft puff of air escapes from me as I continue to hold Jackie's gaze. "She introduced herself at the party on Halloween and pulled me aside for a conversation."

Brooklyn's head swivels toward mine so fast that I'm surprised she doesn't get whiplash. The shocked expression on her face would be comical if there was anything remotely funny about this situation.

"Seriously?"

I jerk my shoulders into a tight shrug, not really wanting to delve into that story right now. Especially with Jackie watching. "Cole never told me what happened between them, and she was kind enough to fill in all the blanks."

"Oh, I just bet she did," Brooklyn grumbles with narrowed eyes and pursed lips.

My voice drops as everything she said circles viciously through my brain again. "Yup."

"Did she also admit to wanting him back?"

Breaking eye contact with Jackie, my head snaps toward Brooklyn in surprise. "How do you know that?"

She rolls her eyes before snorting. "Why else would she be here? Plus, every time she stares at the ice, she gets this sad look on her face."

For some reason, that only makes me feel worse about the situation. Plus, Jackie has Cole's parents on her side, rooting for her.

My bestie slings her arm around my shoulders, tugging me close just as the game is set to start. "You should have told me. Jeez, Cassidy. I always feel like you're keeping me in the dark about what's happening in your life."

She's not wrong.

Maybe I am a bad friend after all.

I force a small laugh. "I feel the same way, Ms. Friends-with-benefits."

A chuckle escapes from her as she shrugs. "What can I say? I was embarrassed."

As the puck is dropped at center ice, I send up a little prayer of thanks that Brooklyn and I have reconnected this year and became even better friends. I don't know what I'd do without her humor and support.

"Liking someone and having feelings for them shouldn't embarrass you," I tell her.

Instead of responding to that comment, she remains silent as we watch the Timber Wolves steal the puck from the other team before racing to their opponent's net. That's one of the things I love about watching and playing hockey—it's fast-paced action from start to finish. There's never a dull moment.

Even though it turns out to be a great game, it's hard to find any enjoyment or pleasure in watching it. My mind is too wrapped up in all the problems that have cropped up in my relationship with Cole.

"I really thought the hard part would be telling Cole about my past. Unfortunately, what we're now dealing with doesn't feel any easier," I admit.

Attention focused on the game, Brooklyn says, "It's just an ex-girl-friend, Cass. You need to remember that Cole loves *you*. Not her. There's nothing to deal with."

I really wish that was the only thing standing in our way.

It feels as if there's a yawning chasm that separates us, and I have no idea how to bridge the growing distance. For the rest of the game, Brooklyn and I munch on popcorn while watching the guys dominate on the ice. Even though Cole is having a good game, I can tell something isn't right.

He just seems...off.

He's playing with a lot more aggression than normal. Over the past few months, I've learned that Cole is a smart player who understands the fundamentals of the game. He hits when it's necessary and advantageous for the team. And his hits are always clean and legal. He's not one to draw a penalty for being a cheap shot.

Just as I think that, Cole slams into one of the other team's forwards. The sheer force of his hit sends them both crashing into the boards. The crowd winces at the reverberation that ripples throughout the chilly arena. I freeze and watch as the other player drops to the ice.

It's not a surprise when Cole receives a penalty for roughing.

To make matters worse, he argues with the ref as he skates over to the penalty box before throwing himself inside. After he slumps onto the bench, one of his coaches rips him a new one.

Stunned, I watch with wide eyes as the older man's arms cut through the air.

Brooklyn leans toward me before whispering, "What's up with him?"

While my friend might not totally grasp the finer points of the game, she knows enough to realize that this isn't a normal behavior for Cole.

I squeeze my eyes closed for a moment, not wanting to believe that the way Cole is playing tonight has anything to do with what happened between us earlier.

Deep down, I know it does.

The rest of the game doesn't fare any better for him or the team. Even though the Timber Wolves started out with a three-goal lead, their opponent took advantage of Cole's two-minute penalty by scoring a goal while he sat in the box. The next one was made on his second trip to the penalty box during the middle of the third period.

As soon as the opposing team ties the game, the Timber Wolves' frustration level becomes almost palpable. It's like a living breathing entity filling the arena. The players aren't the only ones pissed off by the three-goal lead that has disappeared. Fans are on their feet, shouting and booing. All I can do is sit frozen in place and hold Brooklyn's hand, squeezing the very life out of it as nausea churns my belly.

Cole has suceved two penalties for roughing during this game. I've never even seen him draw one penalty. This kind of behavior is so unlike the guy I've gotten to know over the previous few months. I've never seen him be anything less than calm and collected.

Worse than that, he and Luke are getting into it on the ice.

It's impossible to hear what's being said, but it's obvious from the tension radiating off them that their exchanges have become contentious. They're supposed to be a united front on the ice. Right now, they're anything but. The bad energy is affecting the entire team.

With less than a minute and a half to go, the other team charges down the ice. Cole blocks them, slamming into a forward before knocking the puck loose. A scuffle ensues and Luke joins the fray. For a few tense seconds, it's impossible to see what's going on or who has the puck. My gaze flicks anxiously to the game clock.

There are sixty seconds left.

That's plenty of time for the Timber Wolves to score and win the game. In hockey, a team can score with just a few seconds on the clock from the other end of the ice.

The puck is knocked loose from the pile of players as Austin swoops in and nabs it. He digs his blades into the ice and kicks it into high gear. The fans surge to their feet in anticipation. They scream and cheer as Austin races toward the net. Just as Austin closes in, he rips off a lightning quick shot. Everyone within the arena holds their breath, waiting for the puck to hit the back of the net.

Just when it seems like there's no way he won't score the winning goal, the other team's goalie slides, effectively blocking the shot. The game ends in a tie. Even though it's not a loss, the Timber Wolves aren't happy.

And neither is their head coach.

Nerves churn uncomfortably in my belly as we watch both teams file off the ice. Everyone looks pissed off. Even the fans.

"Well," Brooklyn says, drawing my attention to her, "that was one hell of a game."

"Yeah," I mutter.

But it wasn't good.

We rise to our feet, both ready to vacate the cold arena. There's a good possibility that my butt is numb. It feels good to get up and stretch my muscles. Although, I'm undecided as to what to do.

Should I stick around and talk to Cole?

Or wait until tomorrow when we've both had time to get a little perspective?

Brooklyn seems to understand my internal struggle. "Are we waiting around or taking off?"

When I came here tonight, I'd assumed Cole and I would be able to clear the air after the game. That no longer feels like a good idea.

Especially after that game.

It's obvious that he's in a bad mood, and I know it has everything to do with what transpired at the library.

Plus, his parents and ex-girlfriend will probably hang around to talk with him. For all I know, they could have plans to grab something to eat. And then there's Luke. I don't want any further issues arising between them because of me.

But still, leaving without at least saying hello seems wrong. I nibble at my lower lip with indecision.

For better or worse, I decide to stick around. Brooklyn and I are one of the last stragglers to make our way to where the locker rooms are located. We keep to ourselves on the perimeter of the group. The last thing I want is to get sucked into an awkward conversation with Cole's parents or his ex.

"Cassidy?"

Damn.

My heart flips over as I inwardly flinch. It takes effort to plaster a tight smile across my face as I swing around to face her with as much dignity as I can muster. Considering that I've spent the last ten minutes using my friend as a human shield, that's not saying much.

"Hi, Dr. Thompson." Then I nod towards Thomas, Cole's stepfather. "And Dr. Thompson."

Eyes twinkling, he smiles in response. Even though I'm racked with nerves, his easy demeanor manages to ease the thick tension crackling in the air that surrounds us. "Or you could just call us, Dr. Thompson squared."

My lips lift.

He's such a nice man, and yet, all I can focus on is whether he knows that his wife was my psychologist and knows all my deep dark secrets.

"That was a pretty rough game," Thomas comments. "Cole usually plays with a lot more control and finesse. I'm not sure what was going on with him tonight."

I clear my throat. "The whole team seemed to be having issues."

Thomas makes a noncommittal noise in his throat but doesn't say anything more. Since Brooklyn only knows that hockey is played by hot guys, wearing massive shoulder pads and, hopefully, extra-large jockstraps, she can't contribute anything to the conversation, which has become painful.

I'm about to make up an excuse as to why Brooklyn and I have to flee to the bathroom when Cole's mother asks, "Cassidy, could we talk for a moment?"

Everything inside me freezes. I'd rather gouge my eyes out than have a private conversation with Cole's mother.

"What's up, Docs?"

I swing around, never so thrilled to see Austin in my life. I want to jump into his arms and kiss him senseless.

Thomas claps him on the shoulder and tells him that it was a tough game. The rest of us vehemently agree as Brooklyn studiously avoids Austin's gaze. It doesn't look like anything has changed since I last saw them.

At this point, I'm desperately trying to manufacture an excuse as to why we need to make a hasty getaway.

"Where's Cole?"

My heart plummets as my gaze lands on Jackie, who has joined the group.

"Coach wanted to ream his," Austin's gaze catches Dr. Thompson's, "um, talk privately with him. I wouldn't be expecting him anytime soon."

There's no way in hell I'm going to stick around with his parents and ex. Maybe it's better to let everything settle between us and talk in the morning.

Even though I know Brooklyn will probably end up killing me, I don't see any other choice in the matter. We Ubered it here for the game, and I don't want to wait around for another ride. "Austin, would you mind dropping us off at the dorms?"

His gaze slides to Brooklyn as her narrowed one darts to mine.

"Sure, no problem. You ready to take off?"

Relief floods through me.

More than ready.

I nod before turning to Cole's parents. "It was really nice to see you again."

Nothing could be further from the truth.

It takes everything I have to hold the forced smile in place.

The edges of Dr. Thompson's lips also slide upward. Strangely enough, hers looks like the warm one she'd give me in her office. It only makes me wonder if the genuineness and empathy I felt from her was nothing more than a shtick she trots out for her clients.

Cole's stepfather beams at me before closing the distance between us and enveloping me in a warm hug. I can only stand stiffly in his arms until it ends. It's only when the three of us walk through the sliding doors of the ice arena that I can breathe again. The ride back to the dorms is made in silence. As I stare out the window, I wonder how I'll fix this mess with Cole.

When we finally pull up to Washington Hall, I thank Austin before exiting the vehicle. Brooklyn's gaze flickers to me as I wait for her on the sidewalk. Instead of joining me, she remains seated.

"I'm, ah," her voice falters as she breaks eye contact, "going back to Austin's tonight, so don't wait up."

With a nod, I hurry toward the dorm as Brooklyn and Austin take off. I kind of wish Brooklyn had decided to come home with me tonight. I could really use a friend right now. Twenty minutes later, my face is freshly scrubbed, and I've pulled on a pair of well-worn yoga pants and a tank top when my phone chimes with an incoming text.

We need to talk. Can I come up?

17

CASSIDY

I suck in a deep breath as my thumb hovers over the screen of my phone.

I'm scared.

Scared to see him.

Scared to hear what he has to say.

But I know he's right. We need to talk about what's going on between us.

Ok

Two letters.

That's all I'm capable of typing before I hit send. Even though our dorm room is tiny, I pace as I wait. It only takes a few minutes before there's a soft knock on the door. I grab the handle and open it to find Cole standing on the other side of the threshold.

"Hi." Barely can I force out the greeting. Already, everything feels different between us.

He jerks his head as his whiskey-colored eyes collide with mine.

As they do, I realize with a sinking heart that whatever is happening between us is much worse than I originally suspected. Cole's hands are shoved into the front pockets of his jeans. He's wearing a Western Timber Wolves sweatshirt with the hood pulled up

129

over his head. His mouth is a tight slash across his face as unhappiness radiates off him in heavy waves.

"I thought it would be better for us to talk in person," he says before pushing the hood back. His hair is still shiny and damp from his recent shower. I want nothing more than to tunnel my fingers through his thick locks.

Instead, I keep my hands to myself.

"Um, yeah. That's probably a good idea."

Although, it doesn't feel like a good idea.

In fact, it feels like this could potentially be the end of us.

I shake my head to dispel the thought. Have we really reached that point? It seems almost unbelievable.

Unsure of what to do, I step aside so he can enter the room before closing the door behind him. Nerves prickle along my skin as I force myself to settle on my bed as he takes a seat across from me on Brooklyn's. With his knees angled apart, he leans forward, resting his forearms on them. He knots his hands together in front of him. For a long moment, he stares at them as if there are too many thoughts churning through his head for him to organize.

"Cole?" It kills me to see the unhappiness that is written across his face and the tension filling every muscle of his body. What hurts most is that I'm the one who caused it. All I want to do is reach out and smooth away all the hurt and anger filling his eyes.

But I don't.

It's as if there is an ocean of uncertainty sitting between us, and there doesn't seem to be a way to breech it.

Time slowly ticks by before he drags his bruised eyes to mine. A dull ache rips through me. This is the first time I've felt like he'd prefer not to look at me. He inhales, holding the air captive in his lungs for a beat or two before slowly forcing it out.

"I don't like playing games. It's not who I am."

I nod. Cole is one of the few people I've met who refuses to engage in that immature bullshit. It's just another reason I fell so hard for him. He was always so upfront about everything he felt for me and what he wanted. It was as refreshing as it was scary. Even though it took me some time to trust him with the truth of my past, eventually I did. That was a huge step for me. I don't trust people easily.

Not anymore.

That has everything to do with Cole and the kind of person he is. I couldn't have taken that leap of faith with anyone else but him.

I realize that even if he doesn't.

"And I can't be in a relationship with someone who's going to play games with me."

My eyes widen as everything in my world tilts precariously. It's almost as if I can't suck enough oxygen into my lungs.

"I'm not playing games," I whisper.

His expression never falters. "I think there's something going on between you and Luke."

I shake my head in denial. "No. We're just friends. You know that."

He breaks eye contact and stares out the window into the swirling darkness for a painful heartbeat.

"I don't know. It feels like something's going on and I don't want to be the dumbass who gets cheated on again."

"We're nothing more than friends. I had no idea he would be at the library today. It was a coincidence." I stare pleadingly at his profile until his gaze slides back to mine.

"But you weren't going to tell me about it, were you?" It's more of an accusation than a question.

I close my eyes for a moment and try to figure out how to best answer his question. I owe it to both of us to be honest about what I feel, not only for Cole but for Luke as well.

"I'm not sure if I would have mentioned meeting Luke at the library."

Hurt and distrust flash in his golden depths.

I rush to add, "But not because I was doing anything wrong."

"Then why not?" His gaze sifts through mine, searching for answers. "Why not be honest about it?"

My teeth sink into my lower lip as I confess in a very small voice, "I know you don't like when I spend time with Luke." Even though I want to reach out and physically connect with him, I keep my fingers tangled together on my lap.

"You need to tell me the truth, Cassidy." His voice drops, sounding as if it's been scraped from the bottom of the ocean. "Do you have feelings for Luke?"

As much as I want to reassure him by vehemently denying the question, I can't.

What I want most is to be worthy of Cole Mathews. And being worthy means being honest even though it might cause him pain. I take a moment to sift through my feelings for Luke before I give him an answer.

"I feel very connected to him," I admit. "He helped me when no one else would, and I can't let that go. I know he feels the same way about me. We're nothing more than friends."

He leans forward, inching closer to me. It's like we're two opposing ends of a magnet desperately trying to connect with one another.

"You know he wants you, right?"

Even though it's tempting to look away from his probing gaze, I don't.

"Yes," I say with a nod. "He told me that he feels more than friendship for me."

Cole snorts before shaking his head in disgust. "He knew we were together when he told you that."

"Yes."

A heavy silence falls over us before he asks in a clipped tone, "Is he trying to steal you from me or is his plan to undermine our relationship and wait it out?"

My brows pinch together. "Does it matter? What we have has nothing to do with Luke. It shouldn't matter what he wants. You just need to trust me."

He plows his fingers through his damp hair. "Jeez, Cassidy. You have to realize it's not that easy. Even though Luke is my teammate, he's more than willing to screw me over to have you. How am I supposed to trust him both on and off the ice?" He doesn't give me time to answer. "I can't do it." Exhaustion fills every line of his face before he adds, "And it doesn't feel like I can trust you to tell me the truth, either. You could have told me that you two were together at the library, but you chose not to."

My heart flutters painfully before beating into overtime. "I didn't want to upset you," I whisper.

But it sounds bad.

Even to my own ears.

I should have been upfront with Cole.

And now it looks like I might lose him because of it.

The corners of his lips tug downward. He looks as miserable as I feel.

"If Luke hadn't come out of the library with your notebook, you wouldn't have told me that you two spent any time together." The pause that follows has my muscles tensing. "And that's what bothers me most. I have no idea if this is the first time it happened, or if you've chosen to hide it from me because there's actually something going on between you two."

A hot rush of tears sting my eyes. "Nothing is going on between us. I would *never* cheat on you."

"Yeah, well, unfortunately someone else I trusted said those very words to me, and I'm not about to let it happen again." His gaze drops to his fingers. "I think Luke saving you that night has messed with your head, and you either feel beholden to him or you've actually developed feelings that run deeper than friendship." He pauses as his hollowed-out eyes cut back to mine. "You need to figure that out without me getting in the way."

When I shake my head, ready to argue with him, he jerks to his feet. I have no other choice but to do the same. Even though I'm loath to put myself out there, I take a tentative step toward him, only wanting to bridge the distance between us. What I really want to do is hurtle myself into his arms and feel them band around me, holding me tight.

"I love you. You have to know that you're the only one I want to be with."

As the words leave my lips, I know they're the truth.

I feel them deep in my heart.

The fact that Cole feels like he can't trust me, rips me apart inside. I can't help but wonder if maybe, without realizing it, I've sent Luke the wrong message. Did I let him think there would be, at some point, an opportunity for us to be more than just friends?

I don't know.

"Cole, please…" I have no idea what I'm begging for.

Forgiveness?

A second chance to prove that he's the one I love?

The way he shakes his head makes my heart clench painfully.

"I think we both need to take a little bit of time to figure things out. What happened on the ice tonight…" his voice trails off as he glances away. Dull color stains his cheeks. "I can't allow that to happen again. That's not the kind of player I am." He amends softly, "It's not the kind of person I am."

"I know that," I whisper.

I know exactly who Cole Mathews is.

It kills me to think that I've caused this to unfold between us.

"Everything happened really fast with us. Maybe I pushed you too far. I don't know anymore."

"No, that's not it." My voice is so thick with unspent emotion that it feels as if I'm choking on it.

He beelines for the door before saying, "I need to take a step back and clear my head. I think we both do."

My shoulders collapse under the weight of the realization that there is nothing I can say that will change his mind. In a way, his actions don't surprise me. Cole is just being honest and he's doing what he thinks is best, not only for himself, but for me as well.

"That's it then? We're…" No matter how hard I try, I can't wrap my lips around the words *breaking up.*

I'm trying so hard to keep it together, and if I force out those two words, the tears stinging the back of my eyes will fall. I don't think I can bear to hear him say them, either. I don't want him to tell me that it's over and he's moving on with his life.

That I need to do the same.

I can't help but think about the empty shell of a person I was before meeting him. Just going through the motions. Scared to get close to anyone. Afraid of opening up and allowing someone to know the real me. The one who fucked up and made a mess out of her life.

I'm terrified of reverting back to that again.

"If you have feelings for Luke, you need to explore them," he says, cutting into my thoughts. You owe it to yourself to be in a relationship with the person you truly want."

I swallow thickly as he reaches his hand out toward me. Before he's able to make contact, he retracts it.

"We both need to take some time to figure out what we want."

I bite down almost savagely on my lower lip so I won't break down and beg him not to do this. Unable to speak, I jerk my head into a tight nod. Even though it's a small movement, it takes a herculean effort.

Just as I do, his arm snakes out and he hauls me to him so that I'm flush with his hard body. His golden eyes scour mine before his lips crash down onto mine, dragging me under with him. For one blissful moment, I'm consumed by him.

He's all I can taste and feel.

Just as I sink into his caress, he wrenches himself away.

With one last soulful look aimed in my direction, he yanks open my door and leaves the room.

Leaves me.

It's only after the lock clicks into place that my knees buckle and I collapse onto the bed, knowing that I've just let the best thing that ever happened to me walk out of my life.

18

CASSIDY

"Cass, I know you're hurting, but you have to snap out of it." Brooklyn shoots me a concerned glance as we walk across campus before adding, "You're beginning to scare me."

Snap out of it.

If only I could.

If only it were that easy.

It feels like I've been sleepwalking through a dense fog for the past ten days. Other than breaking up with Cole, I don't think I could tell you what else happened. And everything in my life has suffered because of it.

I keep telling myself that I need to pull it together. There is no way I can fail out of school for a second time. Especially when I'm starting to make progress with my parents. Meeting with both of them last week and having everything go smoothly was the only bright spot in an otherwise crappy week.

If I'd held out a tiny scrap of hope that this breakup with Cole would blow over, that hope has been fully extinguished. I've barely seen him. There hasn't been one single text or call exchanged between us. He's pretty much disappeared from my life as if he were never a part of it. Even though we have Psychology 201 together every

Monday, Wednesday, and Friday, he now slides last minute into the back of the lecture hall next to his cousin, Sammy.

"I'm fine. Everything is fine."

That's my new mantra.

Although, I don't think it's working. Otherwise, I wouldn't be such a mess.

It's all I can do to hoist the corners of my mouth into something that hopefully resembles an anemic-looking smile. For the past week and a half, I've been going through the motions. It's just easier that way.

I'd like to think I'm getting pretty good at faking it.

Or not.

With almost a year of therapy under my belt, I've learned how important it is to talk about your feelings, generate a plan, and face your problems head on. Since the breakup, I remember how much easier it is to curl up in a tight ball and ignore the pain that throbs through every pore of my body.

Everything hurts.

Everything feels tender.

It's like an open sore that refuses to heal.

It's like I'm back to square one again in the healing process. It sucks ass.

On the bright side, at least I'm no longer having anxiety issues.

Brooklyn snorts.

We're both bundled up in thick winter jackets, with hats pulled low over our ears to protect them from the icy cold winds that blow through leafless trees and around squat stone buildings. To make matters worse, we had our first snowfall the other day, which made everything feel even more depressing.

"Cassidy, you are so far from fine that it's not even funny." There's a pause before she adds in a serious tone, "I'm worried about you."

I don't bother to argue because the effort seems pointless. There's also the fact that she's spot-on in her assessment of the situation.

I'm not fine.

Even more concerning—I have no idea when I'll be *fine* again.

I'm in such a bad place that I've actually kicked around the idea of popping in to see Dr. Thompson, but the thought of actually coming face-to-face with her makes me gut-sick.

Brooklyn slings an arm around my shoulders before hauling me close as we trudge to our nine o'clock classes.

A small smile tips one corner of her mouth up as she says, "Who would have ever thought that we'd be having so many penis problems."

I shake my head and force out a weak laugh. "I don't think we have problems with penises."

"Of course, we do. Penises are usually at the root of every girl's problem."

"Well, Cole and his penis don't want anything to do with me, and you and Austin's penis are nothing more than—"

"Fuck buddies?" she supplies with a bright smile.

"That wasn't exactly how I was going to describe it but sure, we'll just go with that." There's a moment of silence as we both dwell on our penis problems. "So, how's that situation working out for you?"

She shrugs. "It's not. The whole *sleeping-with-him-to-lose-interest-in-him* strategy hasn't been going according to plan."

I raise a brow, unsurprised by her pronouncement. What does amaze me is that she's admitting defeat. "No? How shocking. I mean, your plan had foolproof written all over it."

She gives me a little shove. "Oh, shut up."

A chuckle slips free from me in response. Although, it sounds a bit rusty around the edges. There hasn't been much to laugh about lately.

I glance over at her. "Does that mean you're going to finally put an end to all this hooking up business?"

She scrunches her nose and gives me a *are-you-off-your-fucking-rocker* look. "What kind of question is that? Of course, I'm going to keep knocking boots with him. The guy is freaking phenomenal in bed." She tugs me closer before whispering in my ear, "And when I say *phenomenal* what I really mean is *freaking amazing.* Remember when I mentioned what he could do with that tongue of his?"

"Yes, I do, and I don't want to hear the gory details again. The first time was mentally-scarring enough."

She rolls her vibrant green eyes. "Oh, whatever."

Plus, I don't need any reminders regarding all the delicious ways Cole uses his tongue, because the thought of him doing that with another girl—or, god forbid, plural—makes me sick to my stomach.

Is that why it's been radio silence from his end?

Has he already gotten together with someone else?

Maybe he's decided to give Jackie a second chance?

I have no idea, and I'm not brave enough to reach out and open up a line of communication.

For whatever reason, Brooklyn decides to bring our conversation back full circle, which I could do without. There is nothing she can say that will make me feel better.

"Listen, Cass, I know you're hurting over the whole Cole situation, and I wish I could tell you that everything will work out in the end, but neither of us knows what will happen. What I do know is that you've worked way too hard to get your ass back into college to let it all fall to shit over some guy."

Ouch.

I wince at her harsh words.

Cole isn't some random dude I got mixed up with. He means so much more than that to me.

He means everything.

She pauses for a moment as if silently debating whether to add the last kick in the ass. But here's the thing about Brooklyn—she's not afraid to give someone she cares about a dose of tough love.

"You two were together on and off since what? Mid-September? I know you really care about him, but it hasn't been that long. If he was willing to simply walk away from you without trying to work it out, then maybe he's not the guy either of us thought he was." She studies me as if to gauge how I'm taking the bitch-slap she's just hit me with. "You know what I'm saying is true. Maybe Cole is a closet douchebag after all."

Even though her comments give me whiplash, that doesn't mean they aren't true. Well, not the douchebag part. Cole is the farthest thing from a D-bag. I don't care what anyone says.

"I know. And you don't have to worry. I'm not going to throw everything I've been working toward away. Whether I'm with Cole or not, my focus is on school." I draw in a deep breath and pray that what I'm about to utter is the truth, because at this point, it doesn't feel like it. "I'll be okay."

Her eyes sift through mine for the truth. "Yeah," she finally says, "I think you will be. It just might take a while for you to actually feel better."

"We'll both be all right," I murmur. Even though my gaze is focused on the concrete path stretched out in front of me and the other students walking past, I don't register any of it. My brain is operating on autopilot.

"Are you going to reach out to him?" she asks.

I shrug. "He doesn't want to see or talk to me right now, and I feel like I should respect that decision."

"Yeah," she says with a sigh, "there's nothing worse than being reduced to a stalker."

Ugh.

"I refuse to go into stalker mode," I mutter. Even if I do kind of want to stalk him. Just a tiny bit. But that would mean jackhammering to a whole new level of pathetic, and I'm not ready to do that.

Yet.

The problem is that I miss the hell out of Cole. I miss our easy comradery. And how much fun we had hanging out. I miss talking with him during the day, and at the end of it. I miss the way he used to look at me like I was his everything. And I miss being held in his arms or lying across his bare chest after making love.

I miss all of it so much that I physically ache for him.

The way he dropped out of my life feels devastating. It's like someone blasted a massive hole through my existence, and I've been left to pick up the fragmented pieces. Even though I have a lot going on with classes, tutoring, and the hockey team, there's a gaping hole where our relationship used to be.

"And Luke?" she asks, cutting into those thoughts.

"We're just friends." I miss Cole way too much to hook up with someone else. He thought I needed to explore my feelings for Luke, but I'm nowhere ready to do that.

Her gaze narrows as if she doesn't believe me. "You two have been hanging out quite a bit lately."

"But that's all we've been doing. I…" my voice trails off as we reach the social sciences building and I catch a glimpse of Cole walking toward it.

She gives me a questioning look as I grind to a halt.

"Cass?"

The wet lump of sawdust lodged in the middle of my throat makes it impossible to speak. My gaze stays pinned to him as heartache tears through me. All the pain and grief I've been trying to keep bottled up inside bursts free, flooding through every cell of my being, making the breakup feel tender and raw all over again.

I just want him back.

"Who's the girl?" Brooklyn asks.

I've been too wrapped up in Cole to notice the pretty brunette he's walking with.

And talking to.

And smiling at.

Just kill me now. I don't think I can deal with anymore of this pain. And seeing him with another girl?

Completely devastating.

From this distance, it's impossible to tell if it's his ex.

"I don't know," I whisper.

"She's probably no one," Brooklyn says. "They're just walking to class together."

"It's not my business who he spends time with," I force myself to say. Maybe if I repeat it enough times, I'll be able to move on as easily as he has. "We're not together anymore."

My fingers rise to gently rub at the spot over my heart, because releasing those words into the atmosphere hurts. It's a physical pain that constricts my chest.

Brooklyn wraps her arm around me before squeezing tight, as if she's trying to force all the air from my body. Or maybe all the heartache. "It'll be okay." She pauses before adding with a groan, "I've got to hustle, otherwise I'm going to be late. You know how much I'd seriously hate to miss a single word of Professor Ling's Calc II lecture."

I force my lips into a slight smile. "Okay. Catch you later for dinner?"

"Definitely." She tosses the response over her shoulder as she jogs toward the mathematics building, which is at least a block away.

I straighten my shoulders and gather my courage before trudging my way to Dorin Hall. Once inside, I head to the first-floor lecture hall where Psych 201 takes place. Cole has thrown me off today. Normally, I'm already seated in the front when he slinks in right before class begins. Most of the time, I don't catch a glimpse of him, and I try not to turn around and seek him out. I don't need to look any more tragic than I already do by staring at him like some pathetic stalker-type-chick who can't move on.

My footsteps stall as I pause outside the lecture hall doors, not wanting to pull them open. I don't want to see him, and I certainly don't want to see him with the girl he walked to class with. I don't need any further confirmation that he's moved on with his life while I'm stuck feeling depressed over the sudden demise of our relationship.

As my hand rises to the handle, I remind myself to keep my gaze trained straight ahead of me. There's no straying to the left or right. No searching for Cole like a heat seeking missile. Just as I'm about to yank open the door, a large male hand reaches around and does it for me. I feel the heat of his body behind me. My head whips around as my gaze collides with his golden, whiskey-colored eyes.

"Cole." Every muscle goes on high alert as electricity zips across my skin.

"Hi, Cassidy," he murmurs.

His gaze holds mine captive for a heartbeat. Before I'm able to think of a way to extend the conversation, the moment ends and I realize other students are piling up behind us, waiting to enter the lecture hall.

He holds open the door as I continue staring up at him like a lovesick puppy. My fingers itch to plow their way through his tousled strands. Instead, I tighten my hand so I won't be tempted to reach out and touch him the way I want to.

I've missed him so much more than I realized.

It's almost painful to be this close to him. To have his masculine scent slyly wrapping its way around me.

It takes effort to shake myself out of the trance that has fallen over me as I force myself to break eye contact and step over the threshold.

"Thank you."

"No problem."

As I walk down the thinly-carpeted steps, I feel him shadow my movements. A tiny spark of hope flares to life within me. Is it possible that he'll sit next to me today? Have we managed to turn a corner in our practically nonexistent relationship?

I wish I had the courage to ask these questions.

"Cassidy?"

I spin around at the sound of my name and find him standing on the step above me. It's the same row his cousin, Sammy, is parked in. I have to crane my neck more than usual to hold his gaze.

"If you're not busy, do you want to grab some lunch this afternoon?"

Even though it feels like we're moving in the right direction, it doesn't necessarily mean we're getting back together.

Although, reining in the smile that curves my lips is impossible. "I'd like that."

A matching expression flashes across his face, but it's by no means a full-blown smile, one that has his dimples peeking out, and I miss them.

"Great. Do you want to meet at the Union around one?"

My heart pumps a painful staccato against my ribcage at the idea of us sitting down and talking. "That sounds good. I'll see you then."

He nods before slipping into the row with his cousin. Hesitantly, I meet Sammy's gaze. She smiles, but much like Cole's, it isn't full-blown by any means. I hate that my breakup with Cole has inadvertently affected my friendship with Sammy. But that's not surprising since they're close, and she did warn me in the beginning not to hurt him.

Even though Sammy and I are teammates, and we skate together three or four times a week on the intramural hockey team, we were just beginning to get to know each other. With the way she's watching me, I can only assume Cole filled her in on what happened between us. Sammy is a formidable chick. She's not someone I want to have an issue with.

Plus, I genuinely like her.

It doesn't escape me that I've lost the people I'd just started to think of as my support system. Cole. Dr. Thompson. And now Sammy.

Instead of concentrating on what professor Mullens is lecturing on, all I can focus on is meeting up with Cole for lunch. Should I even get my hopes up that we'll get back together? Or is he going to tell me that he's ready to move on and I should do the same?

My belly clenches at the thought of those words spilling from his lips.

When our professor finally dismisses the class, I can't help but glance at the half page of notes I've taken. Usually, I type out a solid four pages.

Even worse than that, I have no idea what her lecture was about.

Ugh.

What I need to do is pull my head out of my ass before I fail out of school for a second time. And this time, there's no doubt in my mind that my parents will disown me.

Frustrated with myself, I gather up my belongings before making my way out of the lecture hall. When I look at the spot Cole and Sammy were sitting, their seats are empty. Just like I knew they would be.

As expected, the next three hours drag by as I glance at my phone every five minutes. Unable to focus on homework, I decide to head over to the Union and grab a coffee while I wait.

"Cassidy!"

I swing around on the walking path as my name is called and find Luke pushing through the heard of slow-moving students to reach me.

"Hi." Over the course of the past week and a half, we've become even closer friends.

But that's all we are.

As he falls into step with me, he asks, "Are you on your way to the Union?"

"Yup." I don't mention that I'm grabbing lunch with Cole. For the time being, I want to keep that information to myself.

Since I've been spending quite a bit of time with Luke lately, I've learned a lot about him. Like how easy he is to talk to, and what a great sense of humor he has. The more we're together, the more attractive I find him. And he's a really nice guy on top of all that.

There aren't many people I trust or feel completely at ease with.

He's one of the few.

It's hard not to cling to that.

Or him.

Does that necessarily mean I'm ready to explore the depth of my feelings for him?

No. I'm not ready to give up on Cole. And Luke hasn't pushed the issue. He's been nothing but the friend I've so desperately needed to lean on during this breakup.

"Have you eaten lunch yet?" he asks, breaking into the chaotic whirl of my thoughts.

"No, I was going to grab something now."

"That works out perfectly. We can have lunch together." With a smile, he nudges me in the shoulder. "Maybe you'll even take pity on me and help with some calc homework."

Even though I'd wanted to keep the lunch date to myself, I realize I'm going to have to come clean.

I clear my throat and blurt, "I'm meeting Cole for lunch."

One brow hitches at that bit of information. He's aware that Cole and I haven't spoken in ten days. He also knows how upset I've been about it. "That's a new development."

Since he doesn't sound pissed off, it only reinforces that we really are just friends.

"Yes."

His gaze shifts away from me. "Do you want to get back together with him?"

When I glance at him, his attention locks on me before searching my eyes.

My teeth scrape against my bottom lip as I admit, "Yeah, I do." The last thing I want to do is lead Luke on.

His brow furrows slightly as he nods. "Then I hope everything works out between you two."

Relief rushes through me at his easy acceptance of the situation. Impulsively, I reach out, grabbing a hold of his hand and squeezing it as we continue walking.

"Thank you. Me, too."

As we arrive at the Union, Luke pulls open one of the doors for me. With a smile aimed in his direction, I thank him before walking inside the brick building.

Even though I've arrived early for my lunch with Cole, I couldn't be more aware of Luke's presence beside me. It doesn't escape me that his friendship is the reason Cole pulled away in the first place. The last thing I want to do is exacerbate the situation by being seen with him.

From beneath my lashes, I glance around the open space but don't see Cole anywhere.

As much as it makes me feel like a crappy friend, I want this lunch to go smoothly.

I pause.

When he does the same, I say, "If you don't mind, I'm going to wait for Cole alone."

"Sure." His lips curve into a smile as he leans over and presses a kiss against my cheek. "Text me later and let me know how it goes."

Grateful for his understanding, I beam. This is the first time since Cole walked out of my dorm room that I've allowed myself to be hopeful that we could hash out our issues.

"I will."

After we say our goodbyes, he disappears, getting swallowed up by the thick crowd. The Union is a hub of activity for the students of Western University. There are six different restaurants, a bookstore, a bank, and a couple of different places to hang out at with pool tables, foosball, and air hockey. There's always music playing in the background, and sometimes, on the weekends, there are live bands.

I turn in a tight circle, scanning the sea of students gathered for lunch before spotting Cole on a couch. Air rushes from my lungs as our gazes collide. For a painful heartbeat, my feet feel frozen in place.

The closed off expression on his face makes me realize that he saw Luke and I walk in together. An icy cold fist wraps around my beating heart before squeezing painfully. We haven't spoken one word to each other and already it feels like this lunch is off to a rocky start. I give him a hesitant wave before forcing my feet to close the distance between us.

A heavy weight descends, and I hate it. I hate that this is what our relationship has become. From the beginning, our friendship was always so easy. Even when I was fighting my attraction to him, the comradery was effortless.

This, unfortunately, feels anything but.

"Hi." I keep my voice neutral, hoping we can move past the uncomfortableness that hangs over us.

Part of me is so afraid he'll get up and walk away.

Instead, a slight smile spreads across his face. Even though his dimples remain elusive, I'll still take it. Just like this morning, it feels good to be this close to him.

He rises to his feet before extending his hand out for me to take.

My heart leaps as I place my fingers in his. Energy crackles in the air between us as we make physical contact. Something flickers in his eyes.

Instead of commenting on it, he clears his throat. "What kind of food are you in the mood for?"

Honestly, I don't give a crap what we eat. All that matters in this moment is that we're together.

I shrug. "You decide."

As his gaze roams over the restaurants, I'm able to drink him in while he's unaware of my perusal. "Burgers?"

"Sure, that's fine."

While we stand in line, the fledgling conversation between us stalls.

As I rack my brain for something to say, a flirty female voice says, "Cole! Over here!"

Another voice chimes in. "We haven't seen you in forever! Where've you been hiding?"

I blink as two giggling girls bounce their way over to us.

Neither gives me a second glance.

I should amend that statement, because I don't think I ever got a first glance. I silently watch as he flashes both an easy smile as if genuinely happy to see them.

"What are you two up to?" he asks, attention focused on the girls.

In return, they give him mega-watt smiles before one supplies an answer, "We just stopped by to grab a quick lunch. We've got a class at two."

Not to be outdone by her friend, the other cuts in, "Hey, we heard you guys are having a huge bash this weekend. You need to give us all the details!"

"We're having a party on Saturday night. You should both stop by, I'm sure it'll be a good time."

"Definitely!" one says enthusiastically, practically bouncing on the tips of her toes.

As if realizing there's another person standing with them, one finally slants a look at me. "Is this your girlfriend?"

Cole keeps his attention focused on the girls as he clears his throat. "This is my friend, Cassidy."

His answer is like a slap in my face. All I want to do is melt into the floor.

Was I really so delusional as to think we might be getting back together?

Yeah, I was.

Obviously, that's not going to happen.

Even though it feels impossible, I force my lips into a thin smile before giving a halfhearted wave. "Hi."

The brunette with gorgeous, long wavy hair taps her chest. "Hey, I'm Vanessa." She cocks her head toward her blonde counterpart. "And this is Andrea. We're Taus."

My expression must say it all because she quickly elaborates. "Alpha Sigma Tau, that is."

Oh.

Of course, they're sorority girls. I should have known. They seem exactly like the bubbly ex-cheerleader types with their huge boobs, tiny waists, glossy hair, and lips that look like they could suck the chrome off a bumper.

It only makes me wonder if Cole has experienced either one of their chrome-sucking abilities.

I suck in a steady breath before expelling it.

This is crazy. I seriously need to settle.

Even though it's tempting to reach over and pull out all their lustrous hair, I remind myself that I don't, *technically*, have anything against these girls. Up until five minutes ago, I didn't know they existed.

Since I have zero claim on Cole—as he was quick to point out—he's fair game.

As soon as those thoughts circle through my head, Vanessa reaches over and strokes her sparkly blue talons over his forearm all the while eye-fucking him in front of me.

Unable to stomach the sight, my gaze shifts to Andrea only to see her batting mascara-laden lashes at him.

For goodness' sake, it's one o'clock on a Wednesday afternoon, people. Get a freaking grip on your hormones.

I don't understand if their mentality is *may the best woman win,* or if they plan on sharing him. The mental image of these two getting it on with him makes me sick to my stomach.

You know what?

I can't do this.

I can't stick around and watch these two females rub up against Cole like a couple of cats in heat. Since he's not doing anything to deter them from flirting with him in front of my face, I take it as my cue to leave.

With a quick step in retreat, I force the words from my lips. "I thought lunch would work out, but I've actually got to run." Before Cole can respond, I turn to his friends.

I have to remind myself for the second time that I have no bone to pick with them.

Oh, who am I kidding?

I'd like nothing more than to haul off and bitch-slap the pair of them into next week, where I can then go and kick their asses all over again.

Tamping down those thoughts, I smile. It might be gritted, but I congratulate myself on holding it together.

"It was nice meeting you two, I'm sure I'll see you both around."

They flash identical white smiles before gushing, "You, too!"

And then I swing around and haul ass out of there. Cole calls out my name, but I don't bother to turn around.

To make matters worse, the hot sting of tears pricks the backs of my eyes. But I'll be damned if I allow them to fall. I've spent the last week and a half moping around and mourning our relationship. What's become obvious is that I'm the only one who was hoping we could work things out. If Cole had any interest in getting back together, he wouldn't have let those girls hang all over him in front of me.

I'm done.

Done being depressed.

Done blaming myself for how our relationship fell apart.

Cole Mathews can go to hell and take those sorority chicks with him.

Big breath in.

Slow breath out.

Alright, *now* I'm done.

19

COLE

*W*ell shit.

With my brows pinched together, I watch as Cassidy races from the Union like the hounds of hell are nipping at her heels.

In my head, I saw this lunch working out differently.

I blow out a frustrated breath and turn my attention back to Vanessa and Andrea before glaring at them. "Seriously, what did you do that for?"

They both collapse into a fit of giggles. "It's so fun screwing with these girls who want to get a great big taste of Cole."

I roll my eyes. "Yeah, well, I was kind of hoping to smooth things over with that particular girl. Up until about a week ago, I was seeing her."

Vanessa's eyes widen. "Then maybe you should have said something, instead of letting me paw you in front of her."

Andrea links an arm through her friend's and takes up Vanessa's side. "Yeah, Cole. We thought she was one of those silly groupies who are constantly throwing themselves at you. Usually, you're more than happy when we intervene."

She's right.

Normally, I am.

There have been a lot of times when Vanessa's and Andrea's attention has come in handy.

But not this time.

"I think you blew my chances of getting back together with her to shit."

Andrea shrugs. "It's not a big deal. Just tell her we were joking around."

"Everyone around here knows that we're into chicks, not dicks," Vanessa adds as if it's completely obvious they're lesbians.

I plow a hand through my hair as my gaze slides back to the last place I saw Cassidy before she disappeared through the crowd.

"Well, we've got to get moving." Andrea flashes me an overly bright smile.

"Yeah, see you Saturday!" Vanessa chimes in.

They take off as well, leaving me to stand by myself at the burger place. I'm debating whether to skip lunch when someone steps into my space. For a moment, my pulse picks up speed, hoping Cassidy has returned.

Even if it's to chew my ass out.

"You seriously can't be that much of a douche."

Nope. Definitely not Cassidy.

The urge to squeeze my eyes shut and bang my head against a wall slides through me.

Because yeah…apparently, I *am* that much of a douche.

Luke is the last person I want to deal with. I'm already kicking myself in the ass for allowing Cassidy to think I have any interest in either girl. Those two are only interested in each other, and everyone who knows them is aware of that.

Now…am I above using their antics to get rid of unsuspecting chicks I have zero interest in?

Guilty as charged.

Should I have allowed it to spiral so far out of control with Cassidy that she'd jump to the wrong conclusion?

Guess I really am a douche.

I hate playing games, but that's exactly what I did. I wanted to test the waters and see what her interest level was. I mean, she did stroll into the Union with Luke, and they looked pretty damn chummy while doing it.

What I didn't expect was for her to fly out of here like she did.

"Stay out of it, Wellington," I growl. "It's none of your damn business." The fact that he's here, getting in my face over something that has to do with Cassidy, pisses me off.

It fucking killed me to let her go, but I can't be with a girl who's into another guy. And there's something between Cassidy and Luke. I can feel it simmering in the air around them. What I don't know is how deep her feelings for him run.

I know he wants her.

I see it in his eyes every damn time he looks at her.

Even with all her protests and denials, I expected them to get together as soon as I pulled the plug on our relationship.

The thought of her with anyone else drives me crazy.

And this guy is one of my teammates. He's supposed to have my back, not steal my girl right out from beneath my nose.

Luke's brows snap together. He has the nerve to look as angry as I'm currently feeling. "She likes you, dude," he snaps. "Why would you hurt her like that?"

All his words do is leave me feeling like an even bigger asshole.

And I don't need that.

Especially from him.

I run another hand through my hair while trying to keep a lid on my temper. "Stay out of my relationship with Cassidy." There's a pause before I bark, "What do you even care? I'm sure this is exactly what you wanted to happen."

If he's at all surprised by the accusation, he doesn't show it, which only infuriates me more. When he doesn't bother to deny it, my fists bunch at my sides.

"Cassidy is an amazing girl, and if you're stupid enough to let our friendship get in the way of your relationship, then you're not the guy

I thought you were." His steely-eyed gaze searches mine. "Maybe you don't deserve her after all."

His words are like gasoline poured all over my temper. It takes every ounce of self-control not to haul off and punch this asshole in his face. "You don't have a friendship." I shake my head. "She feels beholden to you because you were there that night and," I force out the rest between clenched teeth, "got her out of a bad situation. All it's done is mess with her head."

Luke steps closer, encroaching on my personal space. I stand my ground as he stays put. I release a steady breath and make a conscious effort to unclench my hands.

Instead of getting any further in my face, he shakes his head as if I'm a total loser. And damn if that doesn't grate against my last nerve.

"I can't believe how wrong I was about you." His eyes narrow. "I was giving you both time to work your shit out, but you know what? You don't deserve her." As if what he just said wasn't bad enough, he continues. "Do I want Cassidy? Damn right, I do. And I'm not going to let you stand in my way any longer." He sneers out the rest. "If you want her, Mathews, then you better step up your game because the gloves are coming off." He stabs a finger against my chest and drops his voice. "And when she's finally mine, I'll treat her so damn good, you'll be nothing more than a blip in her past that she can barely remember."

This fucking guy.

It's taking everything I have inside not to grab him by the shirt-front and throw his ass into the food counter. Instead of giving in to the rage boiling inside me, I take a step back, giving us both a bit of much-needed space. I won't jeopardize my future for a few seconds of gratification. Even if he does deserve it. I've made enough mistakes today.

"Fuck you, Wellington." Unfortunately, there is zero satisfaction in those growled-out words.

His upper lip curls. "Yeah, well…I think you've done a fan-fucking-tastic job of screwing yourself where Cassidy is concerned. Good luck with that, man."

With a clap on the shoulder, he leaves me standing there like an impotent asshole, with my hands clenched and a nasty pit gnawing at the bottom of my gut. What I'm most afraid of is that Luke might be right in his assessment of the situation. I've totally fucked myself with my stupidity and jealousy as far as Cassidy is concerned.

For the first time in my life, I don't know what to do.

2 0

CASSIDY

The ice is the only place where I can lose myself. I pass the puck to one of my wingers and fall back to guard our goal. The last thing I want to think about is how my relationship with Cole has gone up in a burst of flames.

How is it possible that almost a month ago, I couldn't imagine us being apart?

And now—

A hard hit from the left knocks me off my skates. I crash onto the ice and roll to my back. Even with all my padded protection, it hurts like hell. My eyes water as I fight to find my breath. I haven't taken a hit like that in years. It feels like the very life has been knocked from my body.

I open my eyes and stare up into Sammy's narrowed blue ones.

What the fuck!

I can't believe she trucked into me like that!

When I'm finally able to suck enough oxygen into my lungs, it still takes a few moments before I can grit out the question. "What the hell, Sammy?"

She shrugs her broad shoulders, which look even more massive underneath all the padding. "Is it my fault that you weren't paying attention?"

"So, that's a reason to take me out?"

Is there something seriously wrong with this girl?

Like major mental issues?

The number one rule in hockey is that you don't hurt your own teammates. And she just broke it. I just hope that's all she broke.

My gaze swings to the rest of the girls who have stopped skating to form a tight circle around us. It becomes apparent by the way most are shifting uncomfortably and avoiding eye contact that none want to get involved in this skirmish. I can't blame them for that. Sammy is our captain and I've only recently joined the team.

And well…she's Sammy.

I wouldn't want to go against the girl, either. Even though I'm disappointed that no one will stand up for me, I understand it. My entire body hurts as I scramble to my skates, unwilling to keep looking up at her from my sprawled-out position on the ice.

My temper rises as I skate toward her until our face cages are practically touching. What just happened has nothing to do with me being caught unawares, and everything to do with her cousin.

"If you have a problem, take it up with me off the ice." There is so much anger thrumming through me that I'm shaking. "Especially since we both know this has nothing to do with hockey."

Eyes narrowing, she sneers, "And what if I want to take it up with you right now?"

There's no way I can back down from this fight. I'll never be able to hold my head up again with this team and would have to quit.

As much as it sucks, I grit out, "Then let's go." I'm on the verge of tossing down my gloves and whipping off my helmet.

My heartbeat thumps painfully against my ribcage as she holds my gaze for a long, challenging moment. I can almost feel everyone's collective breath being held as the tension in the rink ratchets up another notch.

This won't be the first skirmish I've ever been involved in.

Although, I've never been in a fistfight with a member of my own team.

Sammy cocks her head before saying loudly enough for everyone to hear, "Let's grab something to eat after this, and we'll hash it all out then."

My rigidly held muscles loosen as air rushes from my lungs in relief. I wasn't looking forward to getting my ass handed to me in front of all these girls. I'm not delusional enough to think I could have taken her.

"Fine."

Everyone splinters apart as if a fight didn't almost erupt, and we're back to scrimmaging again. Even though nothing has been solved with Sammy, it feels as if the thick undercurrent of tension brewing between us has been dispelled.

For the rest of our ninety-minute practice, I channel all my energy into the drills. When I get home tonight, I want to be so exhausted that I fall straight into bed and sleep without dreaming about Cole.

Once I'm showered, I wait for Sammy to grab her athletic bag before we walk out of the arena together. Neither of us says much as we slide into her crappy little Honda Civic. When she pulls into traffic at breakneck speed, I'm reminded as to why I scramble for alternative rides to the rink.

Her car should come with a warning label—*not intended for people with heart conditions, high blood pressure, or nervous stomachs.*

The girl drives like she's qualifying for the Indy 500.

Bits and pieces of my life flash before my eyes as she squeals around another turn. Not wanting to encourage her, because I've realized my frantic pointing and high-pitched yelps will do that, I gnash my teeth together to stifle the screams gathering in my throat.

"Dawson's Diner, okay?" She doesn't bother to glance in my direction, instead keeping her gaze focused on the ribbon of dark road beyond the windshield.

Lips pressed tightly together, I reply, "Yup."

Thankfully, it's not far.

No more than two minutes pass by before she pulls abruptly into a parking space in front of the restaurant. Woozy from the manic drive over, my legs shake as I exit the vehicle.

Once we're seated at a small table and my stomach begins to settle, I glance at the menu. The waitress delivers two glasses of water before taking our order and disappearing again.

Now that there's nothing else to focus our attention on, Sammy and I glance warily at each other. She drums her fingertips on the table as I shift uncomfortably in my seat.

With a sigh, she breaks the brewing tension. "Look, Cassidy, I like you."

I tilt my head at her opening line. "I'd hate to see what you do to people you don't like."

One side of her mouth hitches as she smirks. "Actually, you don't want to see that."

She's right about that.

"But," she continues, "my point is that I like you. And I really liked you with Cole."

Thick emotion gathers in my throat as I nod.

"The fact that you were into Luke Wellington the entire time you were seeing my cousin seriously chafes my ass." Fire leaps into her eyes as she leans toward me. "I warned you in the beginning not to hurt him." Her expression fills with disgust as she sits back again. "You're no better than that bitch Jackie."

"Luke and I have never been anything other than friends."

Her eyes narrow. "I thought you two didn't even know each other."

There are three people at Western who know what happened to me last year, and Sammy isn't one of them. Flunking out of college, getting kicked off the hockey team, drowning my sorrows in alcohol, and sleeping around isn't something I'm proud of. Frankly, it's humiliating that I made such a colossal mess out of my life.

As much as I like Sammy, she's Cole's cousin first and foremost. Her allegiance will always be to him, and I wouldn't expect anything less. But her automatically jumping to conclusions without talking to me hurts. I'd thought we were more than just teammates. I'd assumed we were on our way to being friends.

We have a lot in common, hockey being the most obvious.

Her mad driving skills, not so much.

That friendship stalled when Cole and I broke up. And that really sucks. I'd been hoping we could have a relationship independent of him. Obviously, that's not possible.

I spent all my teenage years focused on hockey to the exclusion of everything else, and it had been necessary to sacrifice my friendships along the way. Brooklyn, a neighbor while growing up, was more of an acquaintance than anything else. When I first arrived at Western, I kept to myself, needing to get my life back under control. Making friends hadn't been high on the priority list. Slowly, I've come out of my shell. The tentative relationships I'm now developing feel important, and I don't want to lose them.

A long silence stretches between us as I debate how much to tell Sammy, if anything. There's no way I'm ready to completely spill my guts to her. Honestly, she hasn't earned my trust. But maybe if I give her some of the truth, she'll better understand my relationship with Luke.

At this point, that's all I want.

"Luke and I actually attended the same college last year, and both played hockey."

Sammy's dark blonde brows knit together, but I don't give her a chance to fire off questions at me.

"We weren't friends." I pause before adding, "I only recognized him here at Western after I started seeing Cole."

She cocks a brow. "You certainly seem chummy now."

"Something happened last year—something I'm not going to discuss—but Luke was there, and he got me out of a really bad situation," I add slowly. "Once we sat down and talked about it, it just seemed natural for us to be friends. We've never been anything more than that."

Everything I've just revealed seems to roll around in her head.

Just as Sammy opens her mouth, our food arrives. We both thank our waitress before she takes off to check on other tables.

The smell of my cheese and mushroom omelet hits me and I

realize how hungry I am. Tabling the conversation, we both dig in, demolishing our plates in less than ten minutes. There's no slow, methodical chewing and savoring for either of us. After a ninety-minute practice, we're famished.

Once our plates are scraped clean, we both sit back and sip our waters.

"Why doesn't Cole believe that you two are just friends?" Sammy asks.

Caught off guard by the question, I grapple for an answer before jerking my shoulders. "I guess it's because Luke and I have been spending more time together."

"Okay. Is there more?"

Gaze trained on me, she patiently waits for me to continue. I can't help but fidget under the intense scrutiny, racking my brain for an explanation.

I clear my throat. "He thinks Luke is interested in more than just friendship with me."

Her expression never falters. "Do you think that's true?"

"Maybe." I add hastily, "But nothing has ever happened between us. We're *just* friends."

With a shake of her head, laughter gurgles up from her throat. "Come on, Cassidy! How would it make you feel if your new boyfriend was hanging around with another girl who you knew liked him? A *friend*," she uses air quotes around the word, "who is patiently waiting in the wings for your relationship with Cole to fall apart."

Her face scrunches. "And Luke is Cole's teammate." She takes a lengthy sip of her drink as her expression changes, and she stares at me as if I'm nothing more than a bug smashed across the windshield of her deathtrap.

Heat rushes to my cheeks.

Is that how Cole viewed it? Like he's being betrayed not only by his girlfriend, but by his teammate as well?

I think about all the times he caught sight of us together. At the Union, looking as if I was going to let Luke kiss me. Or when I left the Halloween party and grabbed coffee with him. Right before we broke up, when I was at the library with Luke. Instead of hearing about it from me, Luke was the one who inadvertently let the cat out of the bag, making it look like I was hiding it from Cole. And lastly, I think about how angry Cole was on the ice, and how they almost came to blows.

Shame fills me as I imagine how it feels from Cole's perspective.

Unfortunately, I'm unsure if it's too late to rectify the situation.

Cole could be hooking up with Vanessa.

Or Andrea.

I wince and think about all three of them together at the same time. It's entirely possible the omelet I just wolfed down is going to make an unexpected reappearance.

Instead of saying anything more, Sammy sweeps her tongue across her front teeth as she silently watches me from the other side of the table.

My breath catches at the back of my throat as I realize that I've inadvertently sabotaged my relationship with Cole.

21

CASSIDY

The the week leading up to Thanksgiving break flies by at breakneck speed. There are papers to write, tests to study for, hours spent at the tutoring center, and hockey practice to work myself over in so I can fall into a dead sleep at the end of the day and not spend more time stewing over Cole.

Does it work?

Not really.

I've arrived at the painful conclusion that I screwed up the best relationship I've ever had.

After my late-night dinner with Sammy, I decided to take a giant step back from the situation and focus on the reason I'm at Western in the first place.

Academics.

I'm pouring all my time and energy into my courses, and trying hard not to dwell on Cole or Luke. Until I decided to pull back and get clarity, I hadn't realized how much everything was spiraling out of control.

I think Dr. Thompson would be proud of me for doing what's best for myself and seizing control of my life again. I miss her insightful comments and conversations. Once or twice, I dialed the number to the counseling center before quickly chickening out and hanging up the phone.

Every Monday, Wednesday, and Friday at nine o'clock, I attend my Psych 201 lecture. When I arrive, Cole is never there. I know the exact moment he sneaks in because I get a little prickle at the nape of my neck. Even though I've caught glimpses of him around campus, it's always from afar. Thankfully, I haven't spotted him with Vanessa or Andrea.

Or Jackie.

Catching sight of him, even from a distance, feels devastating.

My heart lurches every single time.

Just like it is at this very moment.

My feet stumble to a halt as my hungry gaze slides over him. It's not a surprise to find yet another girl at his side. I can't tell who she is because she's bundled up against the bracing November wind that's sweeping through campus. He's wearing a navy peacoat and has a dark beanie pulled low over his brow. Pieces of his dark hair stick out from beneath the tight-knit fabric. My hands tighten at my sides. I miss running my fingers through his messy strands.

He couldn't look any sexier if he tried. The girl he's walking with must agree with the sentiment because she's beaming up at him. They look like they're deep in conversation as he says something before laughing. His dimples flash, and my heart constricts because I remember what it felt like to have him look at me the same way.

Unable to watch the interaction for another moment, I swing away before hustling down one of the winding pathways. With my thoughts full of Cole, I don't think about where I'm going, my next class, or all the things on my to-do list this afternoon.

No matter how hard I try, I can't seem to move on or get over him.

Even though it's freeze-your-ass-off-cold, the sun is shining brightly. I blink and find myself standing outside the student counseling center. I try not to think about the irony of unconsciously finding myself outside Dr. Thompson's office as I slump onto a bench.

I pull out my phone and realize that I have an hour before I need to be at the tutoring center for my shift. With any luck, my brain will be too consumed with equations, quadratics, and proofs to dwell on Cole.

After a while, someone settles next to me. I shift my body away, hoping that whoever it is will take the hint that I'm not interested in engaging in meaningless conversation.

At this point, I'd rather pop a vein.

I'm kidding.

Sort of.

"Cassidy?"

The soft voice has me whipping around until my gaze lands on the last person I expected to run into. Although, considering that I'm sitting outside where she works, maybe I should have. A burst of nerves flutter to life at the bottom of my belly.

"How have you been?" she asks.

My brows lift at the innocuous question. Of all the things I imagined her saying to me—I'm so glad you're no longer dating my son, I never realized how fucked up you were, maybe you should consider transferring to another college—that wasn't it.

I suck in a deep breath and try to get my neurons to fire. "Um…good."

Her lips curve into a smile. It's one that's filled with kindness. "I'm glad to hear that."

I can't stop thinking about how weird this feels.

Other than the unexpected meeting at Cole's childhood house and the ice rink, I've never seen Dr. Thompson outside of her office. The fact that we're sitting in broad daylight, on a campus bench like it's the most natural thing in the world, makes this all the more bizarre.

When it becomes obvious that I'm not going to pick up the conversational ball, she says, "I've been hoping you would make another appointment so we could talk."

Unable to hold her steady gaze, mine slices away because we both realize that wasn't going to happen.

"It just felt too weird," I admit.

"Cassidy…" She takes a deep breath but doesn't say another word until I glance back at her. "I realize that discovering your boyfriend's mother is also your psychologist must have been a surprise."

That absurd statement is met with a gurgle of laughter that sounds as if it's being strangled from me.

"For obvious reasons, if you decide to come back for counseling, I wouldn't be able to treat you."

Oh, the horror.

I can't even imagine it.

"No, probably not," I add weakly.

She clears her throat. "It would be a conflict of interest."

To say the least.

"But I want you to know that if you're still interested in receiving counseling services, there are two other therapists who work in the office. Either one would be an excellent fit for you. Or, if you'd prefer to go off campus, I can give you a referral. It's up to you." She reaches out, laying her hand over mine before giving it a gentle squeeze. "My chief concern is making sure you have the support and assistance you need to be successful at Western." There's a pause before she adds softly, "I've been worried about you."

The sincerity of her tone confuses me, but then again, maybe it shouldn't. Dr. Thompson has always been kind, thoughtful, and caring.

My mind tumbles back over the past couple of weeks. My breakup with Cole has been difficult. Even though it was touch-and-go for a while, I managed to handle it on my own. And that feels pretty good. Maybe I didn't realize it at the time, but I was actually able to apply a lot of the tools and coping mechanisms I learned in counseling to the issues I was having.

It's the reason for learning them in the first place.

Huh.

How's that for an *ah-ha* moment?

"You know what?" A hint of a smile plays around the edges of my lips. "I think I'm good."

The fact that I've learned how to deal with my own problems

instead of needing someone to hold my hand feels like a breakthrough.

One I can't help but take pride in.

"Have there been any anxiety attacks?"

The slight smile tilting my lips upward grows as I shake my head. "Nope. None. My chest has tightened up a couple of times, but I was able to breathe through it. And I do a lot of self-checks to assess how I'm feeling. When I need to talk things out, I have a few friends to do that with."

And that's new as well.

Not seeing Dr. Thompson has been difficult, but it's nice to know that I can handle life on my own again. It's a huge step in the right direction, which is kind of an amazing realization considering that these past two weeks have totally sucked.

Although, without them sucking, I wouldn't have realized just how much I'd grown.

She nods, genuine pleasure lighting up her face. "It seems like you have everything under control. I'm proud of you, Cassidy."

My gaze holds hers, and for the first time since she sat down, some of the tension leaks from my muscles. It feels a little like it used to between us, which is nice.

That's the moment I remember that I was sleeping with her son.

"Cassidy," she says, interrupting the freight train of thoughts steamrolling through my head, "it's all right."

I shift on the bench as heat floods my cheeks. "What do you mean?"

"Your relationship with my son has nothing to do with me. It's two separate situations, and although I can't work with you professionally, I want you to know that I have no issues with you seeing Cole."

My mouth tumbles open. "How can you say that?"

I mean, she knows everything about me.

The good, the bad, and the ugly.

"Everyone has issues, whether they see a therapist for them or not. Everyone comes with their own unique set of baggage. I'm not in the business of judging people for what they've been through or the mistakes they've made."

"But you can't possibly want me with him," I whisper.

Cole deserves the best. He deserves a girl with her shit together, and that's not me. I'm still a work in progress. Maybe I'll always be a work in progress. I can't help but stare down at my fingers, which are tangled in the hem of my thick winter coat.

"Cassidy," she says, drawing my attention back to her, "I want my son to be happy and in a healthy, loving relationship. That's all any mother can hope for. Cole is a grown adult, and he's more than capable of making his own choices." There's a pause before she adds, "And his own mistakes. I can't stop that from happening."

I glance away before mumbling, "Does he know I was seeing you?" My voice drops even lower. "Professionally?"

"Of course not. I would never divulge personal information about a client. There are strict laws against that, not to mention ethical oaths I took when I received my license to practice. I take my professional responsibilities very seriously." She gives me a penetrating look. "I hope you realize that. I'd never do anything to harm a client. My role in your life is to offer help and assistance. Now, if you chose to tell him, that's your decision. But I will *never* discuss our relationship with anyone else."

Even though I understand what she's telling me, I can't stop the question from shooting out of my mouth. "Does your husband know?"

She shakes her head. "Absolutely not. He's under the impression that we met for the first time at our house."

That's such a relief.

I force my gaze to hers. "Cole and I aren't seeing each other anymore."

"I know," she acknowledges quietly. "He mentioned it." She clears her throat. "I really hope I wasn't the reason."

I inhale a deep breath before forcing out a response. "No, you weren't."

"Good." She winces before correcting herself. "Well, not good…"

"I know." I force myself to admit, "I messed up our relationship all on my own."

"I guess you need to decide if your relationship with Cole is worth repairing."

If I didn't know better, I'd think she might actually be encouraging me to fix things with her son.

"I don't know if that's possible."

Would he be willing to give me a second chance?

Or has he already moved on?

I've spotted him around campus with several different girls. My heart constricts every time it happens. It's painful to think about him loving someone else the way he once loved me.

"I suppose that's something you'll have to figure out for yourself."

I nod in agreement.

With a glance at her wristwatch, she says, "I need to get back to the office, but it was lovely running into you, Cassidy. I think you've grown tremendously in the short amount of time you've been at Western. You should be proud of all you've accomplished and keep focusing on the goals you've set for yourself." There's a pause. "You should feel good about the person you're growing into. You need to give yourself a bit of grace and stop being so hard on yourself." She gives me a knowing look. "Sometimes we're our own worst critics."

We fall into silence as I allow her words to wash over me.

Emotion gathers in my throat. "Thanks, Dr. Thompson…for everything. I'm going to miss you." As the words fall from my lips, I realize how true they are.

"It was my pleasure. And remember, if you decide you'd like a referral, just give the office a call. All right?" She squeezes my hand for a second time.

"Yes." I smile, feeling less weighted down than I have in a long time.

Closure.

I hadn't realized just how much I'd needed it with her.

She rises to her feet before brushing off the back of her coat. "Good luck." Her gaze holds mine as she adds, "With everything."

"Thank you," I whisper, afraid that if I say anything more, I'll break down and cry before she can disappear inside the counseling center.

22

CASSIDY

"You're really all right with going home for the break? Everything's good with the fam?"

I fold another sweater and place it neatly in my suitcase before glancing at Brooklyn. "Yeah, I think so."

Over the past few weeks, I've gotten together with my parents several times. Our relationship is slowly morphing into one that is comfortable again.

"If you need a breather, just pop on over to my house." She dumps a handful of clothing into her bag. "It's not like anything interesting will be happening at the Bennet household."

"I think everything will be fine. Honestly," I carefully fold a pair of jeans before laying them on top of the sweaters, "I'm looking forward to getting away from campus for a couple of days."

Brooklyn huffs before throwing another armload of clothing into her bag. "I know what you mean. It'll be kind of nice to get the hell out of Dodge."

I can't resist asking, "Aren't you going to miss your little friends-with-benefits buddy?"

I scrutinize her expression, trying to figure out what's going on between them. Brooklyn has been tight-lipped about the entire situa-

172

tion, which isn't her usual style. Under normal circumstances, she enjoys giving me a cringeworthy amount of details regarding whatever guy she's into. I find her newfound reserve disconcerting. I don't even know if they're still sleeping with each other or not.

"First thing, never refer to my benefits buddy as *little*. He guy puts a capital D in dick." She continues as I wince. "And second, I'm pleading the fifth."

My eyes narrow. "Since when?" Since when doesn't Brooklyn want to over-share? TMI is her MO, for goodness' sake.

Shrugging, she remains silent before tossing a few more items into her bag and zipping it up.

She changes the subject by asking, "What time is Luke picking us up?"

I glance at the clock next to my bed. "In an hour."

It was a surprise to learn that Luke lives about twenty miles away from us in a different city. He asked if we needed a ride home for the break, and even though I wasn't altogether sure I should take him up on the offer, I agreed.

It's not like Cole and I are together anymore.

There have been so many times when I've picked up the phone, wanting to shoot Cole a text. Thank god I'm not a drinker, or I probably would have drunk-dialed him half a dozen times.

The conversation with Sammy really struck a chord with me. Even though it's been four days since we sat down and talked after practice, it's still rolling around in my head.

The good news is that Sammy and I have smoothed everything over, and our friendship has fallen back into the easy comradery it once was. I no longer have to worry about her knocking the shit out of me on the ice.

The hour slips by in a flurry of packing, and before I know it, Luke is texting that he's waiting outside. Brooklyn and I take one last look around our room before hustling down to meet him with our bags in tow. As soon as he sees us push through the glass doors of our dorm, he exits his truck and opens the tailgate before setting our bags inside.

"Hey." He greets us with a smile before opening the back door for Brooklyn, and then the front passenger one for me.

As he's walking around the hood of the truck, Brooklyn leans forward and whispers in my ear, "I think someone is happy to finally have you all to himself."

Without even looking at her, I mutter, "We're friends. Nothing more."

"Plus," she teases, "you didn't even call shotgun and you're the one riding up front."

There's no time to respond to that comment as Luke opens the driver's side door and slides in next to me. A moment later, the engine roars to life and we're rolling away from Western's campus. The three of us chat for a while before falling into a comfortable silence as music fills the inside of the vehicle.

A few times during the drive, I find myself studying Luke. With his short blond hair and blue-gray hazel eyes, he's handsome. I'd be lying through my teeth if I didn't admit that I find him attractive. That attraction, coupled with the connection we've already forged, seems to intensify everything I feel for him.

But that doesn't mean I'm ready to take that next step with him.

Because I haven't heard from Cole since our disastrous lunch, I'm guessing that whatever we had is over with. At this point, I don't know if I want to get tangled up in another relationship. I remember my hesitancy about getting involved with Cole in the beginning. It's probably smarter to focus on my classes and take a break from boys.

Lost in the tangle of my thoughts, I don't realize that I've spaced out and am staring at Luke until he turns his head and meets my gaze. Heat creeps into my cheeks as I yank my attention away from him and stare out the window.

"What are you thinking about?"

I force myself to glance at him and say honestly, "That it's probably best for me to focus on classes and not get caught up in all the social stuff."

He nods as if agreeing before his eyes resettle on the road

stretched out in front of him. Mine do the same. "You mean a relationship?"

"Yeah."

He nods as his hand slips around mine. Startled by the connection, my heartbeat hitches as I stare down at our entwined fingers. His thumb rubs soft circles across my flesh.

Unease fills me as I glance over my shoulder at Brooklyn, only to find her sacked out with earbuds in.

"She fell asleep about fifteen minutes ago," he says as if he can read my mind.

"Oh." My mouth turns cottony as I search my brain for something to say.

Whatever is unfolding between us in the front seat of his truck feels dangerous. I'm not sure if I'm ready for our relationship to progress past friendship. When it comes down to it, I'm still hung up on Cole.

His gaze flickers in my direction. "Are you okay with this?" He squeezes my fingers. "I don't want to push you into something you're not ready for."

The last guy to hold my hand was Cole. I'm not sure if I'm ready to feel someone else touching me so intimately. At the same time, I can't deny that it feels kind of nice.

"Cassidy?" he prompts softly. His gaze darts to mine as we continue driving down the highway toward home.

I suck in a deep breath and realize that I don't want him to let go. Just as he begins to remove his fingers, the word shoots out of my mouth. "No."

His movements still. Questions swirl through his eyes. "No?"

"Don't let go," I whisper thickly.

Whether he realizes it or not, this is a big deal for me. I don't allow many people in. Cole was my first real relationship. Even though Luke is only holding my hand, it's a big step for me.

He must understand it as well. For the remainder of the ride, he does nothing more than clasp my hand in his larger one as if allowing me time to get used to the feel of him.

The miles slip by quickly after that shared moment between us. Brooklyn sleeps the entire way, making it feel as if Luke and I are alone. Almost from the beginning, my friendship with Luke has been an easy one. Even though we're holding hands, it doesn't necessarily feel like anything has changed.

By the time we roll up to Brooklyn's house, which is next to mine, she's woken up with a stretch, and Luke is no longer holding my hand.

When he exits the truck to grab her bag, she leans forward and whispers, "Now that was a rather interesting turn of events."

With a wink, she jumps out of the truck and thanks Luke for the ride. Just as I'm about to open my door and get out, Luke slides in beside me.

"I'll drive you over. It's not a problem."

Less than thirty seconds later, he's pulling into my driveway. My gaze locks on the house I grew up in, and my mind tumbles back to when Cole and I snuck in two months ago to retrieve my hockey equipment.

The memory of how angry my father had been when he caught us slices through me. My muscles tense as I continue to stare. It's the feel of Luke's hand squeezing mine that knocks me from the strange paralysis.

"Cassidy? Are you all right?"

"Sorry," I say with a weak smile.

For some reason, sitting here in the driveway of my childhood home, the one I hadn't been allowed to return to after my failure, has all those bad memories crashing around inside my head. And I realize that I'm almost afraid to walk through the front door.

Afraid that this trip home won't turn out to be a positive one.

Maybe that saying *you can never go home again* is true.

The last thing I want is for the next couple of days to be awkward and uncomfortable.

Have I rushed things by agreeing to come home for Thanksgiving, foolishly thinking that everything would magically fall neatly back into place between all of us?

It's a jarring thought.

My chest tightens, making it difficult to breathe. I close my eyes and inhale a deep breath before slowly forcing it out again, all the while desperately trying to rein in my out-of-control feelings.

If I allow my mind to keep tripping down this path, I'll have a full-on anxiety attack.

Relax.

Just relax.

It's the deep timbre of Luke's voice that finally punctures the anxiety spiraling through me.

"Hey," he squeezes my hand again, "are you all right?" His fingers rise to stroke softly over my cheek. "Cassidy, look at me."

He must see the fear and panic rising within my wide eyes, because he slowly tugs me into his arms. I squeeze my eyes tightly shut and rest my head against the solid strength of his chest.

And then I just breathe.

I suck in big gulps of air before slowly pushing them out again.

"Keep breathing," he whispers near the shell of my ear.

I focus on the low cadence of his voice.

It takes about three or four minutes before I find my muscles loosening.

Once I've calmed myself down, he says, "We can leave right now if you want. I'll take you to my house or back to school." He pulls away enough to search my eyes. "Is that what you want?"

For a silent moment, I turn the offer over in my mind, realizing that I don't really want to leave. My parents haven't done anything to make me think that this weekend won't be a step forward for all of us. What frightens me most is that this homecoming has the potential to end in a disaster, leaving my family and me just as broken as we were. There is so much pressure resting on the outcome of these next few days.

I didn't realize I was feeling so stressed about it until now.

"No, I don't want that," I tell him.

I need to give this a chance. I want my family back, and spending time with them is the only way it'll happen.

With his hand resting against my cheek, he continues to gently stroke my skin. "You'll be fine, Cassidy. And if you're not, all you have to do is call me, and I'll drop everything and pick you up. Got it?"

Just knowing that I'm not stuck here if everything tanks makes all the difference in the world.

"Thank you, Luke." Embarrassed by my mini-breakdown, I glance away before mumbling, "Sorry for falling apart like that."

His fingers slip under my chin before turning my face until I have no other choice but to meet his gaze. "We're friends." He brushes his lips across mine. "And friends are always there for each other no matter what."

Even though it was just a fleeting caress, my mind continues to spin.

Before I have a chance to gather my thoughts, he says, "Come on, I'll walk you to the door."

"Okay."

We exit the truck and Luke grabs my bag from the back before carrying it up the brick walkway. Before we make it onto the porch, the door is thrown open as Lexie and Miranda barrel toward us. Both squeal before hurtling their small bodies into my open arms so I can hug them tightly to me.

"We've missed you so much, Cassy!"

My little sisters have always called me Cassy and it brings a rush of hot tears to my eyes to hear them call me that again. It takes a moment to realize that my parents are standing in the open doorway. Both are wearing easy smiles. It's enough to melt away the last of my anxiety.

Dad stretches out a hand toward Luke, who I've completely forgotten about. I straighten and introduce Luke to my parents. He shakes both of their hands before saying hello to my little sisters. They look bowled over by him.

My father sizes Luke up before speculation erupts in his ocean-blue depths. In a subtle movement, I shake my head in response. The last thing I need is for my parents to think that I'm hopping from one guy to another.

That gentle and confusing kiss nudges its way back into my brain.

"I better get going," Luke says.

"I'll walk you to the truck," I murmur, uncomfortably aware that four sets of inquisitive eyes are watching us.

It occurs to me that this is the first time my family has seen me with a boy.

He says goodbye to my family before we walk to the driveway where his vehicle is parked. Once we reach the driver's side door, we pause.

"They're still watching, aren't they?" he asks, a fake smile plastered across his face. His lips barely move.

I mimic his expression. "Of course, they are."

"Well, this is super awkward," he continues, grin held firmly in place.

"I'll be given the third degree as soon as you pull away."

Laughter erupts from him as he drops the fake smile.

His gaze flickers away as he shifts his stance. "I was wondering if you wanted to get together over the break."

As his words and their implication wash over me, I think about the way he calmed me down in the truck. How patient and gentle he was.

Maybe this connection is worth exploring.

My gaze flickers to my family, who continue to stand in the doorway, watching us as if we're putting on a theater production. They couldn't be more obvious if they pulled out lawn chairs from the garage and sat down with a tub of popcorn.

How embarrassing.

When I don't respond, his voice dips. "Is that a *no*?"

I force my attention to him before pushing out an answer that surprises even me. "It's a *yes*."

Even though I'm not over Cole, maybe spending time with Luke— someone I genuinely like and feel connected to—might help with that.

It certainly can't hurt, right?

A big smile breaks out across his face. "Great. I'll text you on Friday with the plans."

"Okay." I nod as nerves gallop across my flesh at what I've set into motion. "That sounds good."

He pulls me in for a hug. With my body pressed against his

muscular one, I'm assaulted by his clean, woodsy cologne. I can't help but think about how different his scent is from Cole's. Before I can decide if I like it, he pulls away and holds me at arm's length.

With a tilt of his head toward my family, he says, "I think everything will be fine. But if it's not, all you have to do is call. All right?"

Unable to contain my smile because, he's right, everything is going to be just fine with my family, I nod. "Thanks for everything."

He climbs into his truck, starts the engine and waves to my family before backing out of the driveway. For a moment, I watch the vehicle until it turns the corner and disappears.

Now that Luke is gone, my sisters race toward me.

"Is that your boyfriend?" Lexie asks.

I shake my head. "No, just a friend."

"He's hot!" Miranda adds.

Hot?

Oh my god. In less than a year, my sisters went from not being interested in boys at all to thinking they're hot.

It looks like we're going to have a lot to catch up on this break, and I'm looking forward to every minute of it.

I wrap my arms around both of them as we head to the house.

2 3

CASSIDY

Thanksgiving Day passes by in a blur of food and extended family that camps out at our house for the day. We wake up early, prep the turkey before shoving it into the oven, and then settle back to watch the Macy's Thanksgiving Day Parade on the big screen. As I sit on the couch with my sisters, my dad relaxes in his recliner and my mom putters around in the kitchen, it feels just like it used to before I flunked out of school last December.

And I'm seriously loving every single moment of it.

A little more than a month ago, I was barely in contact with my family, and now I'm home, celebrating the holidays with them. Stranger than that, it actually feels normal. Even though I was unsure what to expect, I feel stupid for getting so jacked up in Luke's truck.

Lexie, who is fourteen, makes a comment about one of the choreographed routines, and suddenly both her and Miranda are jumping off the couch and copying the dancers on TV. As my gaze darts between the parade and my sisters, I realize they're both able to imitate the performers perfectly.

My jaw drops as pride fills me. "Wow! When did you two become so good?"

"We're both in competition dance troupes," Lexie says as she follows the steps.

"I didn't know that."

It's surprising how much they've grown up over the past year. Both are more mature than when I left for college fifteen months ago. As I watch them, I silently vow never to lose contact with either one of them again. It's like I blinked, and they grew up.

And I missed it.

Even though I'm thrilled to be home again, I wish I hadn't missed so much of their lives.

"Dance with us, Cassy!"

"Yeah, come on. It's easy," Lexie chimes in.

I snort. "Easy for you maybe, but not me," I reply from the comfort of the couch. I'm still lounging in my pajamas, which also happens to be another tradition. We don't get dressed until after the parade is over.

"Cassy, please?" Miranda sends a pleading gaze my way.

"I can't dance like you guys." I burrow further into my blanket, thoroughly enjoying the show these two are putting on.

Dad glances up from the newspaper he's reading on his tablet. "She's a hockey player, girls, not a dancer. Totally different skill set."

My sisters laugh before continuing to beg me to join them. Even though I'm nowhere near their level, I decide to give it my best shot.

And just like I expected, I'm terrible.

Horrible, even.

I can dance my ass off at a frat party with a bunch of drunken college students, but next to my sisters who have serious skills, I look like an uncoordinated clod. For the most part, I'm just swinging my arms and legs around.

But you know what?

I'm having the best time.

We all are.

My dad looks up again, barely able to suppress his laughter. Mom stops what she's doing in the kitchen and comes to stand next to my father. From the corner of my eye, I watch them share a private look and smile.

After about a minute, the dance number, thankfully, comes to a close. My sisters end in the same pose as the dancers in the parade. Since there's no way I can pull off the grand finale, I twirl before adding some jazz hands.

Because who doesn't like jazz hands?

My sisters laugh hysterically, and I can't help but join them as they pile on top of me in the middle of the family room.

Later that evening, after the grandparents, aunts, uncles, and cousins have headed home, I'm in bed, scrolling through Insta when there's a knock on the door.

Mom peeks her head around the corner. "Are you busy?"

I scooch up on my bed. "No, just scrolling through stuff online."

She settles on the mattress next to me. "Today was nice, wasn't it?" Before I can answer, she shakes her head and purses her lips. "Your cousin nearly ate an entire pumpkin pie by himself. The poor guy was groaning all the way to the car. I really hope he doesn't throw up like he did last year."

We both smile because that kid does the same thing every year. It's just another tradition, I suppose. Sure, we could stop him, but who really wants to mess with tradition?

Once she sobers, she says, "It's nice to have you back home, Cassidy."

Her words set off an explosion of all the nostalgic emotions plaguing me today as tears prick my eyes. "It's good to be back," I finally whisper.

"We really missed you. All of us." She nips her bottom lip with her teeth. "Especially your father."

Today has felt like a gift. I'm so happy that we've been able to work through our issues. It occurs to me that without Cole contacting my father and invited him to my first hockey scrimmage, this homecoming-of-sorts wouldn't have happened.

I owe him so much.

My heart constricts as that thought rolls unwantedly through my head.

"I want you to know that I'm really proud of you," Mom says, drawing my attention back to her.

My brows draw together as I force out an uncomfortable laugh. "For what? Flunking out of school and getting kicked off the hockey team?" Unable to hold her eyes, I focus on a picture on the other side of the room.

It's only when her hand settles over mine that my gaze cuts back to hers. "No, for picking yourself back up and having the courage to try again."

I jerk my shoulders into a shrug. "I wish I could have gone to school and done well like everybody else. Instead, I made a big mess out of everything and disappointed both of you."

"Oh, honey. We shouldn't have sent you to your grandparents' house after you came home from school. I think we were just in a state of shock and didn't know what to do. Here we send our daughter off to play Division I hockey at a prestigious college, and she ends up flunking out, getting kicked off the team, and..." her voice trails off awkwardly.

"Yeah," I mumble. "We don't need to rehash what happened."

"Well," she says with a sigh, "it happened. And there's no way to go back and undo it. You have to learn what you can from the experience and continue moving forward. And that's exactly what you've done." There's a pause. "What I'm trying to say is that I'm proud of you for turning it around." She quickly amends, "Both your father and I are proud of you for working hard this semester."

I inhale a deep breath before pushing it out.

What she's saying really means a lot to me.

My mom and I don't have a super close relationship. While Dad and I were at the hockey arena, she was with Miranda and Lexie at dance competitions. It feels good that she's here, telling me how proud she is.

That we're kind of having—not to sound all sappy—a moment.

"Thanks for saying that."

She closes the distance between us and tugs me into her arms. At first it feels a little uncomfortable, but after a moment, I allow myself to melt into her embrace. It's been difficult to find the silver lining in what happened last year, but maybe this new relationship with my mom is one.

She pulls away just enough to meet my gaze. "I was wondering if you wanted to go shopping with us tomorrow morning?"

In all the years I lived at home, Mom and my sisters would get up super early and hit all the Black Friday sales. Normally, I'd be playing in some turkey shootout tournament, but that's not the case this year, and suddenly, I'm glad for it.

"I'd like that. Thanks for asking."

"Great." Her eyes take on a sly look before she asks, "So, any plans with that foxy boy who gave you and Brooklyn a ride home yesterday?"

My mouth drops open as I repeat with a fair amount of horror, "*Foxy?* Did you seriously just say that?"

Her brows draw together as she says, "Isn't that the hip lingo all the kids are using these days?"

I shake my head. "Um, no. And quite frankly, I don't want to hear that word come out of your mouth ever again." I shudder. "It's so wrong, it can never be right."

Her lips twitch. "How about sexy? Is that better? Like we're just a couple of gals trying to keep it real?"

I slap my hands over my ears before howling, "Oh my god, that's even worse!"

She perks up before asking, "What about *hot?*"

Unable to bear another moment, I point to the door. "You need to leave. Now."

When a chuckle escapes from her, I can't help but join in.

"Oh, wait, I know—*smoking!*" There's a pause. "*Smoking hot!*" She nods as if she's totally nailed it this time.

"Are you trying to scar me for life? Because that's what's happening here."

She waves a hand. "All right, all right. Sheesh. I'll stop. I just wanted to know about the cute boy who drove you home."

Unsure if I want to discuss Luke with my mother, I flop onto my bed before nibbling at my lower lip.

"He was quite studly."

I shake my head. "You are seriously killing me. You know that, right?" Giving in, I throw her a tiny crumb of information, hoping she'll refrain from using any more hip lingo. "He's just a friend."

She rolls her eyes. "It certainly seemed like more to me. He looked smitten."

Smitten?

Nope, I'm not even going to touch that one.

"We're just friends," I repeat. For a moment, I debate whether to tack on *right now,* but then decide not to because who knows what will happen between us.

It's kind of amazing that my mom and I are even having this kind of conversation. We've never talked about boys before. Even though it feels like the tips of my ears are burning with embarrassment, it's kind of nice.

When I remain silent, she waggles her brows. "He's quite a handsome young man." She leans a bit closer before adding in a loud whisper, "and he had a nice butt on him."

I shriek again, because I absolutely do not want to hear my mother talking about a guy's backside.

With a chuckle she says, "I'm old, Cassidy. Not dead. There's a difference."

Clearly.

We both dissolve into another bout of laughter.

"Is Luke the boy who invited your father to the hockey game?"

The laughter dies a slow death on my lips, and I shake my head. "No, it was Cole who called Dad."

Confusion flickers across her face. "Is he still in the picture?"

The laughter of moments ago is totally forgotten as sadness fills me. "I don't think so."

She searches my eyes carefully before asking, "You like Cole a lot?"

It's not really a question I have to think about. "Yeah, I do."

Understanding seems to dawn across her expression. "So, Luke really is just a friend?"

"I'm not sure what we are anymore," I admit.

"But he'd like to be more than friends?"

"Yes, I think so. I started something up with Cole in the beginning of the semester, and it took a long time for me to lower my guard and trust him. I still have feelings for him."

Almost absently she runs her fingers through my hair, and it reminds me of when I was a small child and she'd tuck me in at night. She always ran her fingers through my hair before kissing me goodnight. I'm not sure when she stopped doing that. But I'm glad she's here now and that we're talking.

Really talking.

I've always had a close relationship with my dad. Now, I'm wondering if it came at the expense of the one I could have had with my mom. It's not something I ever thought about before.

Maybe I should have.

"That's understandable."

"Plus," I add, "I have a lot going on with school. I don't want to do anything to jeopardize my success."

"You're right. You do have a lot going on, but you also seem to be handling it well. The best advice I can give is to take things slow and do what feels right. Maybe that's being on your own right now." She sifts her fingers through my hair again. "You know, I never worried about you when it came to boys because you were always so focused on hockey to the exclusion of everything else. Most of the time, it was a relief. Even though your life took a slight detour last year, you're back on track again. Whatever decision you make will be the right decision. I believe in you, Cassidy."

This time, I take the initiative by leaning forward and wrapping my arms around her. "Thanks, Mom." I close my eyes and inhale the sweet scent of her rosemary mint shampoo. It catapults me back to a time when life felt simpler.

"Anytime, sweetie."

As we break apart, my phone chimes with an incoming message. I glance down at it, surprised when I see Cole's name pop up.

Mom peeks at the screen. "Cole, huh?"

My wide eyes dart to hers and I drop my voice as if it's possible for him to hear us discussing him. "We haven't talked in a while."

"Then it sounds like you two might have a lot to say to one another." She smiles before rising to her feet and walking to the door. "Oh," she adds, swinging around to face me, "the minivan pulls out at four."

I wince at the idea of hauling my ass out of bed at three-thirty in the morning just to go shopping. I can't help but wonder what I've gotten myself into.

"Having second thoughts?"

I meet her questioning gaze and realize that I'd get up at any ungodly hour of the morning if it means spending more time with my family.

"Nope."

"Good. If you make it to noon, I'll treat you to lunch."

My eyes widen. "We're planning to shop for eight hours?"

"At least. We have to find all the deals."

My brows knit together as I stare in shock. "You're kidding, right?"

She points to the solemn expression she's wearing. "Does this look like the face of someone who isn't a serious Black Friday shopper? My advice is to wear comfortable shoes, dress in layers, and pack a few snacks in your bag."

My mouth drops open as she closes the door behind her with a wide smile. I stare for a few seconds before remembering the message from Cole.

Hope you had a good turkey day with your family.

Something in my heart warms as I read over the text half a dozen times. It only reminds me how much I miss him. It takes at least ten minutes and roughly thirty drafts before I get my message just right and hit the send button.

Had a great turkey day with the fam—thanks to you. Hope yours was just as good.

As soon as the message is rocketed into space, I wonder if I should have written something else. Maybe I should have played it a little cooler.

Ugh. I really hate this kind of stuff.

I'm not good at it.

When fifteen minutes drag by, I consider chucking my phone across the room. Just when I figure he won't respond, the cell chimes with another incoming message.

Glad everything went well. Mine was good too. Playing hockey tomorrow. How about you?

A smile tips the corners of my lips as I flop onto my bed. Again, I compose about twenty different responses before actually hitting send. It's tortuous.

Shopping with my mom and sisters. Not sure what I just got myself into :0

I release a pent-up breath when he responds within a few minutes.

It's kind of unbelievable that after a full week of silence, Cole and I are conversing through text messages. What I don't know is if it means anything. Cole is such a nice guy. I could see him wondering if everything's going all right for me after not speaking to my family for almost a year. When I think about it like that, it makes perfect sense that he would reach out.

Which probably means I shouldn't read too much into this gesture.

It's Cole just being…well…*Cole.*

I'm glad the break is going well. Have fun tomorrow.

I nibble at my lower lip and debate what to write. It's completely obvious that he was just concerned how I was faring.

Have fun playing hockey. See you when—

I'm about to finish the sentence with—*I get back,* but I have no clue if I'll see him. Are we going to start talking again?

I don't know, and I really don't want to put myself out there by implying it.

Instead, I end up composing a friendly—yet not too friendly—message in return.

Have fun playing hockey and enjoy the rest of your break.

My thumb hovers over the send button for a moment as I read the message at least a dozen times before firing it off into the atmosphere.

With a huff, I collapse onto the mattress and wish everything could be different between us.

24

CASSIDY

It's slammed home Friday morning that getting up at the ass-crack of dawn to fight an overzealous crowd of crazed shoppers for a few sweaters and a cute pair of ankle boots is not my idea of a good time.

Not only do we hit a few malls, but then I'm dragged against my will to Target and Walmart for more of this tortuous thing called Black Friday shopping.

If I never hit another store for the rest of my life, it'll be too soon.

The only thing that makes the experience bearable is the steady supply of caffeinated beverages shoved in my hand. Brooklyn also accompanies us on this miserable excursion. Unlike me, she seems to thoroughly enjoy the thrill of the hunt and excitement over every new discovery as much as the other demented people who are out and about before the sun has risen in the sky. In other words, she fits in perfectly with my mom and sisters.

I have two words to sum up this day—

Never.

Again.

I don't think I've ever felt more exhausted in my life. By the time we return home around two o'clock in the afternoon, the only thing I want to do is crawl into bed and sleep for the rest of the day. And since I have no plans, that's exactly what I do. I pass out for three blissful hours, getting up around dinnertime.

With a yawn, I grab my phone and realize there are a few messages. My heart skips a beat, wondering if Cole texted again. As I scroll through them, I see two are from Brooklyn and one is from Luke.

Nothing from Cole.

Rationally speaking, I shouldn't be disappointed.

But I am, which only makes me crabbier than I already am.

I read through Brooklyn's texts, asking if I'm up for going out tonight.

Ugh. Not really.

I'm still exhausted from the ridiculous amount of shopping we did. And no, having lunch at the Cheesecake Factory did not make any of it better. But I know Brooklyn will end up harassing me for being lame if I give her a firm negative at five o'clock in the evening. I send her a noncommittal response that I can back out of in a couple of hours.

I scan Luke's text.

Are you up for a party tonight?

I gnaw on my lower lip as I contemplate the question.

Even though I don't really want to go out, I wonder if maybe I should. I got my hopes up with the few messages Cole and I exchanged. It seems obvious now that he was just checking in to make sure I was okay, because that's the kind of guy Cole is. It's one of the reasons I fell so hard for him. He's so considerate and nice.

Then again, so is Luke.

And I do like him…as a friend. Maybe I owe it to myself to explore the connection between us. I don't know. Maybe I won't know until I try.

Before I can overthink the invitation, I type out a response.

Sure. Can Brooklyn come?

I actually feel pretty good about killing two birds with one stone.

If nothing else comes out of tonight, at least it'll get Brooklyn off my back.

His text pops up almost immediately.

Sure. I'll pick you both up at 9.

See you then.

There.

Done.

I'm moving on with my life.

As I suck in a deep breath, I can't help but wonder if I've made a mistake.

Five hours later, we're at the house of Luke's high school friend. There are a ton of people, none of whom I know. Luke has been at my side the entire evening, introducing Brooklyn and me to his friends.

After a couple of hours, Luke slips my hand into his. I stare down at the connection, trying to decide if moving in this new direction with Luke feels right. When my gaze collides with his, something jolts insides me. His lips tilt up at the corners, and I can't help but return the expression with a hesitant smile of my own.

He leans toward me so I can hear him over the pulsing beat of the music. "Do you want something to drink?"

My usual MO is to stick with water. Occasionally, I'll have a beer. The remnants of last year and the trouble I got myself into are never very far from my mind. Plus, I've discovered that I like being in control of myself and my surroundings. It's hard to be in control when you're totally wasted.

I shake my head. "No, I'm good."

Understanding floods his eyes and I'm reminded that Luke knows everything—all the ugly little details of last year—and still accepts me for who I am.

For the rest of the night, we dance, laugh, and have a good time. By the end of the evening, it's evident how well-liked Luke is among his friends. Brooklyn also seems to have fun. She's been off dancing with a couple of different guys.

It's the reason I do a doubletake when Austin walks through the front door. For a moment, I can't figure out what he's doing here. My gaze narrows suspiciously on Brooklyn.

She doesn't look surprised in the least to see him.

As I make my way over to them, Austin rips his attention away from her long enough to meet my gaze.

"Hey, Cassidy. How's it going?"

"Pretty good." I raise my brows. "I didn't expect to see you here tonight."

He glances at the tall blonde before shrugging. "I'm giving Brooklyn a ride home."

I can't resist needling the pair, because their relationship has seriously moved beyond ridiculous. Clearly, this is more than just a booty call, or friends-with-benefits situation, or whatever the heck they're now trying to call it.

"Oh, you live close by?" I give him a wide-eyed look because I know damn well that he doesn't.

A dull flush creeps into Austin's cheeks as he clears his throat. "Not that far. About an hour or so."

Liar. More like two and a half. I take pity on him, because he really must care for her, and decide not to call him out.

Brooklyn studiously avoids my searching gaze.

"That was nice of you to drive all the way over here to take Brook home," I say.

That remark is met with deafening silence.

Brooklyn must have decided that she's had enough of my comments and shoots me a well-honed death glare.

As soon as Luke joins our trio, the air shifts, making it feel charged and uncomfortable. Even though Austin and Luke are teammates, the strain between them is palpable. The issue between Cole and Luke has obviously bled over.

Austin gives him a stiff chin lift. "What's up, Wellington."

Luke causally drapes an arm around my shoulders, making it clear that we're together. "Not much. How about you?"

A hard glint enters Austin's eyes as he takes in how close Luke and I are standing. "Brook called, so I'm going to take her home." His narrowed gaze shifts to me. "You need a lift home, Cassidy?" He nods his head toward Brooklyn. "Since you're next door, we can drop you off."

Unease blooms in the pit of my belly as I shift, wanting to defuse the thick, suffocating waves of tension that have fallen over the group.

From beneath my lashes, I glance at Luke. At this point, we're just friends, but I'm sure Austin assumes differently. My heart trips, wondering if he'll mention it to Cole.

Just as quickly, I wonder if it matters.

My guess is that it doesn't.

"I'll take her home," Luke replies before tugging me a bit closer.

It feels as if I'm in the middle of a pissing match between these two, which is ridiculous. Austin has no reason to be angry with Luke. Cole and I aren't together anymore. If the wide variety of girls I've seen him walking around campus with is any indication, then Cole has moved on with his life.

And I should probably do the same.

"Luke will drive me home later." I hold my breath when it looks like Austin might argue.

Instead, he nods before grabbing Brooklyn's hand. "See you at school, Cassidy." He flicks a hard look at Luke. "Wellington."

I nod, relieved that Austin and Brooklyn are taking off. "Yup."

Once they walk out the door, I release the pent-up breath clogging my lungs as my gaze finally drifts to Luke's. "That was kind of weird. Is there a problem between you two?"

He shrugs, his eyes becoming shuttered. "Nope, not at all." He changes the subject. "Are you ready to take off?"

"Yeah, I am."

"All right, let me say goodbye to a few friends and then we can head out."

It's another thirty minutes before we leave. On the ride home, thoughts of Cole circle through my head and a little prick of sadness fills me.

"Are you all right?" His gaze flickers to me as we drive through the darkness. "You've been really quiet."

I don't realize just how tangled up in my thoughts I'd become until he pulls the truck into my driveway. Instead of cutting the engine, he leaves it running before turning to me.

I nibble at my lower lip and debate whether to tell him the truth. Luke and I are friends. It's important that I'm honest with him. "I was thinking about Cole."

His expression never falters. If he's bothered by my answer, he doesn't show any outward sign of it. "Is that because Austin showed up tonight?"

I jerk my shoulders. "I guess." But Cole has been on my mind since...I try to think of a time when I haven't been consumed with thoughts of him, and I can't.

"Have you talked with him lately?"

"We exchanged a few texts yesterday," I admit.

He glances away for a heartbeat before his gaze pins mine in place. A moment later, he reaches out and takes hold of my fingers. As I stare at our clasped hands, I can't help but notice how small, almost delicate, my hand looks in his larger one. I also realize that every time he does it, it feels more natural.

"I know you're still getting over Cole," he says. "And I realize that you're not ready to get involved with anyone else just yet, but I'll wait, Cassidy. For as long as it takes, I'll wait."

My eyes widen as his words wash over me. "Luke, I—"

He squeezes my hand gently before shaking his head. "Don't say anything right now. I know you need more time. But there's something between us. Ever since that night..." His voice trails off as my mind tumbles back in time.

To him.

"I haven't been able to get you out of my mind." There is an ocean of emotion swimming around in his eyes. It arrows through the heart of me as he whispers, "I want to be with you."

"Luke..." His name rolls softly off my lips, but I'm not sure how to respond to the enormousness of his words or their meaning.

His other hand rises to tenderly stroke my cheek, and even though it feels different than when Cole has done the same thing, it doesn't feel bad. It actually feels nice. I squeeze my eyes closed as my mind somersaults.

"Give us a chance to be more than what we are," he pleads.

"I still love him," I force myself to admit, wanting him to understand what he's up against.

His fingers continue to touch my cheek. "I wish you didn't."

When I finally lift my lashes, our gazes collide. "I know."

Something indescribable sparks to life between us.

He leans forward, gradually closing the distance. I realize that he's giving me time to stop this from happening. Part of me wonders if this is what needs to occur.

Maybe this is what I need to get over Cole.

His lips ghost over mine. He brushes my top lip before giving the same attention my bottom one. Gently, he kisses the corners of my mouth. It's only when he pulls back that I realize I'm not ready to let him go. His gaze searches mine for a second before he closes the distance between us again. His lips drift over mine with soft seductive strokes.

We kiss for a few more minutes before he ends it.

When I finally open my eyes, he whispers, "I want you to think about that, Cassidy."

Every thought flees from my head, making speech impossible.

"Come on, I'll walk you to the door."

With that, he exits the vehicle, jogging around the front of his truck. Once he reaches the passenger side door, he opens it and helps me out. As we face one another on my front lawn, he pulls me close until I'm wrapped up in his arms. I rest my head against the solid wall of his chest and breathe him in.

"I'm not going to push you into anything, Cassidy. You're the one who needs to decide what you want." He pauses before adding, "You need to decide *who* you want." He pulls back enough to holds my gaze in the darkness. "I think we could be good together. Give me a chance to prove just how good we could be. If I'm the one you want to be with, then it's up to you to make the next move."

My mind whirls with the implication of his words. "Okay."

Just when I wonder if he'll lean in for one last kiss, he turns and tows me to the front door. Once we're standing under the bright porch light, he tugs me into his arms and holds me close.

"I'll pick you up on Sunday around two so we can head back to school. Let Brooklyn know."

Still unable to speak, I nod.

His gaze holds mine as he presses a kiss to my mouth. A few heartbeats later, he retreats down the steps to the driveway. And I'm left standing on the front porch with the cold swirling around me.

As he walks backwards down the brick pathway, his gaze stays pinned to mine. "Go inside, it's cold."

I nod, feeling strangely scattered. Once inside, I lean heavily against the front door before releasing a breath.

I can't remember a time when I've felt this conflicted.

2 5

COLE

"Someone's at the door, can you please answer it?" Mom yells from the kitchen where she's baking Christmas cookies.

Already.

That's not a complaint.

It means I'll have more food to take back to school when I leave tomorrow afternoon. I pause, unable to rip my attention away from the big screen TV as the final seconds of the first quarter play out. The bell rings for a second time as the ball is being passed and—

"Cole?" she shouts again.

Except this time there's exasperation lacing her voice.

And that's never good.

"I'm on it!"

But not really.

Fumble.

Damn.

With a shake of my head, I jog to the door and throw it wide open. Almost immediately, I wish I'd ignored it.

"Hi, Cole." The edges of her lips lift tentatively.

When I remain silent, she shifts from one foot to the other before stuffing her hands into the pockets of her jacket.

"Hey," I force myself to say. If she thinks enough time has passed for me to forget about what happened between us, she's in for a rude awakening.

She clears her throat. "If you're not busy, I was hoping we could talk."

"Ummm…" I rub the back of my neck and try to come up with a plausible excuse as to why that's not a good idea. Unfortunately, I've got nothing. "I'm kind of in the middle of something."

Like an entire day of football. Make that an entire weekend of football. Just because I play hockey doesn't mean that I don't love college ball. That being said, it wouldn't matter if I was bored off my ass, I still wouldn't want to hash out all this shit with Jackie. Because let's face it, that's exactly what she wants to do.

And I'm over it.

I've moved on.

One brow rises. "I'd lay odds that you're in the middle of watching the Ohio State-Michigan game."

That's exactly what I'm in the middle of, and the fact she so easily guessed it leaves me feeling irritated. I don't like that after a year spent apart, she can still predict my behavior. I cross my arms across my chest and casually lean against the door frame. I'll be damned if I invite this girl inside my home.

"So, what if I am?"

Her shoulders slump as her teeth sink into her bottom lip. It makes me feel like a prick. Treating girls like crap goes against everything my parents instilled in me.

I grit my teeth and grudgingly swing one arm toward the living room, where I'm camped out for the day with Gatorade and enough snacks to last me for a week.

"You can come in," I grumble before tacking on, "if you want." That's about as gracious as it's going to get.

Hope lights up her eyes as she nods and steps over the threshold and into the entryway.

"Who's winning?"

I glance toward the living room as she removes her jacket before tossing it over one end of the couch. "Michigan."

Her lips quirk as she murmurs, "Go Wolverines."

A little bit of my annoyance dissolves as one side of my mouth hitches. Michigan is one of my favorite teams, and Jackie knows it. While some things change, others stay the same.

She settles on a chair as I gravitate back to the couch. An awkward silence descends, and our gazes drift toward the seventy-inch screen as the second quarter gets under way.

A few minutes slowly tick by. The tension filling the atmosphere is enough to make me regret inviting her in. There's uncomfortable… and then there's sucking ass.

Make no mistake—this sucks major ass.

It's almost difficult to believe that we were ever best friends and spent so much time together. That thought is quickly followed by sadness and then anger.

"Who was at the door?"

I stifle a groan when Mom walks into the living room, drying her hands with a dish towel. Her feet grind to a halt as her gaze lands on Jackie. The way her eyes widen would be comical if this situation wasn't so painful.

"Jackie!" She claps her hands together as happiness lights up her face. "It's so good to see you again!"

My ex's entire demeanor changes as she jumps from the chair and hurls herself into my mother's outstretched arms. When they finally pull apart, my mother's deep brown gaze fastens onto mine in question. She's encouraged me over the past year to sit down and talk with Jackie dozens of times, and I've always shut down the conversations, refusing to do it.

I shrug. "She stopped over."

I'm sure my mother can read between the lines enough to realize this wasn't my idea.

"It's good to see you two talking again." Mom gives her one last squeeze before releasing her. "It's just like old times, isn't it?"

While Jackie grins in response, I remain silent. There's no way I'm going to touch that loaded question.

I mean…what the hell am I supposed to say?

We all know that this is *nothing* like old times.

"All right." She clears her throat. "I need to run to the store to pick up more flour. I should be back in about thirty minutes."

Her gaze bounces between us before she exits the room.

Longing fills Jackie's eyes as she stares after my mother. "I've really missed her," she murmurs.

"You could always see if she'd be willing to go out with you." The comment shoots out of my mouth before I can rein it back in again.

She huffs out a breath before dropping down onto the chair. "Where's Thomas? Is he around?"

My gaze stays glued to the action unfolding on the screen. "He's at the hospital."

Another stretch of uncomfortable silence falls over us. As much as I want to enjoy this game, that's not going to happen.

Five more tortuous minutes pass by before I mutter, "What did you want to talk about?"

The last time I saw Jackie was at the hockey game where I lost my shit. It's also the night Cassidy and I broke up. I grumbled out a quick hello to my ex after I came out of the locker room, but was in no mood to converse after having Coach ram his size twelve boot up my ass.

She nibbles at her lower lip as if silently debating how to proceed.

We might have been incommunicado for a year, but I still know every expression that flits across her face. Every nervous gesture. I guess that's what you get with a solid decade of friendship under your belt.

"I was hoping we could talk about what happened." She gulps before pushing out the rest. "Maybe start over again." Her voice drops. "We were always such good friends. I miss that." There's a pause. "I miss you."

I straighten on the couch before swiveling toward her. "You have some nerve showing up at my door after you screwed me over. And now you want to sweep it under the rug and pretend it never happened so we can magically go back to being friends again?" I shake my head. "You're the one who shit all over our friendship. Not me." Anger bubbles up inside me. "You weren't just my *girlfriend*, you were my *best friend*. What you did cut deep, and there's no coming back from that."

When she remains silent, I snap, "Did you really think it would be that simple? That all you'd have to do is waltz in here and decide we should be friends again, and poof—we would be? That it could all go back to the way it was before you cheated on me?"

If I'm not careful, I'll start frothing at the mouth. That's how pissed off I am. It's the reason I didn't want to sit down with her in the first place. It's the reason I've been avoiding her.

A dull blush crawls up her cheeks as moisture gathers in her eyes. There was a time in the not so distant past when the sight of her tears would have me backing down and apologizing, but that's no longer the case.

This girl ripped my heart out last year.

And then she stomped all over it.

"I'm so sorry, Cole," she whispers in a thick voice overflowing with unspent emotion. "I never meant for any of this to happen."

My shoulders slump as some of the anger drains away. "What do you want from me?"

She gulps before whispering, "I want your forgiveness."

I shake my head as laughter gurgles up in my throat. Either she's lost it, or I have. I can barely look at her, much less absolve her. "I don't think I can do that."

"It's been over a year. Can't we at least try to move on?"

"I know exactly how long it's been." Even though I'd thought I was completely over her and what happened, I realize that it's still festering inside me like poison.

"I screwed up." Her eyes turn pleading. "And I hurt my best friend in the process."

What sucks most is that Jackie had been my closest friend.

I'd been ten years old when my dad died, and she's the one who sat up in the tree house with me for hours while I sobbed like a little girl. I still remember what it felt like to have her scrawny arms wrapped tightly around me, holding onto me for dear life as if I might float away if she didn't anchor me to the earth.

I can picture her sitting on one of our lawn chairs while I slapped thousands of hockey pucks at the net in our driveway, attempting to channel all of my anger and rage toward something other than the drunk asshole who stole my father from me.

In middle school, I made sure no one messed with her. Even though I wasn't a fighter, I kicked anyone's ass who gave her shit. Somewhere toward the end of my sophomore year in high school, I realized that Jackie was the girl I wanted to be with, and that what I felt for her went beyond friendship.

It's the reason her betrayal cut to the bone and hurt like hell.

Maybe it still does.

I suck in a deep breath as another tear rolls down her cheek. There's nothing that makes me feel more helpless than female tears. Even though I know the magic words that would make them stop, I can't force myself to say them.

"I can't do this right now. I'm sorry."

The only positive in this situation is that my mom isn't here. She'd probably want to have an impromptu therapy session so we could discuss our feelings in a healthy manner and come to a resolution.

No, thanks.

Her tongue darts out to moisten her lips. "Cole—"

"Why?" It's a question that's been gnawing at the back of my mind since I found out about her cheating. "Why did you do it?"

Her eyes widen before she glances away. Another thick silence tries to suffocate the very life out of us.

When she remains silent, I wonder if she'll bother to answer. Maybe she doesn't have one. At least the one she's willing to share with me. But then her gaze locks onto mine. Even though I want to be indifferent to the pain that throbs and pulses in her dark depths, that's impossible.

"When I left last year, I thought I'd be gone for four years, get my degree, find a good job, and then we'd settle down somewhere and start our life together." When I remain silent, her voice fills with emotion. "And I wanted that. I wanted you. There was never a time when I didn't."

My brows pinch together. What she's saying doesn't make any sense. "What happened to change that?"

She swipes at another tear before jerking her shoulders. "I want you to know that I never set out to cheat on you. A few weeks into the semester, I met this guy in class and at first, we were just friends. I wasn't clicking with my roommate or other girls on the dorm floor, so it just felt easier to hang out with him. You'd been my best friend for so long that being friends with another guy just felt normal. But the more time we spent together, the more my feelings grew and changed. It confused me to feel such an intense pull toward him. Especially when I'd only ever felt that way about you. It made me question our relationship and my feelings."

Her explanation sends a fresh wave of pain crashing over me. It takes effort to keep my voice level. "Then you should have been upfront with me about that. You should have pulled the plug on our relationship instead of stringing me along while you hooked up with this other dude."

She shakes her head as more tears slide down her cheeks. "At first, I was going to tell you. I was going to break it off." Misery fills her expression. "I really thought I loved him."

I can only stare at her in shock. We've known each other for so long and yet, right now, it feels like I'm staring at a stranger. Not once did I ever question our relationship.

"I was wrong," she whispers. "It wasn't real. We were together for a few weeks and then it ended." Her gaze drops to her lap as her voice dips. "I just wanted to pretend it never happened. Being with him showed me how much I loved you. Even though I knew I should come clean, I didn't want to lose you."

My head spins that she would even consider keeping all this from me.

"But then I found out I was pregnant, and knew I couldn't pretend it didn't happen."

I'd thought it wasn't possible to be anymore pissed off about the situation.

I was wrong.

Her shoulders collapse as she whispers, "It took weeks for me to work up the nerve to tell you."

My mind tumbles back to the call I'd received from her before Thanksgiving break. I'd been too shellshocked to do anything other than shutdown. I'd sat in my darkened room, holding the phone in my hand, feeling blindsided. None of it felt real.

My girlfriend would never cheat on me.

My best friend would never betray me like that.

But she did.

I don't realize that my fingers are curled and digging into the couch cushions until pain shoots through them. Only then do I loosen my grip.

"What I did was wrong," she says quickly. "I was an idiot to doubt what we had for even a second. I should have just attended Western instead of going away." She swipes at the wetness on her cheeks. "I think we'd still be together if I'd done that. Hurting you and ruining what we had will always be my biggest regret. If there were a way to go back and change what I did, I'd do it in a heartbeat. I hope you realize that."

All the hopes and dreams we'd talked about roll through my head. Even though we'd been young, we'd still planned out our future.

It takes a moment to realize that when I now think about the years stretched out on front of me, it isn't Jackie standing beside me, holding my hand.

It's Cassidy.

We might not be together, but that doesn't mean I don't think about her all the time. Or that I don't still love her. Maybe it's too early to be thinking about a possible future for us, but we have a connection that needs to be explored. And I'm nowhere near ready to let that or her go.

That's when it hits me that if Jackie and I were still together, if she'd actually attended Western freshman year, I wouldn't have met Cassidy. We wouldn't have had the chance to get to know one another or fall in love.

Maybe there's a reason why Jackie and I ended the way we did. It hurt like hell, and made me question everything, but that doesn't mean it wasn't for the best. It's almost a surprise when the anger and resentment festering inside me dissipates.

As I stare at Jackie, I realize that it really is over between us.

Even though I don't love her anymore, I no longer hate her. This is the first time in a year I've been able to think that.

"Is there any chance that we can start over?" she whispers.

Here's another startling realization—I don't want to hurt her. Maybe a different kind of guy would be relishing this moment and looking to mete out a little justice, but that's not me.

I shake my head. "No, there's not." I'm not sure why I say the words, but they feel right slipping off my tongue. "I'm sorry. It's just not going to happen."

She squeezes her eyes closed as a few more tears trek down her face. "I didn't think so, but I had to ask."

Unsure of how to respond to that, I nod.

"Is it because of the girl you're seeing?" she asks in a small voice.

For a moment, I remain silent, reluctant to share any private information with her. My personal life is no longer her business. But then, I decide that regardless of Cassidy, Jackie and I are still over, and nothing will change that.

"We're not together right now."

Emotion flickers in her eyes. "But you love her?"

"Yes," I admit softly.

I honestly can't imagine *not* loving her. I suck in a breath as that thought rips through me. Today has been a day for revelations. And like everything else, maybe that needed to happen as well.

She glances away from me before nodding in understanding.

Another heavy silence falls over us.

Just when I wonder if this will turn awkward again, she says, "If you love her, don't let her go. Don't make a mistake you'll end up regretting for the rest of your life."

My eyes widen as they lock on hers.

"I won't."

As I stare at Jackie, I know without a shadow of a doubt that there was a time when I loved this girl more than anything else. But that time is over. What we had has run its course, and there's no going back and trying to salvage it. Choices were made that sent us both spinning down different paths. Our connection no longer exists.

But it doesn't have to be that way with Cassidy.

There's still time for us to reclaim our relationship. I thought I was doing what was best for both of us when I ended things. I wanted to give her time to sort out her feelings. But, maybe the truth is that I'd been scared of getting my heart ripped out for a second time. Maybe I'd allowed fear to consume me.

Maybe what I wanted was for her to prove that she wanted me more than she wanted Luke Wellington.

In hindsight, all I'd done is push her into the other guy's arms.

"You're a good guy, Cole," she says. "You deserve to be happy."

"So do you." As the words slip free, I realize that I actually mean them. "I hope you find someone who makes you happy."

Her lips lift at the corners. "Thank you."

Before I can overthink the offer, I ask, "Do you want to hang here and watch the game?" I nod toward the kitchen. "Mom was just baking Christmas cookies."

Her smile grows brighter, and she finally looks like the girl I grew up with. Even though we'll never recapture what we once had, maybe we can forge a new relationship.

"You know nothing would make me happier than watching Michigan get their asses handed to them," she says with a smirk.

I shoot her a dirty look before pointing to the door. "Get out."

A chuckle slips free from her as she settles on the chair. For the next couple of hours, we watch the game and scarf down way too many Christmas cookies.

Our friendship doesn't feel as easy as it once did, but it is kind of nice.

Maybe Mom is right.

Maybe there's something to be said for closure.

Although, I won't be admitting that to her anytime soon.

2 6

COLE

"So, what's the deal between you two?" Austin asks. "You two aren't together, are you?"

The suspicion in his voice is clear.

My gaze flickers to his. "No, we're just friends." Sort of. I guess. Maybe. It's all a bit tentative right now. And weird. But it's much better than hating her guts.

His brows furrow as we walk to class.

I'm aware of how Austin feels about Jackie.

And none of it is good.

He might not know her personally, but he was there when shit hit the fan last fall. He's the one who encouraged me to get back out there again. Up until that point, I'd never been with anyone else but her. For a couple of months, I made up for lost time in that department before deciding that random hookups weren't for me.

He gives me a bit of side-eye. "You sure about that?"

"Yup." I have zero desire to travel down that road again.

When I say nothing more on the topic, his muscles gradually loosen. "Glad to hear it."

To fight off the wicked cold blasting through campus, we both have our hockey jackets buttoned up to the collar.

"I ran into Cassidy this weekend," he says casually.

Even though I'm the one who walked away, Austin understands that I'm still hung up on her, just like I know he's still chasing after Brooklyn.

"Where?" The word slips out before I can stop it. Or, at the very least, before I can temper my voice so I don't sound so desperate.

My mind spins, trying to come up with an answer. I know Cassidy went home for the first time in almost a year, which means he didn't run into her somewhere around here. The other detail I'm aware of is that Brooklyn lives next door to her.

You add those two things up and you get—

"I picked Brooklyn up from a party on Friday night, and we hung out for a while."

Yeah. Right.

"I think what you're trying to say is that you drove two and a half hours to get laid." This doesn't surprise me at all. I think Austin would drive five hours one way to be with that girl. He's got it bad.

"I'll have you know that it was way more than a hookup. I spent the night on her couch and met the fam in the morning. Ate a tasty stack of pancakes with Janie and Richard." A shit-eating grin slides across his face. "They love me, by the way."

A chuckle escapes from me. "I guess that's progress. Good job."

"Exactly," he agrees. "Slowly but surely. That's what I'm all about."

I'm still waiting to hear where this Cassidy-sighting occurred. "I'm guessing you saw Cassidy at this party."

His smile dims. "Yeah, she was there all right."

My gut clenches as I wait for the next bomb he's about to drop. From the pinched expression on his face, I can feel it coming.

"With Wellington." He shakes his head in disgust. "That guy is such a tool."

Even though I shouldn't be surprised by this information, I am. After all, I practically gave her my blessing before shoving her in his direction. If there's a tool around here, it's probably me.

"Oh, yeah?" It takes effort to keep my voice level.

"Yeah. I offered to take her home, but Wellington was quick to shoot down that idea. I guess he picked them up earlier. The party was at his high school buddy's house or something like that." Austin pauses before adding, "I wanted to give you a heads up."

At least I can count on Austin to have my back.

Luke Wellington…not so much.

My gaze slides to his before I lift my chin. "I appreciate it."

"Later, dude." He jerks his head to the left where the science building is located. "I'll catch you at practice."

"Yup."

Even though I miss Cassidy like crazy, I feel like the lessons I learned from my relationship with Jackie have been pounded into my brain. The last thing I'm looking to do is get my heart stomped on for a second time. Maybe the connection I have with Cassidy isn't enough. Maybe what she feels for Luke is deeper.

If she spent her break with him, then he must be the guy she wants to be with. As painful as that realization is, it's better to figure it out now rather than later when I'm in even deeper.

With my head so full of the dark-haired girl, I'm startled when she materializes before my eyes. As our gazes collide, I lift my hand in tentative greeting. The edges of her lips lift as she stops and waits for me to catch up with her. Even though I want to play it cool, it feels like I'm starving for the sight of this girl.

When she unleashes a smile, my heart beats into overdrive, and I realize that I'm in so deep that I'm practically drowning.

"Hi," she says.

I might be mentally beating myself up for letting her go, but I flash her a smile in return because it feels so damn good to see her. I have to resist the urge to yank her into my arms and kiss her.

I've missed her so damn much.

I miss the way her soft body feels stretched out beneath mine.

I miss being inside her tight heat.

And I miss the breathy little sounds she makes when she comes.

Those memories are enough to have me stiffening right up.

I clear my throat and attempt to refocus my thoughts. "Hey, it's good to see you. How was your break?"

We fall into line and continue walking to class.

She glances at me from beneath the dark fringe of her lashes.

Cassidy has the most beautiful blue eyes I've ever seen.

"It was pretty great. I really enjoyed being home again and spending time with my family. It made me realize how much I missed being a part of their lives." A chuckle escapes from her. "You wouldn't believe how grown-up my two younger sisters are."

"I'm glad it went well." Before I can stop myself, the words are shooting out of my mouth. "I thought about you a lot over the break."

Damn. Could I sound more desperate?

My mind spins as I quickly backtrack. "You know, wondering how it was going with your family and hoping you were doing okay. Things like that."

Whether Cassidy realizes it or not, I spent a lot of time thinking about her. Especially after my conversation with Jackie. That's when I realized I couldn't let her go without a fight.

Although, after what Austin divulged, maybe it's too late and I've already lost her.

The corners of her mouth spring upward. "I owe you a huge thank you."

I shake my head. "You don't owe me anything." The last thing I want is her gratitude. Sometimes, I wonder if that's what binds her to Luke.

What I want is her heart, not her gratefulness.

When she reaches out and takes a hold of my fingers, my wide gaze darts to hers.

She looks equally startled by her own actions, but our hands remain clasped. The need to yank her into my arms surges through me for a second time.

"If you hadn't reached out to my father, we probably wouldn't be talking. And I wouldn't have spent my vacation with them. What you did means a lot to me, and I wanted you to know that."

Even though we're still walking, our gazes stay locked and something electrical sizzles between us.

"You're welcome." Again, I want to kick my own ass for encouraging her to explore her feelings for Luke.

As we reach the social sciences building where our nine o'clock class is held, she pulls me to the side, out of the way of student traffic. There are a few grumbles as we cut across the sidewalk to the lawn.

Her gaze darts away before she straightens her shoulders and forces it back to me. "I was wondering if we could get together sometime this week." She bites down on her lower lip.

She has no idea just how much it makes me want to nip at her mouth.

"What did you have in mind?"

"Maybe we could skate like we used to?" When her expression turns hopeful, something leaps to life inside me.

"Sure." My mind quickly sifts through everything I have going on for the week. "Does Wednesday work?"

The corners of her lips lift as tension leaks from her. "That sounds good."

"I'll pick you up at five."

She's practically beaming. "Okay." She glances at Dorin Hall. "I guess we better get moving before class starts."

If given the choice, I'd blow off our lecture so we can continue talking.

With a nod in agreement, we jog up the stairs. As I reach the glass door, I pull it open for her. We hustle down the corridor and enter the lecture hall just as the professor walks up to the podium. Even though I'm tempted to follow her, I decide it's probably best to park myself beside Sammy.

"I'll see you Wednesday morning," Cassidy says as I move into the row next to my cousin.

"Yup."

Sammy gives me a speculative look as I slide into my seat. Even though she doesn't say a word, I see the questions brimming in her curious eyes.

I give my head a little shake as I pull my laptop out of my backpack. "We're just skating together."

She snorts. "Whatever you say, loser."

I narrow my eyes.

"Tell me that you don't want her."

I huff out a breath.

There doesn't seem to be any point in denying it. "I can't do that."

For a long moment she remains silent. Just when I think she's dropped the subject, she says, "Good. I like you two together."

A small smile tugs at the corners of my mouth, because that makes two of us.

27

CASSIDY

I've spent most of today camped out at the library, with the exception of two classes. Now that Christmas break is right around the corner, it seems like almost every course has a paper due. My books are spread out all over the table as I tap away on my laptop.

Every time I begin to feel overwhelmed, I close my eyes and inhale a deep breath. Once it no longer feels like my heart is being squeezed in a vise grip, I look over the list I've compiled to prioritize all my assignments.

It's taken a lot of hard work to get my grades up to where they were before Thanksgiving break. I refuse to blow it now that we're in the homestretch. After my breakup with Cole, I'd let some of my classwork slide. Thankfully, Brooklyn was there to slap some sense into me, and I've been able to bounce back.

Getting through that experience was tough, but it made me realize that life will always have its ups and downs. What's important is that you push through the bad times until they're behind you.

Unfortunately, curling up in bed and crying into a pint of Ben and Jerry's isn't an option.

All right, it is an option.

And a tasty one at that.

But it isn't a long-term solution to not flunking out of school.

I'm proud of myself for getting through the situation without shutting down and falling apart. Even more than that, I'm excited to put this semester behind me, and to show my parents that I'm not the screwup they assumed I was when I crashed and burned last year. They've both made a point to tell me how proud they are, but it'll still be nice to show them the tangible proof.

And it'll be nice to see it for myself.

I'm three hours in, editing my psych paper, when I realize that someone has sidled up to my table. I glance up, startled to find Jackie. The muscles in my belly contract as I brace myself for this unwelcome conversation. We haven't spoken since the Halloween party, and quite frankly, I don't really need a repeat of that.

Especially since Cole and I aren't together.

What surprises me even more than finding her here is the tentative smile curving her lips. "Do you mind if I sit down for a minute? I've been hoping we would run into each other."

"Ahhh…" My voice trails off as my brain spins. I have no idea what we could possibly have to talk about.

Her smile falters as she whispers, "Please?"

That's all it takes for me to cave.

I gesture halfheartedly to the chair parked across from me and mutter, "I'm in the middle of writing a paper."

She settles on the chair before tucking a few strands of hair behind her ear. Her gaze skitters away from mine before returning. "I wanted to apologize for ambushing you at the Halloween party. It was wrong, and I shouldn't have done it."

My brows rise in surprise. Whatever I was expecting her to say, that wasn't it. Not by a long shot.

I clear my throat. "Um, okay. Thanks."

"At that point, I guess I was still hoping Cole and I could work everything out between us." She shrugs. "Maybe even pick back up where we left off before I…" her voice trails off awkwardly as color rushes to her cheeks.

Since I can't blame her for wanting Cole back, I nod in understanding.

Who wouldn't want to be with him?

He's one of the best guys I know.

And it's obvious that Jackie feels the same way.

"So…you tried to work everything out with him?" I ask softly.

Sadness seeps into her eyes. "Yeah, we actually had a really good conversation last weekend."

When she falls silent, my muscles tighten, and it feels like I'm waiting with bated breath for her to continue.

"But it's not going to happen. I…" She blinks and glances away.

For one horrible moment it looks like she might actually break down.

There's no way I can console this girl about not being with the guy I want.

Thankfully, she rallies at the last second before the tears can fall.

"I really screwed up and there's no way to repair the damage I inflicted. Hurting Cole is something I'll regret for the rest of my life." She searches my gaze for a long moment. "I hope you realize what an amazing guy he is."

Even though I'm loathe to admit it to her, I say, "Cole and I aren't together."

I have no idea what prompts me to be honest with her. The girl is Cole's ex. I don't owe her anything…but still.

"He told me."

I'm taken off guard that she would know about the demise of our relationship. For all I know, she's here to gloat.

I search her gaze, half-expecting to see victory or happiness dancing gleefully in her eyes. Surprisingly, there's no pleasure in her expression.

"Then whatever you need to say is moot."

She straightens before pressing forward. "Is it?"

I blink, unsure how to answer her.

"I don't know," I whisper.

Her lips flatten into a tight line as she rolls her eyes.

Yeah, that's right. The girl actually rolls her eyes at me.

Cole's ex-girlfriend. The one who desperately wanted him back. She's annoyed with me for not knowing if a relationship will work out between us.

It's definitely a little strange.

Maybe more than a little.

"If you love Cole and want him back, then do something about it." Sorrow flashes in her eyes. "If he's the best thing that ever happened to you, then don't let him slip through your fingers." She rises to her feet. "I'll let you get back to work." After a couple of steps, she swings back around. "Don't make the same mistake I did. Don't let him go."

I'm not sure why Jackie felt compelled to seek me out, but I'm grateful she did. "Thank you."

Even though a smile tips the corners of her lips, unhappiness shimmers around her. "You're welcome."

Before she can disappear around a bookshelf, I say, "Jackie."

This time, when she turns, one dark brow is raised. And I realize all over again how pretty she is, and how perfectly suited she and Cole are for each other. In my mind, I can imagine them together.

"Are you still in love with him?"

"I'll always be in love him," she says. "Somehow, I need to find a way to live with my mistakes and move on."

Even though I shouldn't ask, the question trips off my tongue. "How do you know he won't change his mind?"

Her shoulders collapse under the weight of her answer. "Because what we had is over and there's no going back."

In a weird way, I can sympathize with her pain.

"I'm sorry. I understand what it's like to live with regrets. To pick up all the pieces and try to glue them all back together again. It's not easy."

With a tilt of her head, her gaze sharpens on mine. She smiles as if seeing me for the first time. "Under different circumstances, I think we could have been friends."

"Maybe," I say in return.

In a small way, we're kindred spirits. We've both made mistakes and have regrets. We're also working to put our lives back together again.

She jerks a thumb over her shoulder. "I need to get going. It was nice talking with you, Cassidy. Good luck."

"You, too."

For a long stretch of minutes, everything Jackie said churns through my head. Decision made, I grab my phone and fire off a message. There's something I need to take care of before I meet up with Cole tomorrow morning.

Something that never should have flared to life.

CASSIDY

A smile lights up Luke's face as he pulls me into the warm circle of his arms. "I have about thirty minutes before I need to be at practice. What's up?"

For a heartbeat I allow him to hold me before untangling myself from his embrace. "Do you mind if we grab a coffee and talk?"

"Sure."

After we order our drinks, Luke hands the barista a few bills before I can grab the money from my purse.

"I've got it," I say, quickly digging through my wallet. "I'm the one who invited you for coffee. I should pay."

"You can get the next one." When he winks at me, the barista sighs. "Don't worry, I'll hold you to it."

A few minutes later, he grabs our coffees from the counter, and we head to a table nestled in the corner. Once settled, we both take a few sips from our mugs. The weather has only grown colder, and it feels good to warm up.

"How are classes going?" he asks. "All caught up?"

Luke understands how stressful my breakup was with Cole because he was there. It was his and Brooklyn's shoulders that I cried on. They held my hand and made sure I was doing what needed to be done in school. I'm lucky to have them in my life.

"Yup. It took a while but I'm finally back on track again." A tiny smile springs to my lips. "Although, I'm pretty sure the library staff is going to start charging me rent. I've been living there since Thanksgiving break." I take another small sip of coffee. "How about you?"

He shrugs as his gaze remains focused on me. His blond hair has grown out, and I realize the longer length looks good on him. As I glance around the space, I notice that I'm not the only one who thinks he's handsome. Several girls are checking him out.

"I'll be glad when this semester is over," he says. "I'm a little burnt-out right now. I could use a break."

I think about all the papers and exams I have coming up. "Me, too."

I've been working around the clock, and can't wait to return home and spend more time with my family. The relationship I'm building with my parents feels so much better than even before I left for college the first time. Even though the year apart sucked, it allowed my dad and me to break the dysfunctional patterns we'd established. Not only that, but I also feel closer to my mom. We've talked on the phone a few times since I returned to school, and we text every day. It's nice.

Actually, it's way better than that.

"Maybe after exams are wrapped up, we can get together and celebrate. A successful first semester at Western for both of us."

I smile at the thought. "It can't come soon enough."

As we drink our coffee, a comfortable silence falls over us. Over the past couple of weeks, I've had time to sort out my feelings for both Luke and Cole. Even though I feel tied to both of them, it's obvious who my heart belongs to.

And there's no changing that.

I have no idea how it'll turn out with Cole, but I can't let Luke think that our relationship will ever be anything more than friendship.

"Cassidy?"

I blink to awareness, not realizing I've become tangled up in my thoughts until he says my name. For the first time since we've sat down, I see the questions swimming around in his eyes.

"Sorry. Guess I spaced out there for a moment."

His lips lift into a smile, but it's no longer full-fledged. "No problem. I know you've had a lot going on with school."

I nod, but that's not the issue, and I have to wonder by the way his smile dims if he realizes that, too.

As much as I don't want to hurt Luke, I need to be honest about what I feel. "There has been a lot going on, but I wanted the chance to talk to you."

His shoulders tense and his eyes darken. "You're choosing Cole, aren't you?"

My heart thumps against my breast as I nod. "I love him." That's the bottom line, and there's no getting past it or around it.

I love him.

I'm still *in* love with him.

And I can't let that go.

I can't let *him* go without a fight.

Luke's gaze drops to his coffee as silence falls over us. He's turned out to be a such a good friend and I don't want to lose that, but I can't give him anything more than that, either.

"You've worked things out with him?" he finally asks.

"No." I shake my head. "Not yet."

His brows slide together as his attention settles on me again. "And if he's not interested in getting back together, what then?"

That could be a definite possibility.

"Then I move on with my life."

It's a scary prospect.

Honestly, I'm already at that point. Cole and I aren't together, and I have no idea if we'll be able to work through everything standing in our way, but I have to try. I don't want to walk away from our relationship with any more regrets than I already have.

"And you don't think you could move on with me?" he asks, voice dipping.

I release a steady breath. "I've been doing a lot of thinking since

Thanksgiving break, trying to sort out my feelings for both of you. I like you, Luke. And I care about you. I'm so thankful that you're in my life, but my feelings for you aren't romantic in nature." I reach out, gently covering his hand with my own. "I don't want you to wait around for me when I don't think anything will ever come of it."

"I wish you'd give me a chance to show you how good we could be together."

"I can't." I nibble at my lower lip. "I never meant to lead you on, and if that's what I did, I'm sorry."

He twists his hand beneath mine until his fingers lock around mine.

"You never led me on. You were always upfront about your feelings. I guess I'd hoped that at some point, you'd feel about me the way I feel for you."

"It was never my intention to hurt you."

"I know," he acknowledges with a slight smile.

"I'm—"

He shakes his head. "Don't say it."

I fall silent as my lips quirk.

He draws in a breath before slowly releasing it. As he does, I get the feeling that everything will be all right between us.

"You don't have anything to be sorry about."

My hesitant smile grows as I squeeze his hand. "Thank you."

Even though I don't love Luke the way he wants me to, I still have deep feelings for him. I think I always will. What happened between us—the experience we shared—bonded us together. I don't think it's a connection that can ever be broken.

Luke's gaze clings to mine. "I told you before that no matter what you decide, you wouldn't lose me, and I meant it. We're friends, Cassidy. And we're always going to be friends."

29

─────

CASSIDY

"*Pass it to me!*"

I wind up and hit the puck to Cole who flies across the ice. The rubber disk lands right on the end of his stick as he races with it to the goal and flicks it into the net. We've been here for about thirty minutes, and it feels just like it used to. I love spending time with Cole on the ice, and over the last month, I've missed it.

Missed him.

As difficult as it was talking with Luke yesterday, I'm so glad I cleared the air. Even if nothing changes with Cole, I know that remaining friends with Luke is what's best for both of us.

After I thought about it, I decided that maybe Cole was right, and I was allowing what happened last year skew my feelings for Luke. I didn't want to believe that was a possibility, but when I tried to separate my emotions for him, I wasn't able to do it.

They were too deeply intertwined.

"Water break?"

I nod as we skate to our water bottles on the bench. After removing our gloves, we toss them onto the long stretch of wood before guzzling down our drinks.

When I finally come up for air, the words slip from my mouth before I can stop them. "I've really missed spending time on the ice with you." Everything inside me freezes, hoping that I haven't ruined the moment.

Heat fills my face as one heartbeat passes and then another.

Just as I open my mouth to backtrack, a smile curves his lips. "Me, too."

Relief rushes through every cell of my body as my muscles loosen. I realize that if I'm going to be honest and tell him how I feel, it needs to be now before I lose my nerve.

"What I've missed most of all is our relationship." Those nine little words are the most difficult ones I've ever had to say. As soon as they escape from my mouth, I want to snatch them out of the air.

I've never been good at putting myself out there.

But Cole is worth it.

He's worth the risk of rejection.

His gaze searches mine as the silence stretches between us. When he doesn't respond, air gets clogged in my throat, making it impossible to breathe. My heart pounds harshly against my ribcage. That's the moment I wonder if maybe too much has happened, too much time has passed, and it really is too late for us.

Is it possible that I let the best guy I've ever known slip through my fingers?

My flight response kicks in, telling me to flee before I embarrass myself any further.

As I retreat a step, he reaches out and takes a hold of my hand. It's the cool feel of his skin sliding over mine that jolts me into remembering how I'd placed my hand over Luke's in the same manner, wanting to let him down as gently as possible.

My gut twists with nerves until it feels like I might throw up.

"Cassidy..."

Oh god, this is bad.

Only now do I realize that he doesn't feel the same way. He's moved on while I'm still in love with him. He must think I'm so pathetic.

Is there anything worse than giving your heart to someone who no longer wants it?

"I'm sorry," I gasp on a strangled breath. Unable to stay here, I stumble back another step. I need to get out of here. "I shouldn't have said anything."

Before I can formulate an exit strategy, he grabs my arm and pulls me toward him. For a fraction of a moment, my mind tumbles back to the night we met. Only this time, my body doesn't seize up the same way it did in August, because I know Cole would never do anything to hurt me.

"Cassidy, wait! Just give me a second to catch up." The patient smile that plays around the corners of his lips only intensifies the growing ache in my heart.

Instead of running away, I straighten my shoulders and force out the rest through stiff lips. Maybe it is too late for us, but I want him to know exactly how I feel.

I've come too far not to finish it.

"I love you, and I'm sorry if I made you feel like I wanted someone else more than I wanted you. I don't. I couldn't possibly. You were right about my feelings getting tangled up for Luke because of what happened. You're the only guy I've ever wanted, and I really hate myself for screwing up our relationship."

There.

Done.

Just as I open my mouth to plead my case and tell him why I deserve a second chance, he yanks me to him. My eyes widen as his lips crash onto mine.

And then I'm lost in the taste and feel of him.

It's been so long, and I've missed him—and this—so much.

He barely draws away, just enough to whisper, "Haven't you realized yet that I'm still in love with you?" His lips stroke over mine before he murmurs, "It was taking everything I had inside to keep my distance."

My head spins. I'd really thought I lost him. That I squandered the possibility of an us.

"I'm so sorry for pushing you away," I whisper.

He nods as uncertainty flickers in his eyes. "Are you absolutely certain about your feelings for Luke?" There's a pause as his voice dips. "I can't go through that again, Cassidy. I love you, but I need to know there's nothing going on between the two of you."

"I'm positive. We're nothing more than friends." My teeth sink into my lower lip as a thought occurs to me. "Are you all right with that?"

As much as I like Luke, and as connected as I feel to him, I realize that it's nothing compared to my feelings for Cole. I love Cole more than anything. The enormity of those feelings is so much deeper than what I could possibly feel for Luke.

"As long as I'm the one you want, the one you love, then I trust you."

My fingers curl into the collar of his warmup jacket before tugging him closer so that my arms can wind around his neck. I've missed the feel of him so much.

"It's always been you." My conversation with Jackie tumbles through my head and I add, "And I won't mess that up again."

He untangles my arms from around his neck before stepping away and locking his fingers around my wrist, pulling me toward the heavy metal door that leads off the ice.

"Where are we going?"

His heated gaze collides with mine, but he doesn't stop moving. "To my place."

A shiver of anticipation dances down my spine at the thought of being alone with him.

"And FYI—you'll be there for a while," he adds as if I might argue.

My thighs clench as need crashes through me.

"Can you really wait that long?" It'll be at least twenty minutes.

He grinds to an abrupt halt before tugging me into his arms again.

"The real question is, can you?"

Well…the rink *is* closed to the public for another thirty minutes.

"I don't know," I whisper as his mouth strokes over mine. "I really want you."

The tip of his tongue dances across my lips before slipping inside to mingle with my own. A soft groan fills the silent rink.

I'm pretty sure it came from me.

How many weeks has it been since I've felt the slide of his cock deep inside my body?

Way too long.

"We can go into the office," he offers.

It's tempting.

So tempting.

But a quickie isn't what I need right now.

I shake my head. "Once I get you naked, you aren't going to be putting your clothes on for a while. Let's head back to your house."

A wicked gleam ignites in his eyes. "I like the way you think, baby. Let's go."

And then he's once again dragging me off the ice.

We make quick work of shedding our skates and hockey gear before shoving it all into our bags. With my hand held securely in his, we sprint out of the rink. The ride to his place takes just fifteen minutes, and I can't keep my hands off him.

By the time he parks his Mustang in front of the Victorian he shares with five other guys from the hockey team, I want to tear the clothes from his body. I think he must feel the same way since his fingers are already slipping beneath my shirt as we race up the porch stairs and barge through the front door. It bursts open, reverberating on its hinges before Cole slams it shut. And then we're running up the staircase. We're both laughing so hard as our fingers grasp for one another.

"Hey." Alex lumbers out of the living room wearing a pair of boxers. "I'm glad you're—"

"Not now," Cole yells over his shoulder as he leads me to the second floor. "And probably not for a while. Anyone bothers us, they're getting their ass kicked. Got it?"

"Yeah, man. I got it."

Even though I don't turn around to see his expression, I can hear the humor that simmers in Alex's deep voice. He knows exactly what's about to happen.

And you know what?

I don't care at all.

Right now, all I can think about is the feel of Cole's hands drifting over me and his muscular body settling on top of mine.

Once we're inside his room, he twists the lock and pounces, catching me around the middle and pressing me to him. When his hands settle on my ass, he hoists me up so that my legs can wrap around his waist. A growl rumbles up from his chest as I grind myself against him.

His lips crash onto mine, and there is nothing gentle about how this kiss unfolds.

"Too much clothing," I gasp.

"Agreed."

His hands leave my bottom as I drop to the floor. My palms stroke over the solid planes of his chest before my fingers grip the hem of his T-shirt and I whip it over his head, tossing it over my shoulder. In the blink of an eye, my shirt also disappears. He removes my bra as I work the button and fly of his jeans. Even though his erection is still covered by his boxers, it springs forward. My thighs clench as I stroke my fingers over the hot length.

I've missed this so much.

Impatiently, he pushes the thick denim material down his hips and thighs before kicking it away. His hands settle on the elastic band at my waist, and before I can suck in a breath, the leggings are yanked down, pulled away, and tossed aside.

Now that most of our clothing has been shed, we stare at each other for a long heartbeat. He's still in his boxers and I'm in nothing more than my panties.

His eyes darken as they lick over my nearly naked body, taking in every dip and curve. The way he stares makes me feel beautiful.

"I've missed you so damn much, baby." His gaze singes my flesh with their golden intensity. "And I've missed this."

It feels as if there is a magnet pulling me to him as I close the distance between us until the tips of my breasts are pressed against his chest. I lift my hands until my palms can cup his cheeks.

"I'll never be able to apologize enough for hurting you," I whisper. It makes me sick that I allowed something—someone—to come between us.

And I could have lost him.

With his gaze holding mine, he leans into my touch. "It's behind us now, and we don't have to talk about it anymore."

I reach up, stretching on my tiptoes until I can press my lips to his. "I love you more than anything." One hand falls away from his cheek and trails down his hard body before slipping inside his underwear until I'm able to hold a different part of him.

He groans as I tighten my grip around his rigid length. A moment later, he's thrusting his hips, moving against me. It's such a turn-on to watch his whiskey-colored eyes cloud with pleasure.

"I won't last very long if you keep that up," he groans as I continue stroking him.

Before I can torment him any further, he sweeps me up into his arms and walks us to the bed, depositing me in the middle of it. He crawls onto the mattress and up my body until I'm stretched out beneath him. Hovering above me, he reaches out and strokes my breasts, plucking at my nipples until I'm the one making desperate noises deep in my throat and shifting with need. When I can't stand another second, he leans forward and kisses a stiff tip before giving the same attention to the other one.

His mouth licks and sucks a hot trail down my ribcage to my navel until he arrives at the elastic band of my panties. Cole knows exactly what I like and how to touch me to elicit the most pleasure.

And I love it.

Love the way he worships my body so completely.

My breath catches as he lowers the pink cotton material down my hips, bearing me one tortuous inch at a time. My heavy-lidded gaze stays locked on him. I love the possessive look filling his eyes as he stares at me.

Once my panties have been stripped away, he places a gentle kiss against my pussy. My hips arch off the mattress in response. All I can think about is the feel of his lips caressing me, nuzzling me, licking me with long, deliberate strokes.

"I've missed you so much, baby." His gaze flicks upward until it captures mine as his tongue slides over my flesh. "Mmm. You're already so nice and wet for me."

My head lolls back as sensation explodes inside my body. I widen my legs, wanting to feel him lick every inch of me. I've missed this just as much as he has.

"You taste so damn good."

He nibbles at my delicate flesh until it feels like I might lose my mind. Pleasure ratchets up inside me as his tongue strokes over my clit, circling the tiny bundle of nerves. A whimper escapes from me as he continues to lap at me. My body vibrates with the need he's stoked to life.

I arch against him, needing to get closer. I'm so close to splintering apart. So close to screaming with the thick tension coiled tightly in my core.

"Do you want my cock or tongue?"

The growled-out question sends a spasm of arousal shooting through me and pushes me closer to the precipice.

All I want is *him*.

Cole.

My mind cartwheels. I'm not even sure I can string together a passable sentence. "Cock," I gasp, "I need your cock."

With a final kiss pressed against me, he rises to his feet and quickly sheds his boxers. My gaze fastens onto his groin as his cock springs free.

He reaches into his nightstand drawer and pulls out a condom before sheathing himself in it, and then he's back on the bed, kneeling between my spread thighs. Not a heartbeat later, the blunt head of his cock nudges my entrance.

Bliss.

Pure bliss.

There are no other words to describe the feeling he instills in me.

"You're so fucking tight," he groans through clenched teeth, carefully inching his way inside me.

As my inner muscles lock around him, waves of pleasure wash over me. I lift my hips, arching toward him, needing him to fill me to the brim. We both sigh as he slides deep inside me before pulling out and then thrusting back in.

Ten strokes.

That's all it takes before he's spilling himself inside me and I'm shattering around him.

Once the condom has been disposed of, Cole gathers me into his arms and pulls me to him until I'm sprawled out across his chest. The steady thumping of his heartbeat fills my ears.

I sift my fingers through the sprinkling of dark hair across his chest before trailing them over his nipples. When they harden, I lean over, licking and sucking each one into my mouth.

"You're going to kill me," he groans.

A grin springs to my lips as I continue to play with his body. From the corner of my eye, I watch as his thick shaft stirs to life again.

"I really missed you," I tell him between kisses.

His fingers settle beneath my chin before he lifts it until my gaze locks on him. "I missed you, too. Maybe that's what we needed to go through in order to find our way back to each other."

I allow his words to roll around in my brain before nodding. "I don't want anything else to come between us."

"It won't." His hands lock around my ribcage before he pulls me the rest of the way on top of him. "I love you."

"I love you, too."

When I spread my legs, his hard shaft slips inside me and we're making love all over again. As amazing as it was the first time, this is even better, because it's long and slow, and perfect.

The sensation of him filling my body, making me feel complete, is the most beautiful part.

I can't imagine sharing myself like this with anyone other than Cole.

3 0

CASSIDY

wo hours later, we finally leave his room to scrounge up some food.

After making love three times, I'm famished. I'm so hungry that my belly is rumbling and growling in protest.

Once in the kitchen, Cole fills two bowls with cereal before saturating the flakes in milk.

"Eat up," he says with a wink before shoveling a spoonful into his mouth. After he swallows it down, he adds, "You're going to need all your energy."

A giggle slips free as I spoon Frosted Flakes into my mouth. As we finish our bowls, his phone chimes with an incoming message. He picks up the slim device and glances at the screen.

His gaze flicks to mine. "It's my mom. She's going to drop off some laundry I left at the house over the weekend."

My heart stutters as my eyes widen.

Dr. Thompson, who also happens to be Cole's mother.

My teeth sink into my lower lip as an internal debate gets waged in my brain.

Do I tell him that his mother was my psychologist?

Or do I bury it in the back of my mind since I'm no longer one of her clients?

"Cassidy?" My gaze jerks back to him, and I see all the questions that now swim around in his golden depths. "Are you all right?"

"Umm, yeah." A fresh wave of nerves skitters across my flesh. "I'm fine."

The problem is that I can't have any more secrets sitting between us.

His brows pinch together. "Are you sure?"

Heat fills my cheeks as I force out the words. "There's something I need to tell you."

I blink as Cole swallows up the distance between us and sweeps me up into his arms before settling at one of the kitchen chairs. His arms stay wrapped protectively around me as he holds me close.

"So, tell me," he murmurs against my hair.

I stare at my fingers, which are knotted together on my lap. "The dinner at your house wasn't the first time I met your mother."

His body stills beneath mine.

I push the rest out in a jumble, "I had met her in August at the counseling center." There's a pause. "She was my psychologist."

Air gets wedged in my throat as I sit frozen on his lap and wait for his reaction. My muscles are locked so tight that it feels as if I could shatter into a million jagged pieces. The idea of getting back together for a few short hours only to lose him all over again would very likely kill me.

"I didn't know she was your mother. You don't have the same last name. It never occurred to me that she might be related to you."

When he remains silent, fear slides down my spine and I begin to babble. "She knows everything about our relationship, Cole. Like us sleeping together, and that we were using condoms. But, umm, I haven't seen her professionally since I realized she was your mother." There's a pause before I add, "Actually, I saw her on campus before Thanksgiving break and we cleared the air."

I really wish it were possible to sink into the floor and disappear.

It's the shaking of his body that has me glancing up. A frown tugs at the corners of my mouth as my brows pinch together. He can't possibly be…

Laughing.

Oh my god, the guy is actually laughing!

"Cole!" I screech. All the embarrassment from moments ago ebbs as anger fills the void instead. "Are you seriously laughing about this?"

"Sorry." His shoulders tremble. "I knew something had to be wrong. That dinner went to total shit as soon as my mom walked through the door, but I couldn't figure out what it was."

When he continues to chuckle, I slap his T-shirt covered chest before trying to jump off his lap.

"It's not funny," I seethe. "She knows everything about our relationship because I told her! I talked to her about going on the pill." I drag a hand over my face. "Do you have any idea how mortified I was when she walked through that door, and I realized that the woman I'd been confiding in was none other than my boyfriend's mother?"

A fresh wave of humiliation crashes over me again, making me feel even worse.

Before I can get away from him, Cole tightens his arms around my wriggling body. They feel like steel bands holding me firmly in place. Even as I continue to fight, I know the struggle is futile. I won't be going anywhere until he decides to release me.

"Do you want to know what's even more embarrassing than that?"

Lips smashed together, I refuse to respond.

When it becomes obvious that I'm not going to answer, he says, "Having your mom barge into your room when you're balls deep in your girlfriend and seconds away from blowing your load. Trust me, that's a lot worse. And because that experience wasn't mentally scarring enough, I had to sit down with her and my stepfather to discuss the ramifications of what Jackie and I were doing with our bodies. It unfortunately ended in an overly graphic PowerPoint presentation regarding STIs and pregnancy." He shudders. "The only thing that would have made it worse is if she'd decided to give me a few pointers and tips before finally allowing me to slink back to the scene of the crime."

A smile trembles around the corners of my lips as laughter explodes from me.

His arms tighten around me as he grins. "Oh, so that's funny, huh?"

When his dimples pop, my heart melts.

"I didn't have sex for two months after that fiasco." He shakes his head at the memory.

I'm dying as I imagine Dr. Thompson sitting down to have an in-depth sex talk with a teenage Cole.

After my giggling subsides, he says, "So, do I think it's a catastrophe that my mother knows I'm having sex with someone I love, and that we're trying to be responsible about it?" He shakes his head. "No. Honestly? It doesn't bother me at all."

I shoot him a look from beneath the fringe of my lashes. "She knows about my past, Cole. She knows *everything* about me."

He shrugs. "Who cares? You've worked hard this semester to overcome everything and I'm proud of you for that, Cassidy. In the grand scheme of things, nothing else matters."

His words ring throughout my head as I release a steady breath. "You're right." I press my lips to his. "I'm sorry if I made a big deal out of it. I just don't want there to be any more secrets between us."

His mouth ghosts over mine. "I don't care about any of that." His tongue slips inside my mouth as his hands slide under my T-shirt before settling on my breasts and stroking my nipples.

Just as my head rolls back, a deep voice says, "Breakfast and an X-rated show! Now that's how you start off the morning."

We swing around and find Alex wearing a huge smile. When Cole growls, he raises his hands in a gesture of surrender before backing out of the kitchen, leaving us alone again.

I duck my head and press my face against the curve of Cole's neck.

"Maybe we should take this X-rated show back up to the bedroom."

I lift my face to meet his gaze. My cheeks feel like they're on fire. "Is this one of those embarrassing stories we now get to tell?"

"Sure, but it'll probably take a couple of months before it seems funny."

Before I can say anything else, he rises to his feet with me held securely in his arms and strolls out of the kitchen and back up to his bedroom. Once the door to Cole's room is closed, I realize we've missed our nine o'clock class.

I guess we'll have to borrow Sammy's notes.

As Cole slides his thick erection inside me, the world around us falls away. It doesn't take long before we're both splintering apart.

Last year, when I got kicked off the hockey team and failed out of Dartmouth, I couldn't imagine anything good ever coming out of it. But that's exactly what happened. If my life hadn't taken a detour, I wouldn't have found Cole, or fallen in love with him. And I wouldn't have this opportunity to forge a new relationship with my mom, and an even better one with my father. Brooklyn and I wouldn't be roommates or best friends. And I wouldn't be playing hockey on a team that I actually enjoy.

Even though last year was painful and it felt like I'd lost everything important to me, I actually ended up gaining more than I ever imagined possible.

Unable to help myself, I reach up and brush the hair out of Cole's eyes. One side of his mouth hitches at the corner.

I honestly couldn't love him more.

"What are you thinking about?" he asks as we lay spent in each other's arms.

For a moment, my mind is filled with all the good that has found its way back into my life.

"I was just thinking that everything happens for a reason, and you, Cole Mathews, are my everything."

A smile spreads across his face before he takes my lips in a kiss that sears every single part of me.

I'm sure you can guess what happens after that.

Total.

Bliss.

EPILOGUE

COLE

 *our years later...*

"Hurry it up, babe," I call from the living room of our high-rise apartment in downtown Chicago. "Or we'll be late."

I just got home from a team practice with the Blackhawks, and now we're heading out to meet up with friends for dinner. Austin and Brooklyn are in town for the weekend. And so is Luke and his new girlfriend. It might have taken time for the two of us to iron out our friendship, but it happened.

Eventually.

"I'm coming."

A low whistle escapes from me as she walks out of the bedroom wearing a little black dress that clings to her every curve. Even after spending a couple of hours on the ice, my dick stiffens right up.

Damn, but my fiancée is hot.

"Is it possible to cancel our plans for the evening?" There's a beat of silence. "Because I'd much rather stay here and strip you out of that gorgeous dress. It would look perfect draped over the chair in the corner of our room."

Color stains her cheeks as she does a little twirl. "You like?"

My gaze falls to her backside. "Umm, I don't just like it. I *love* it."

Cassidy has never been one for slinky outfits or overly girlie things. So, this is a total surprise. One I'm absolutely loving.

"You know we can't cancel," she says. "We haven't seen Brooklyn and Austin, or Luke, in months. I've missed them. We have a lot of catching up to do."

As much as I was looking forward to getting together with our friends, it's tempting to keep Cassidy here, all to myself.

"I suppose not," I grumble.

She closes the distance between us before stretching onto the tips of her toes and pressing a kiss against my lips. "I promise to make it worth your while when we get home tonight."

My lips lift into a grin. "Deal."

I smack her bottom when she turns away from me. "You ready to head out?"

Her gaze darts to the open bedroom door as she nibbles at her lower lip.

I know Cassidy well enough to realize something's up. "What's going on?"

She clears her throat. "We need to wait for a few more minutes before we can leave."

"Why is that?" My gaze searches hers, looking for the answers she hasn't given me.

Silence descends before she finally admits, "I just took a pregnancy test."

My brows shoot up as my mouth falls open. Out of all the things I thought she might say, that wasn't one of them.

"A pregnancy test?" It takes a moment to wrap my lips around the word as I swallow up the distance between us and yank her into my arms. "Do you really think you could be pregnant?"

"I'm two weeks late," she murmurs, "so there's a good possibility."

Two weeks.

She's been keeping this to herself for that long?

"Why didn't you tell me?"

Her tongue darts out to moisten her lips. "I just wanted to make sure before I said anything." There's a moment of hesitation. "It just seems like such bad timing. I'm in graduate school and you're on the road with the team."

Joy explodes inside me as my hand slips between us to settle on her gently curved belly. "No matter what happens, we'll figure it out. Everything will be fine. Promise."

"We're not even married yet."

I lift her left hand so she can stare at the ginormous engagement ring adorning her finger. "Close enough."

Her teeth scrape against her lower lip as she searches my gaze. "You're really happy about this?"

"Not just happy, *thrilled*." I press a kiss against her mouth. How could she possibly think otherwise?

When the alarm on her phone goes off, her eyes widen. "That's the timer for the test." There's a pause. "I'm nervous."

"Don't be. We have each other, and no matter what happens, we'll get through it. All right?"

She nods as her muscles loosen.

"Should we find out if we're going to be parents?" I ask.

Excitement sparks to life in her eyes. "Yes."

With her hand secured in mine, I pull her through the bedroom into the attached bathroom where the test sits on the granite counter. Our gazes stay locked for a long heartbeat before she carefully picks up the white stick and stares at it.

When a few seconds tick by and she remains silent, I shift, anticipation building inside me until it feels like I'm about to explode.

"Well?"

She turns the stick toward me until I can see the two windows on one end. I'll be honest, I have no idea what I'm looking at. Or what it means. It's a couple of pink lines.

Wait a minute...

Does that—

"Are we pregnant?"

She nods as a gurgle of laughter escapes from her. "Yup, we're pregnant."

I let out a loud whoop before picking Cassidy up and swinging her around in a tight circle.

I can't believe this.

We're going to be parents.

My mind tumbles back to the first time I saw Cassidy sitting in our Psych class. I had no idea that this was the girl who would end up changing my life. But that's exactly what she did.

And now, I can't imagine a single day without her filling it.

This girl is my everything.

And nothing will ever change that.

The End

HATE TO LOVE YOU

BRODY

Dude, I thought you'd be back earlier." Cooper, one of my roommates, grins as I walk through the front door. There's a half-naked chick straddling his lap. "We had to get this party started without you." He shrugs as if he's just taken one for the team. "It couldn't be helped."
I snort as my gaze travels around the living room of the house we rent a few blocks off campus. Even though there are only four of us on the lease, our place seems to be a crash pad for half the team. By the looks of the beer bottles strewn around, they've been at it for a while. I'm seriously thinking about charging some of these assholes rent. Although, I guess if I were stuck in a shoebox of a dorm, I'd be desperate for a way out, too. I played juniors straight out of high school for two years before coming in as a freshman at twenty. I skipped dorm living and went straight to renting a place nearby. There was no way I was bunking down with a bunch of random eighteen-year-olds who'd never lived away from home. Not to mention, having an RA up my ass telling me what I could and couldn't do.
That sounds about as much fun as ripping duct tape off my balls. Which is, I might add, the complete opposite of fun. Hazing sucks. And for future reference, you don't rip duct tape off your balls, you

carefully cut it away with a steady hand while mother-fucking the entire team.

My other two roommates, Luke Anderson and Sawyer Stevens, are hunched at the edge of the couch, battling it out in an intense game of NHL. Their thumbs are jerking the controllers in lightning-quick movements, and their eyeballs are fastened to the seventy-inch HD screen hanging across the room.

I can only shake my head. Every time they play, it's like a freaking National Championship is at stake.

I arch a brow as the girl on Cooper's lap reaches around and unhooks her bra, dropping it to the floor. Apparently, she doesn't mind if there's an audience. Cooper's lazy grin stretches as his fingers zero in on her nips.

I'd love to say this scene isn't typical for a Sunday night, but I'd be lying through my teeth. Usually, it's much worse.

Deking out Luke with some impressive video game puck handling skills, Sawyer says, "Grab a beer, bro. You can take over for Luke after I make him cry again like a little bitch."

"Fuck you," Luke grumbles.

I glance at the score. Luke is getting his ass handed to him on a silver platter, and he knows it.

"Sure." Sawyer smirks. "Maybe later. But I should warn you, you're not really my type. I like a dude who's packing a little more meat than you."

My lips twitch as I drop my duffle to the floor.

"Hey, you see that bullshit text from Coach?" Cooper asks from between the girl's tits.

I groan, hoping I didn't miss anything important while I was out of town for the weekend. I'm already under contract with the Milwaukee Mavericks. My dad and I flew there to meet with the coaching staff. I also got to hang with a few of the defensive players. Saturday night was freaking crazy. Next season is going to rock.

"Nah, didn't see it," I say. "What's going on?"

"Practice times have changed," Cooper continues, all the while playing with the girl's body. "We're now at six o'clock in the morning and seven in the evening."

Fuck me. He's starting two-a-days already?

"You think he's just screwing around with us?" I wouldn't put it past Coach Lang. I don't think he has anything better to do than lie awake at night, dreaming up new ways to torture us. The guy is a real hard-ass.

Then again, that's why we're here.

But six in the morning...that sucks. Between school and hockey practice, I already feel like I don't get enough sleep. And it's only September. That means I'll need to be up and out the door by five to make it to the rink, get dressed, and be on the ice by six. By the time eleven o'clock at night rolls around, I'll fall into bed an exhausted heap.

Sawyer shrugs, not looking particularly put out by the time change. Cooper pops the nipple out of his mouth and fixes his glassy-eyed gaze on me. "Can't you have your dad talk some freaking sense into the guy?"

Luke grumbles under his breath, "I can barely make it to the seven o'clock practice on time."

"Nope." I shake my head. I'd do just about anything for these guys, except run to my father with anything related to hockey. Coach and my dad go way back. They both played for the Detroit Redwings. I've known the man my entire life. He helped me lace up my first pair of Bauers. So, you'd think he'd have a soft spot for me. Maybe take it easy on me.

Yeah...fat chance of that happening.

If anything, he comes down on me like a ton of bricks *because* of our personal relationship. I think Lang doesn't want any of the guys to feel like he's playing favorites.

Mission accomplished, dude.

No one would ever accuse him of that.

"Then prepare to haul ass at the butt crack of dawn, my friend." With that, Cooper turns his attention elsewhere, attacking the girl's mouth.

Luke eyes them for a moment before yelling, "Hey, you gonna take that shit to the bedroom or are we all being treated to a free show?"

Not bothering to come up for air, Cooper ignores the question.

Luke shakes his head and focuses his attention on making a comeback. Or at least knocking Sawyer's avatar on its ass. "Guess that means we should make some popcorn."

I pick up my duffel and hoist it over my shoulder, deciding to head upstairs for a while. I love hanging with these guys, but I'm not feeling it at the moment.

"Hi, Brody." A lush blonde slips her arms around me and presses her ample cleavage against my chest. "I was hoping you'd show up."

Given the fact that this is my house, the chances of that happening were extremely high.

I stare down into her big green eyes.

"Hey." She looks familiar. I do a quick mental search, trying to produce a name, but only come up with blanks.

Which probably means I haven't slept with her recently.

When it comes to the ladies, I've come up with an algorithm that I've perfected over the last three years. It's simple, yet foolproof. I never screw the same girl more than three times in a six-month period. If you do, you run the risk of entering into the murky territory of a quasi-relationship or a friends-with-benefits situation. I'm not looking for any attachments at this point.

Even casual ones.

I'm at Whitmore to earn a degree and prepare for the pros. I'm focused on getting bigger, faster, and stronger. The NHL is no place for pussies. If you can't hack it, the league will chew you up and spit you out before you can blink your eyes. I have no intention of allowing that to happen. I've worked too hard to crash and burn at this point.

Or get distracted.

In a surprisingly bold move, Blondie slides her hand from my chest to my package and gives it a firm squeeze to let me know she means business.

I have no doubts that if I asked her to drop to her knees and suck me off in front of all these people, she would do it in a heartbeat. Other than a thong, the girl grinding away on Cooper's lap is naked.

My first year playing juniors, when a girl offered to have no-strings-attached-sex, I'd thought I'd hit the flipping jackpot. Less than five minutes later, I'd blown my load and was ready for round two. Fast forward five years, and I don't even blink at a chick who's willing to drop her panties within minutes of me walking through the door. It happens far too often for it to be considered a novelty.

Which is just plain sad.

When I was in high school, I jumped at the chance to dip my wick.

Now?

Not so much.

It's like being fed a steady diet of steak and lobster. Sure, it's delicious the first couple of days. Maybe even a full week. You can't help but greedily devour every single bite and then lick your fingertips afterward. But, believe it or not, even steak and lobster become mundane.

Most guys, no matter what their age, would give their left nut to be in my skates.

To have their pick of any girl. Or, more often than not, *girls*.

And here I am...limp dick in hand.

Actually, limp dick in *her* hand.

Sex has become something I do to take the edge off when I'm feeling stressed. It's my version of a relaxation technique. For fuck's sake, I'm twenty-three years old. I'm in the sexual prime of my life. I should be ecstatic when any girl wants to spread her legs for me. What I shouldn't be is bored. And I sure as hell shouldn't be mentally running through the drills we'll be doing when I lead a captain's practice.

I pry her fingers from my junk and shake my head. "Sorry, I've got some shit to take care of."

And that shit would be school. I have forty pages of reading that needs to be finished up by tomorrow morning.

Blondie pouts and bats her mascara-laden lashes.

"Maybe later?" she coos in a baby voice.

Fuck. That is such a turnoff.

Why do chicks do that?

No, seriously. It's a legitimate question. Why do they do that? It's like nails on a chalkboard. I'm tempted to answer back in a ridiculous, lispy-sounding voice.

But I don't.

I'm not that big of an asshole.

Plus, she might be into it.

Then I'd be screwed. I envision us cooing at each other in baby voices for the rest of the night and almost shudder.

"Maybe," I say noncommittally. Although I'm not going to lie, that toddler voice has killed any chance for a later hookup. But I'm smart enough not to tell her that. Chances are high that she'll end up finding another hockey player to latch on to and forget all about me. Because let's face it, that's what she's here for.

A little dick from a guy who skates with a stick.

Just to be sure, I run my eyes over the length of her again.

Toddler voice aside, she's got it going on.

And yet, that banging body is doing absolutely nothing for me. Which is troublesome. I almost want to take her upstairs just to prove to myself that everything is in proper working order. But I won't.

As I hit the first step, Cooper breaks away from his girl. "WTF, McKinnon? Where you going?" He waves a hand around the room. "Can't you see we're in the middle of entertaining?"

"I'll leave you to take care of our guests," I say, trudging up the staircase.

"Well, if you insist," he slurs happily.

My bedroom is at the end of the hall, away from the noise of the first floor. As a general rule, no one is allowed on the second floor except for the guys who live here. I pull out my key and unlock the door before stepping inside.

My duffel gets tossed in the corner before I open my Managerial Finance book. I thought I'd have a chance to plow through some of the reading over the weekend, but my dad and I were on the go the entire time. Meeting people from the Milwaukee organization, hitting a team party, checking out a few condos near the lakefront. Just getting the general lay of the land. On the plane ride home, I had every intention of being productive, but ended up sacking out once we hit cruising altitude.

Three hours later, there's a knock on the door. Normally an interruption would piss me off, but after slogging through thirty pages, my eyes have glazed over, and I'm fighting to stay awake. This material is mind-numbingly boring, and that's not helping matters.

"It's open," I call out, expecting Cooper to try cajoling me back downstairs.

When that guy's shitfaced, he wants everyone else to be just as hammered as he is. I've never seen anyone put away alcohol the way he does. It's almost as impressive as it is scary. And yet, he's somehow able to wake up for morning practice bright-eyed and bushy-tailed like he wasn't just wasted six hours ago. Someone from the biology department really needs to do a case study on him, 'cause that shit just ain't normal.

When I suck down alcohol like that, the next morning I'm like a newborn colt on the ice who can't keep his legs under him.

It's not a pretty sight. Which is why I don't do it. Been there, done that. Moving on.

The door swings open to reveal Blondie-With-The-Toddler-Voice. And she's not alone. She's brought a friend.

I raise my brows in interest as they step inside the room.

In the three hours since I've seen her, Blondie has managed to lose most of her clothing. The brunette she's with appears to be in the same predicament. They stand in lacy bras and barely-there thongs with their hands entwined.

My gaze roves over them appreciatively.

How could it not?

Their tummies are flat and toned. Hips are nicely rounded. Tits jiggle enticingly as they saunter toward the bed where I'm currently sprawled.

I should be a man of steel over here. I haven't gotten laid in three weeks. Which is almost unheard of. I haven't gone that long without sex since I first started having it.

But there's nothing.

Not even a twitch.

Which begs the question—What the hell is wrong with me?

It must be the stress of school and the skating regimen I'm on. Even though I'm already under contract with Milwaukee and don't have to worry about the NHL draft later this year, I'm still under a lot of pressure to perform this season.

National Championships don't bring themselves home.

I'd be concerned that I have some serious erectile dysfunction issues happening except there's one chick who gets me hard every time I lay eyes on her. Rather ironically, she wants nothing to do with me. I think she'd claw my eyes out if I laid one solitary finger on her.

Actually, all I have to do is stare in her direction, and she bares her teeth at me.

Maybe these girls are exactly what I need to relieve some of my pent-up stress. It certainly can't hurt.

Decision made, I slam my finance book closed and toss it to the floor where it lands with a loud thud. I fold my arms behind my head and smile at the girls in silent invitation.

And the rest, shall we say, is history.

Want to read more of Brody & Natalie's story? You can buy it here -)
https://books2read.com/u/bPXN6x

CAMPUS PLAYER

DEMI

"*M*orning, Demi!" Gary, one of the stadium custodians, calls out with an easy smile and wave as he saunters toward me. "Up and at 'em bright and early this morning, I see."

My heart jackhammers beneath my ribcage from the twenty-minute run as I flash him a grin. "Always!"

"You have a good one! I'll see you tomorrow!"

Since I've already moved past him, I holler over my shoulder, "Same place, same time!"

Even with *The Killers* pumping through my earbuds, I almost hear the deep chuckle that slides from his lips. Our morning greetings are a ritual three years in the making. I've been running through the wide corridor that leads to the stadium football field since I stepped foot on campus freshman year. This will be something I miss when I graduate in the spring. Five days a week, I'm up at six, logging in a four-mile run before returning home, jumping in the shower, and heading off to class.

At this time of the day, the stadium is still relatively quiet, with only a few people wandering the hallways. There's something both serene and eerie about it. I've been here on game days when there are thirty thousand fans packed shoulder to shoulder, rooting on the

Western Wildcats football team. Three-fourths of the stadium filled with black and orange is an amazing sight to behold. Football is a religion at Western. Unfortunately, the same can't be said for the women's soccer team. We're lucky if there are a couple of hundred spectators in the stands.

I've come to terms with it.

Sort of.

I keep my gaze trained on the light at the end of the tunnel and push myself faster. As soon as I burst out of the darkness, bright sunlight pours down on me, stroking over the bare skin of my arms and shoulders. It's late August, and summer is still in full swing. A whistle cuts through the silence of the stadium, and my gaze slices to the field. Nick Richards has been head coach of the Wildcats for the last decade. He also happens to be my father.

Two days a week, the guys are up at six in the morning for yoga. Dad is a big believer in flexibility. Even though I'm winded, a smirk lifts the corners of my lips. Watching two-hundred-and-eighty-pound linebackers contort their bodies into Downward-Facing Dog, the Warrior II Pose, and the Cobra is enough to bring a chuckle to my lips. Some of the guys actually like it, but most grumble when they think Dad isn't paying attention. Little do they know that he sees and hears everything.

My father catches sight of me and flashes a quick smile along with a wave in my direction. He has a black ball cap pulled low and aviators covering his eyes. There's a clipboard in one hand as he paces behind the instructor.

When I point to the field, he shakes his head. He might make the guys do yoga, but he refuses to participate. Something about old dogs and new tricks. Every once in a while, I'll tell him that he needs to get out there and set a good example for the team. He usually shoots me a glare in return.

Every Wednesday night, Dad and I get together. Our weekly dinners became a thing when I moved out of the house and into the dorms freshman year. He's busy coaching football, and my schedule is packed tight with school and soccer. Getting together once a week is the best way for us to stay connected. It doesn't matter if we're in the middle of our seasons; we always make time for each other. Especially since Mom lives in sunny California. After eighteen years of marriage, she got fed up with being a distant second to the Western University football program. She packed up her bags and walked out. I hate to say it, but Dad didn't notice her absence for a couple of days. Which only proved her point. Now she's remarried, learning to surf, and is a vegan. I visit for a couple of weeks during the summer before soccer training camp starts up at the end of June.

Even though it's only the two of us, our weekly dinners are set for three people.

I tell myself to stare straight ahead and not glance in his direction.

Don't do it!

Don't you dare do it!

Damn.

My gaze reluctantly zeros in on him like a heat-seeking missile. Long blond hair, bright blue eyes, sun-kissed skin, and muscles for miles. And he's tall, somewhere around six foot three.

I'm describing none other than Rowan Michaels.

Otherwise known as the bane of my existence.

My dad discovered the talented quarterback the summer before we entered high school and took him under his wing. Which has been...aggravating. In the seven years since, Rowan has become an irritatingly permanent fixture in my life. He's the brother I never wanted or asked for. He's the gift I wish I could give back. He's the son my father never had but secretly longed for.

On a campus with over thirty thousand students, one would think that avoidance would be easy to accomplish. That hasn't turned out to be the case. Somehow, we ended up in the same major—Exercise Science. I get stuck in at least one class with the guy each semester. This time it's statistics, which is a requirement. Three times a week, I'm forced to see him. And then there are the weekly dinners at Dad's house.

Every Wednesday, Rowan shows up without fail.

It's so annoying.

No, *he's* annoying!

Our gazes collide, and electricity sizzles through my veins before I immediately snuff it out and pretend it never happened.

I am not attracted to Rowan Michaels.

I am not attracted to Rowan Michaels.

I am not attracted to Rowan Michaels.

Maybe if I repeat the mantra enough times, it'll be true. That's the hope I cling to. I've made it through the last seven years trying to convince myself of this. I only have to get through our final year together, and then we'll go our separate ways—me to graduate school or maybe to the Women's National Soccer League, and Rowan to the NFL. He's one of the most talented quarterbacks in the conference. Hell, probably the country. There is little doubt in my mind that he'll be a first-round draft pick come next spring.

Trust me when I say that Rowan Michaels fever is alive and well at Western University. His fanbase is legendary. The guy is a major player.

Both on and off the field.

Girls fall all over themselves to be with him. They fill the stands at football practice, show up at parties he's rumored to be at, and basically stalk him around campus.

It's a little nauseating. Don't these girls have any self-respect when it comes to a hot guy?

I wince at that unchecked thought.

Fine...I'll begrudgingly admit it; he's good-looking.

I shake my head as if that will banish the insidious thoughts currently invading my brain. Enough about Rowan. It's time to focus on the reason I'm at the stadium at this ungodly hour. I rip my gaze from him as I hit the cement staircase. After half a flight, all thoughts of the blond quarterback vanish from my mind. How could they not when my quads, glutes, and calves are on fire, screaming for mercy as I force myself to the nosebleed section. By the time I finish, my legs are Jell-O, and I still have a two-mile run back to the apartment I share with my best friend off-campus.

I give Dad a half-hearted wave before leaving. It's the most I can muster. His lips quirk at the corners as he shakes his head. He thinks I'm crazy. At the moment, I can't argue with his assessment of the situation. Although, it's the extra training I put in that helps me run circles around the other team in the second half of the game.

The jog home feels like it will last forever. By the time I unlock the apartment door, I'm ready to collapse. I beeline for the shower and jump in before it's fully warm. My skin prickles with goose flesh, but it feels so damn good. Twenty minutes later, I'm dressed and ready to take on the day. My hair has been thrown up in a messy bun, and I'm making a protein smoothie that will fuel me for my morning classes.

Just before taking off, I poke my head into Sydney's room. I know exactly how I'll find her, and that's buried beneath a small mountain of blankets. She doesn't disappoint. We met the summer before freshman year in training camp and have been besties ever since. She's the yin to my yang. The peanut butter to my jelly. The Thelma to my Louise. Where I'm more introverted and cautious, she's loud and boisterous. She's been known to leap without necessarily looking at what she's jumping into. Every so often, it gets us into trouble. Sydney and I have lived together since sophomore year. I gave up trying to cajole her ass out of bed for a six o'clock run after the first week of us cohabitating when she nearly took my head off with an alarm clock.

"It's that time again," I sing-song obnoxiously, "rise and shine."

There's a grunt and then some shifting from under the blankets that tells me she's alive.

When I chant her name repeatedly, each time escalating in volume, she growls, "Get the fuck out!"

"Awww," I mock, "that's so sweet. I love you, too."

Sydney snorts before a hand snakes out from beneath the blankets to give me a one-fingered salute. Then she grabs a pillow and tosses it in my general vicinity. It falls about five feet short of its mark.

I stare at the dismal attempt. "If you're trying to cause bodily harm, you'll have to do better than that."

"Piss off."

"All right then." I shrug. "See you after class." With that, I close the door behind me.

My farewell is met with another indecipherable mouthful. If this weren't something we went through on the daily, I'd worry she was in the midst of a stroke. Sydney is definitely not a morning person. She's more of an early afternoon person. Another thing I've learned over the years? The action of waking up to a brand-new day is a gradual process. She's like a bear rousing prematurely from hibernation. It's not a pretty sight. She's lucky I don't take her insults personally.

I grab my backpack from the small table crammed into the breakfast nook area along with a coffee before heading out the door. The apartment I share with Sydney is located three blocks from campus, which is highly sought out real estate. We're fortunate Dad is friends with the guy who manages the building. It's probably one of the only perks of having a father who is a head coach of a college football team.

You'd think there would be more, but you'd be wrong. Honestly, being Nick Richard's daughter is more of a hindrance than anything else. People assume you receive special treatment on campus, from professors, or that you have an in with all the football players.

Or worse...

Much worse.

After a bunch of ugly—not to mention untrue—rumors circulated freshman year, I've done my best to distance myself from the Wildcats football team. They're a great bunch of guys, but I don't need all the ugly gossip and speculation that comes along with being friends with them.

As I reach Corbin Hall, the mathematics building for my stats class, my gaze is drawn to a clump of students standing around outside the three-story, red-brick building. In the center of that crowd is Rowan. I don't have to see him physically to know that he's close. The muscles in my belly contract with awareness. It's like a sixth sense. One I wish would go away. He's the last person I want to be cognizant of.

As I jog up the wide stone stairs to the entrance, my gaze fastens on him. A smirk twists the edges of his lips, and my eyes narrow before I drag them away and yank open the door to the building.

Relief rushes through me as I step inside the air conditioning and disappear from sight.

"Hey, Demi, wait up!"

I turn at the sound of my name before slowing my step. The dark-haired guy jogging to catch up smiles before falling in line with me.

Justin Fischer.

He's a baseball player and teammates with Sydney's boyfriend, Ethan. We've been seeing each other for about a month. It's still casual at this point. With school and soccer, I don't have a ton of time to invest in a relationship. He seems to understand that and isn't pushing to be more serious.

When he leans in for a kiss, I angle my head. At the last moment, he tilts in the opposite direction, and we end up bumping teeth instead of locking lips. With a grunt, I pull away and chuckle. My fingers fly to my mouth to make sure I haven't chipped a tooth.

Maybe I've been reluctant to admit it to myself, but that kiss sums up our relationship perfectly.

Awkward and a step out of sync with each other.

"Sorry," he murmurs with a slight smile. I search his face and wait for any telltale sign of sexual chemistry to ping inside me. Unfortunately, my insides remain completely unfazed, which is disappointing but not altogether unexpected. I had a sneaking suspicion when we first got together that it might turn out this way.

"No problem," I say, hoisting my smile and brushing aside those thoughts.

"I haven't seen you for a couple of days," he remarks as we turn a corner and continue walking.

"It's been busy." Which isn't a lie. School might have recently started, but the academics at Western are rigorous. And being a Division I athlete is more like a job. If you're not ready to put in the work, don't bother showing up. There's no half-assing it around this place.

"When's your next game?" he asks.

"Tomorrow at six." My gaze flickers in his direction. Not that I expect him to come, but...

Fine, so maybe I do. If he wants to be my boyfriend, then he needs to show a little support.

His dark brows draw together. "That sucks. I've got a mandatory study hour I have to attend."

I shrug off the disappointment. It's another nail in the coffin of this relationship as far as I'm concerned. "That's cool. It's not a big deal."

"But I'll see you tonight?"

Oh. Right.

Tonight.

Well, damn. In a moment of weakness, I threw out an invitation to join our Wednesday evening dinner. It's one I now regret. If only there were a gracious way to rescind the offer.

"If you're busy, I totally understand—"

"Are you kidding? No way." With a grin, he shakes his head. "I wouldn't miss it for the world. I'm looking forward to meeting Coach Richards."

Great. So this is more about my father than me? Exactly what every girl wants to hear.

I force a brittle smile. "Awesome. He's excited, too."

That might be something of an overstatement.

Justin nods toward the end of the corridor. "I better get moving. Professor Andrews is a real stickler for punctuality."

"Yup. See you later."

This time, when he leans in, our lips align perfectly. The kiss is nothing more than a fleeting caress. There and gone before I can sink into it.

And I'm left feeling...absolutely nothing.

I bury the disappointment where I can't inspect it too closely before giving him a wave as he takes off. For a moment, I stand rooted in the hallway and watch as he disappears through the crowd. There's nothing to distinguish Justin from the thousands of guys who look exactly like him on campus. He's of average height and build with dark hair and espresso-colored eyes. He's nice enough. Although, if I'm completely honest, he's a little self-absorbed. He talks about baseball all the time. If Ethan hadn't introduced us, he's not someone I would have looked twice at. We don't have a ton in common.

As much as I hate to admit it, this relationship has probably reached its expiration date.

Now it's a matter of pulling the plug.

Ugh. I hate breakups. Although, it's doubtful this will end up destroying him. I'll have to make it through tonight and figure out the rest.

With a sigh of resignation, I head to the classroom and find a seat tucked away in the far corner of the small lecture hall. A lanky guy I recognize from a few of my other classes settles beside me. He flashes a dimpled smile as we empty our backpacks.

The tiny hair at the nape of my neck rises seconds before Rowan enters the room. It's like my body knows when he's within a thirty-foot radius. I glance at him from beneath the thick fringe of my lashes before shifting away. Air becomes wedged in my lungs as I wait for him to take a seat. And it won't be next to me because I'm—

"Hey man, would you mind moving?"

Surrounded on both sides.

Damnit. I'm hoping the cutie next to me will tell Rowan to go take a flying leap.

What? It could happen. Not everyone at this university is enamored of the football-playing god. Although I realize the odds aren't stacked in my favor. Rowan is the most recognized athlete on campus. People fall all over themselves to accommodate him.

It's a little sickening.

Okay, maybe more than a little.

"Sure, no problem, Michaels." The guy next to me hastily packs up his books before vacating the desk. Unable to ignore him any longer, I glare as Rowan slides onto the seat next to me.

"Did you really think you could evade me that easily?" Laughter brims in his deep voice. A voice, I might add, that does funny things to my insides.

"One can always hope, right?"

"Oh, answering a question with a question." He leans closer, eating up some of the much-needed distance between us. "I like it."

I roll my eyes as his lips stretch into a satisfied grin. Irritation bubbles up inside me when sexual tension blooms at the bottom of my belly. Or maybe that tension has settled a little lower.

It's definitely lower.

I'm tempted to swear like a sailor. How is it possible that I feel nothing for the guy I'm actually dating, and yet my pulse skitters out of control for someone I don't even like? It's so freaking ironic. It's been this way since we met, and nothing I do stomps it out. I can try to fool myself into believing it's not there, but that doesn't make it any less true.

It's a relief when Professor Peters takes his place at the podium and clears his throat. Once he's captured everyone's attention, he delves headfirst into the probability of dependent and independent events.

Grateful for the excuse to ignore Rowan for the next fifty minutes, I open my textbook and concentrate on the lesson. Just as the blond boy fades into the background, his bare knee bumps into mine. Electricity ricochets through my entire being. I glance at him to see if he's noticed the strange energy we always seem to generate and find his ocean-colored gaze fastened to mine.

My guess is that he does.

Damnation.

Want to read more of Demi & Rowan's story? You can do it here -)
https://books2read.com/u/mYAxqV

ABOUT THE AUTHOR

Jennifer Sucevic is a USA Today bestselling author who has published twenty New Adult novels. Her work has been translated into German, Dutch, and Italian. Jen has a bachelor's degree in History and a master's degree in Educational Psychology. Both are from the University of Wisconsin-Milwaukee. She started out her career as a high school counselor, which she loved. She lives in the Midwest with her husband, four kids, and a menagerie of animals. If you would like to receive regular updates regarding new releases, please subscribe to her newsletter here-
Jennifer Sucevic Newsletter (subscribepage.com)
Or contact Jen through email, at her website, or on Facebook.
sucevicjennifer@gmail.com
Want to join her reader group? Do it here -)
J Sucevic's Book Boyfriends | Facebook
Social media links-
https://www.tiktok.com/@jennifersucevicauthor
www.jennifersucevic.com
https://www.instagram.com/jennifersucevicauthor
https://www.facebook.com/jennifer.sucevic
Amazon.com: Jennifer Sucevic: Books, Biography, Blog, Audiobooks, Kindle
Jennifer Sucevic Books - BookBub

www.ingramcontent.com/pod-product-compliance
Lightning Source LLC
Chambersburg PA
CBHW051145190726
48290CB00006B/2003